DEATH OF AN IMMORTAL

ELI HINZE

REGALE PRESS

Copyright © 2021 by Eli Hinze
All rights reserved. This book or any portion thereof may not be reproduced
or used in any manner whatsoever without the express written permission of
the publisher except for the use of brief quotations in a book review.

Cover by Psycat Studio

Published by Regale Press

"The trouble is, you think you have time." — *The Buddha*

1

WATCHER AT THE WINDOW

I check my pulse for the third time today and release the tension I didn't realize had gathered in my shoulders. Perfectly normal, as always. Small an act as it seems, this sort of repetition is the glue that holds me together. Sustains me. For some people such mundanity is the death of them, but those are the people that don't have their lives together. Not like I do.

A reclaimed-fabric clad customer walks up to the counter, the side of her hand smudged with graphite. For a millisecond, my eyes flick up to her for assessment: a community college student pulling an all-nighter and in desperate need of caffeine. Those are the only customers a coffee house like this gets at eleven PM. Why the hell are we even open that late? And doesn't she know all-nighters will ruin your health? Too much sleep can be lethal too, though. There have been studies on it. Seven and a half hours is thought to be the best amount, so that's what I aim for every night of my life, trimming and lengthening my natural rhythm with meds and alarms and whatever else necessary.

"Did you get that?" my all-nighter-because-I-can't-plan-my-life customer asks.

But judge her all I want, I'm the one who spaced out.

"Sorry, could you repeat that?" My hands shake as I punch in her order for an iced horchata latte. *Stupid.*

She thanks me despite my ineptitude and waits for the barista to whisk together her drink.

I give an inward sigh as I glance at the coffee-cup clock, the spoon-shaped minute hand crawling towards the end of shift. Eleven o'clock strikes just as the door swings open, the chimes above it banging in a cacophonous rattle. I force my eyebrows to stay down as a scraggly old man walks through the door, bits of food enmeshed in his beard and his teeth a putrid yellow. Colors may not have a smell, but it gives me that impression all the same. I don't even want to think about the bacteria a man like this plays host to.

"We're closing in two minutes, sir," the other barista, Nick, says as he slings an espresso-stained towel across his shoulders. He has less patience than I do when it comes to late customers, or at least doesn't bother with bending over backwards for them. If it weren't for him, I'd probably let these people keep the shop open all night, too afraid to upset anyone should they complain to the manager. Not that she would've liked staying open late, either.

"Then I'll take two minutes."

Nick masks his irritation well, then goes to the register. "What can I get you?"

"Are you Eugene?" he asks.

I look him up and down from across the counter. It's not possible that I've met him before—is it? I've never seen this man in my life.

"Nope, not me," Nick says.

"Well, I need him to take my order." He points a dirty fingernail at me. "I guess that's you."

Nick blows out a half-stifled laugh, making it seem almost like a cough. It takes him a minute to step away from the register though, almost like he's wary. Waiting for something. It's likely just my imagination.

"Good luck," he mutters as I pass him.

"What would you like, sir?" I ask. Working food service for the past two years, I've learned how to school my features into pleasantness even if I don't feel it.

"Don't know. Don't like coffee much."

"Oh." I pause. He stares at me, face blank. "Well, we have a selection of teas available, if that's something you'd like."

He shrugs. "I want the cheapest thing you have. Only got five bucks for the night."

Homeless then, though I'm not sure late night treats are the best use of his money. Not that it's my place to say as much. I eye the red glass bowl of individually wrapped caramels near the card reader, marked for 50 cents apiece.

"That would be these, sir."

He grunts and roots around in the bowl with those cracked and tobacco-stained nails. A queasy feeling skitters through me.

"One of these, then," he says.

I punch it into the machine. "That'll be fifty three cents."

"I thought you said fifty?"

"Sales tax, sir." I force my breathing to stay even, to not cower in the face of his annoyance—though I don't quite look him in the eyes as I say it.

With a huff, he hands me a single five dollar bill, crisp and clean despite his appearance. I blink. Either someone was very generous to have given him a full five, or he isn't as hard-pressed as I thought. I take it and fish around in the drawer for his change.

"I'm sorry, sir, but I was just wondering." I glance down at where my name tag should be, but that my work doesn't provide. Apparently labeling people doesn't mesh with the pseudo-bohemian vibe of the cafe, even if it's as innocent as stating one's name. "How did you know my name?"

"Some woman out in the parking lot."

I wait for him to continue. He doesn't. "Some woman in the parking lot…did what?"

"Gave me money, told me to get some food." He scratches at his stomach and his stained shirt rides up. "So long as I asked for you."

I falter as I slide the change towards him. My patience for the evening is wearing thin, anxiety beginning to replace it. The later I leave work, the less time I have to tend to my evening routine, the more likely the next day is to get thrown out of whack, and so on. The gentleman in front of me certainly isn't going to help get things back on track, either. Best not to indulge him.

"Here you go, sir."

The door bangs open, the chimes tied to it rattling in the quiet air.

"We're closed," Nick says from over his shoulder as he wipes down the milk frother.

The woman who just entered makes no move towards the counter, doesn't even glance at the overhead menu. I try to assess her like all the others, to anticipate what she'd want, but instead draw a blank. Her eyes, golden like raw ocher, graze over the homeless man before locking onto me. I squint. It's been a while since I've seen someone wear colored contacts, at least those of such an unnatural color. It would be jarring if they weren't so transfixing. She nods at Nick in what I guess is acknowledgement of what he said, then makes a sharp turn out the door, black hair whipping behind her. Weird, but one less customer for me to contend with—one who respects closing time, no less. A rarity. Her silhouette climbs into a car under the parking lot's buzzing light, but she makes no move to pull out, just sitting there. I turn away. Better for her to dawdle out there than in here.

The congregations of students begin to file out, the dull murmur of chatter leaving with them and the parking lot emptying car by car. The homeless man leaves too. Nick tosses his rag into the sink and slings an arm around my shoulder.

"I don't want to say I hate late customers," he sighs, "but I hate late customers."

I chuckle, but keep it low in case the manager is listening in. Never mind that she left an hour ago. "I feel that. Had a lot of them this week."

He nods. "How many hours does this make for you? It's gotta be something wild."

"I don't mind," I say even as I stifle a yawn. I take in a lungful of the coffee bean scent in hopes it'll revive me.

"You're probably beat. Anyone would be, with your schedule." Nick shakes his head and closes down the register. While I've never had an older brother, Nick seems like the person who'd make a great one. Protective, slightly annoying, and very much a hardhead. It's an endearing combination. "I can lock up today. You head home, alright?"

"No, I'll stay. It's not fair to leave you with all the closing stuff." In truth, I just don't want to be thought of as someone who coasts at their job, someone who'd jump at the chance to take it easy. If word were to get back to my boss, all my future job or college plans could shatter. In any recommendation letters or references, she could toss a wet blanket right onto my prospects with two short words: *he coasts.*

"Might be for the best," Nick says as he collects the cappuccino cups. Their chipped porcelain clinks together in his hands as he sets them in the sink. "Last thing this town needs is another Brendon Watts."

I quirk an eyebrow up at him. "Am I supposed to know who that is?"

He quirks one right back at me and turns away from washing dishes. "Are you serious?"

"Yeah, why?"

"Do you not watch the news or something?"

"Celebrity news doesn't count as news."

"Are you for real right now?"

"Uh, yes?" I stammer as my pulse quickens.

"Brendon Watts." He says it like a statement, not a question, but I still can't tell what he's getting at. Nick leans in, elbows on the flecked granite countertop and eyes bright like a child with a secret he's not supposed to share—but who plans to anyway. "Dead kid?"

My expression remains blank, though I kick myself on the inside. Apparently this is a name I should know, and while it's somewhat familiar, 'somewhat' doesn't cut it. I've tried to get into the habit of making flash cards from unfamiliar names and facts to sharpen my memory, but it's remembering to do so that I forget.

Nick continues. "Two days ago, someone named Brendon's found shot dead in a parking lot just north of town. Some guy in my finance class, his old man works with county PD, and word is that it was brutal. Like, execution style. No motive, no evidence, nothing. Things are still kinda hush-hush because they don't want to freak everyone out, but I think it's a bit late for that."

An involuntary chill scuttles down my spine. Never would I have thought something like that could happen here. Sure, no place is ever totally insulated from violence, but still. Austin is known for being safe, and while the growing population has seen our crime rate increase, it's still low.

Nick shakes his head and clicks his tongue before turning back to the cups. "Crazy world out there, man."

"Yeah." I grab a clean rag from the drawer, mind elsewhere, lingering on his words. "Sure is."

I wipe down the counters and look out the window again, into the vast blackness of the parking lot. The black-haired woman's car is gone.

Death of an Immortal

NICK and I walk to the back employee parking lot together. As we finished cleaning the cafe, he'd taken it upon himself to divulge the gory contents of every last Brendon-Watts-related rumor that's ever graced his ears, and nineteen though we may be, now neither of us feel all that safe walking into an unlit, unsurveilled lot at night. From the pallor of his face, it's safe to guess Nick regrets psyching himself out too.

Tragedy though it was—I really do feel for his family's loss—I throw off all thoughts of Brendon and step into my paint-chipped sedan. I hit the lock three times before I buckle my seatbelt, a habit my older sister ingrained into me. The car rumbles to life, and after double-checking my rearview mirror, I see a third car in the employee parking lot—despite that only Nick and I were on-shift. *Loiterers.* Before I sit long enough to look suspicious—the hell do I have to look suspicious for? I'm the one at work—or to contemplate the dim outlines in the car, I speed away.

Fifteen minutes later I'm home, having averaged a responsible gas-mileage and never daring to edge near the speed limit. Once the doors are double-bolted and I've ingested enough calories to maintain my weight, I open my email on my phone. My eyes drift to one message in particular and I tap it.

> *Beautiful here as always! Abuela says to make sure you're eating and sleeping enough. How're things on your end? Try to relax and enjoy this summer!*
> *XO - Mom and Dad*

Attached is a photo of my dad and his mother, my abuela, with his finger blurring the upper corner of the lens. Their sun-kissed cheeks are flushed with a rosy tint and wide smiles eclipse their faces. Currently my parents are off in Spain visiting my father's family, well into their fourth week by now. They'd tried to drag my older sister along with them, but she was toiling away on her graduate thesis and would've sooner swallowed glass than get onto an airplane. I had chosen to stay so I could work and invest in my mutual funds, that way they could grow while I was busy with whatever degree I pursued. Which I definitely would pursue—once I decided what to do with my life. My parents, however, still feel bad about leaving, and have been sending messages since.

I pull the coffee-and-soap-scented shirt over my head and toss it into the hamper, then throw in the shirt for my other job as well. Realizing the name tag is still on it, I bend over to pluck it off. *Eugene Reyes*, it reads. Such a godawful name, uptight and weak, but it fits me. Lanky, not that outspoken, a completely anal basket-case, and with a mess of black hair that skims down my neck like a sodden mop.

By the time I floss and swallow my sleep aids, the clock reads 11:32. Two minutes later than my norm, but…I'll survive without bumping my alarm ahead. Two fewer minutes of rest won't be the end of me, so long as I don't indulge the behavior. I flop onto my bed and give a small sigh, pulling my thick-framed glasses from my nose. Thank god the hipster style is in. Contacts pose too great a risk of papillary conjunctivitis for my liking.

I tug the bedside lamp string and the room goes dark, the shadows bleeding in like ink through cotton. As I lie there, eyes closed and slowing my breathing, my mind flicks back to Nick's words. No evidence, he'd said.

Stop thinking. I picture a blank wall and try to focus on it, attempt to clear my thoughts, but to no avail. Execution style, he'd said. My mind's eye conjures up the image of some poor soul's lifeless body, left to be discovered in an alleyway or parking garage. What kind of person could do that? Try as I might to picture a wall instead, I can't shake the image. I roll onto my side, then my back, then around again until my legs tangle in the sheets, but the thoughts remain.

Death of an Immortal

What was Watts doing to draw a killer's attention to him? Was he in with a rough crowd? No, Nick said they hadn't found a motive, not yet at least. Was he just not being conscious of his safety? Blaming the victim is never in good taste, but sometimes you wonder: if they acted differently, would things have turned out the same?

At the very least, I know that I'm in the clear. I live in a safe neighborhood. My jobs are in reputable areas of town. I take care to watch my back, and I'm hyper-vigilant in almost every aspect of my life. Unexpected though the unexpected may be, that sort of tragedy is the last thing I'll ever have to worry about—one of the many benefits of making my life predictable to a T.

Eased by the thought, I curl around the comforter and drop into sleep.

2

SPIRITED

I BOUNCE on the balls of my feet, back and forth, back and forth as I wait for the crosswalk to give me the light. Even though there are no cars at the intersection, you never know when one might come around the corner, but I don't want to lose my momentum either. Waking up early just to further torture myself with a run is bad enough as is. Catching every standstill crosswalk doesn't help. I check the morning's humidity level on my phone and try to calculate how much water I'll need to drink to replenish my fluids. And what amount of electrolytes I'll need to consume to keep my water intake from diluting my stores. And how to fit it into my daily caloric allotment.

I wish I could just let things go sometimes, but my mind refuses.

The white pedestrian icon lights up. I trot across the intersection, still careful to check both ways for cars. There aren't many on the road at this time on a Saturday. My thigh muscles burn. I pound across the pavement. Sweat runs along my bony spine. Save a few hiccoughs, these moments are some of the only times my brain is quiet. Relaxed. I've certainly been told exercise will fix my problems often enough for me to give it a try. It doesn't, but it comes with its own benefits. The baggy shirt swings around my form with each stride, a collar of sweat darkening the neck of it. I pull it from my skin with a finger and duck my head to give myself a sniff. I cough. As if there was any doubt that I reeked.

While I'm not trying to impress anyone, I scan the area all the same. No one's there. I hear the rush of vehicles on the main road a few blocks off, but nothing closer save for some chatty squirrels. Yet while I don't see anyone…

No, that's just the paranoia from last night kicking in. It's only natural after what happened to Brendon, but that's all it is. Fixable panic.

Eyes press into my back. I turn around one more time, more like a startled cat's jump. No one's there. Of course not. I wipe my sweaty hands on my running shorts then head back home, and still I can't help but look over my shoulder every twenty seconds. My sister Moira quirks up a brow from upon the couch as I walk through the door.

"Still running?" she asks.

"Still coming over to leech off Mom and Dad's cable?"

She shrugs, the glare from the TV illuminating her blocky glasses. "I can't stream local news from my apartment."

"Since when do you watch loc—"

The macabre image that flashes onto the screen shuts me up. Even through the blurred pixels, there's still enough horrible context clues to show me more than I ever wanted to know. Splatters fleck the brick wall near where Brendon's body was found, and I'm not sure it's all blood. My stomach curls in on itself in a bout of nausea.

"Why're you watching that?" I turn away and head into the kitchen. The photograph dampened my appetite, but if I wait for my muscles to go through post-workout break down, I'll get even skinnier than I already am. I rummage through the cabinets for an easy source of protein. Scooping unprocessed peanut butter from the jar, I then pop it in my mouth.

"I'm sorry, do you not want me to be informed?" Moira shoots back.

The reporter's voice, strangely warm despite the subject, details the time and place of the incident. "Authorities still have no suspects or theories regarding the death of young Brendon Watts, and are holding his body for further examination before he is interred on Saturday morning. The Watts family has asked that donations be made to local charities in lieu of flowers."

The anchor continues on, but I try to tune out her voice. "Can you shut that off?"

"This is why I came over here," Moira says with a shrug, still looking ahead.

I huff out a sigh and move to head for my room, but hear the TV click off before I make it to the end of the hall.

"Eugene?" she calls. When I don't respond, she repeats herself with that demanding, big-sister tone. "*Eugene.*"

"Yeah." I come back out to the living room and lean up against the wall, head tilted at an awkward angle between the plaster and my shoulder to avoid eye contact.

"Something's wrong," she says, eyes dragging over me like she's trying to sniff out clues. "Tell me."

"It's nothing. Don't worry." My standard response to everything. When my parents ask why I'm wound so tight, when my classmates want to know if they could get some control over our projects... The list goes on.

"I *will* sit on you, stupid."

That she will. I sigh, and she smacks the leather couch cushion beside her. Resigned, I plop down onto it. We sit in silence for one moment, then two.

"It's just all the Brendon stuff," I say.

"Eugene." She rolls her eyes and rubs at them. I know how this conversation will go. "We've talked about this. Every time something happens, even something minor, you spiral—"

"He was *killed*."

"Yes, he was and it's horrible and I hope they catch the monsters who did it. *But*. You can't rev yourself up about it so badly that you can't sleep or eat or function. We've been there too many times before."

"How can you distance yourself like that?" My voice raises by a fraction, but not at her. "How is everyone not locked up in their houses and—"

"Listen," she says, putting a hand on my shoulder, "it was a tragedy, but stuff like this happens. It's unlikely anything will happen again for quite some time, especially in a neighborhood like this. Okay?"

"But you can't be sure."

She takes her hands off me to run them through her hair, pin-straight like mine, but maintains her composure. I don't know how she finds it in herself to tolerate me, but I appreciate the effort. Even if I never voice it. "No one can ever be one-hundred percent sure of anything, alright? Now I want you to make plans, put this out of your mind, and go have fun. No working, no worrying, just fun. It's summertime, for god's sake."

"It's not—," I sigh. "It's not just the news. That's bothering me, I mean."

Her eyebrows arch up, an invitation for me to go on. I try to swallow down what I want to say, and find myself second guessing my thoughts from last night and this morning. Maybe I am being ridiculous, but could it hurt to mention it?

"I think someone's following me."

Moira blinks. Before she can laugh or object, the words rush out of me.

"Well, more like someone's watching me. I don't know exactly, but I've just had this really weird feeling—"

"Don't do this, Eugene." She now grips both hands around my shoulders and turns me to face her firm expression, older and more certain than my own. "I know it's hard.

But you have to let this anxiety stuff go, or else it'll always be something that's got you looking over your shoulder. That's no way to live."

I purse my lips together, biting down my retort. *That's exactly the point*, I want to say. When anxiety becomes your natural state, you don't know what actually warrants being afraid anymore. What if this is one of them?

"Call me if you ever need anything or just want to talk, alright? But as for this," she gives me a light shake, "relax. Promise?"

Despite that I'm not sure it's a promise I can keep, I nod all the same.

I WIPE a sheen of sweat from under my ball cap, then pull it off to fan myself. The air hangs heavy with the scent of grease scrapings and a salty tang, and while I know my skin isn't *actually* coated in a film of oil, I can't help but imagine one. I sling a dishcloth over my shoulder and look out over the few straggling Chicken Bucket patrons as they file out, stained plastic trays and crumpled receipts in their wake. It's been an uneventful night. The evening chaos aside, no one got any snippier than usual, and no threats walked through our doors. My shoulders are no longer so tight, so tense up around my ears.

After a few minutes I gather the trash, grateful no one has stayed too long past closing. I bend over a booth's linoleum tabletop to sweep off grains of salt. They stick to my hand. I shake them off and my reflection catches in the window, the glass panes showing me the drab brown interior, the tiled floor, the particle board tables.

Something shifts again in the window—this time from the other side, in the pitch dark night.

My heart stops. It's too bright in here for me to see

Death of an Immortal

whoever—or whatever—is outside. But anyone can see inside, as easy as staring into a goldfish bowl. I lunge towards the glass, cup my hand around it, and peer out. Nothing stares back at me, at least not that I can see. These night shifts always used to be my ideal; quick-paced and with a free meal.

Since yesterday, my opinion has shifted ever so slightly.

I step back and stare, eyes tight. It could have been a grackle for all I know, but I'm not going to stick around to find out. After the half hour it takes me to clean the soda machine, restock the napkins and straws for the morning, and make the next day's coleslaw, I'm back in my car, doors promptly locked and shift complete.

As I take off my hat to rub where its cheap material has chafed my ears, I realize I'm out of bananas at the house. I curse under my breath. While not a calamity, it *is* an inconvenience. I have another early morning run scheduled for tomorrow, and my tried-and-true pre-exercise snack has been a banana for the past eight months. Making a whole separate trip for it would be a waste of gas and breaking from the repetition of today's routine isn't an idea that thrills me, but better to throw off today—a day that's almost over—than flubbing tomorrow before it even gets off the ground. I turn the keys in the ignition. There's only one grocery store still open at this time of night, but it isn't far. Throwing my arm over the passenger seat's cracked shoulder to back out, I make for the main road.

It takes me less than a second to see the sedan hurtling my way, screaming through the lot. A rush of heat seizes me. My mind scrambles. Slam the breaks and hope it overshoots me, swerve and hope we miss each other, or punch the gas and get the hell out of the way. Before I can consciously decide, my foot slams on the gas as I peel out of the parking lot and onto the road. No one else is driving in the far right lane, leaving me with a safe out.

Relief bleeds through my chest, the throbbing fire in my

veins lessening as I pull over and take in a deep gulp of air. I glance in my rearview mirror to see what the other driver did, if he's drunk or texting at the wheel. I cock my head to the side. Another driver cut him off. Parking lots have gotten more hectic since the area has grown, but rarely do they descend into total chaos. Until now, I guess. I shrug off what tension remains then drive on, trying to keep my eyes ahead.

Whatever happened, no one was hurt. Uncrushed limbs and an undeployed airbag are the only two items on my checklist for this evening. And bananas.

I reach the store. Tonight the parking lot has an unsettling clarity, a crispness to it compared to the filmy smog hanging over the highways, spewed out by construction vehicles en route to the newest high rise or strip mall. The street lamps buzz like whirring cicadas overhead and stray grocery carts litter the parking spaces. Being in the service industry myself, I feel for the poor soul who'll have to collect these.

I step through the painfully bright front doors and grab a cart out of habit. Might as well pick up a few other things while I'm here, so long as I keep my costs down. It'd be inefficient otherwise. I take a mental tally of what the house is out of and head to the produce section, first to the left. The wheels of my cart squeal with each rotation, met only by the occasional cash register chirp or slap of a mop against the concrete floor. The store is almost deserted at this time of night, 10:27, save for a few college students and service workers. I rub the goosebumps puckering along my forearms as I draw closer to the chilled section. Jewel-toned cabbages sit clustered together, outer leaves withered, herbs a row above them. I throw a bag of romaine lettuce in my cart, then pluck three bananas from their cardboard box, and as I look sideways at the appetizing display of tubers, shallots, and peppers, I push my cart all of two feet before a woman seizes the front of it. I nearly jump backwards.

It's her. The woman from the coffee shop. Her eyes, inex-

Death of an Immortal

plicably golden, stab through me sharper than any blade. My sights dart down to see her fingers clenched through the wire front of my cart, white knuckled.

"We need to leave," she says before I can utter a word.

I blink twice. "Uh, what?"

"Leave your cart and come with me. You're—"

"Listen, ma'am." I try to move my cart and she holds it in place. What exactly do you say when someone does—well, whatever this is? "I'm sorry, but I think you have the wrong person."

"I don't."

I push forward, but she doesn't budge. In her all-black ensemble—boots with what looks like a hell of a lot of traction rubber at the soles, form fitting pants—she manages to look intimidating despite her petite height, in no small part due to her bared, corded arms. Even though it's clipped to the back of her head, dark hair spills over her shoulder, stretching to reach her ribcage.

"This isn't some damned gallery." She jerks the cart towards her and leans in. "If you don't come with me right now, you will die. Tonight."

My insides go cold.

I search her eyes. Unreadable. Unfathomable. Who would lie about something like this? Is this some sick threat? But no, she wouldn't kill me.

Would she?

I think back to the only other time I've seen her before, in the coffee house all of twenty-three hours ago. She'd only looked at me—then left once she saw I wasn't alone. It was *her* who'd sent in the homeless man to figure out who I was. Oh god, how long has she been planning this? Just tonight I thought there was someone outside the restaurant window, someone I couldn't see. A car had sped after me. I saw an extra car in the employee parking lot the night before. A roiling wave of nausea hits, making me feel light-headed and like cement all at once. It's no mistake that she's here.

"Have you been…following me?" I know the answer before the words even leave my mouth.

She glances towards the entrance behind me ever so quickly, too fast for me to make a run for it, and while I'm a runner, I have a sinking feeling that I'd be outmatched here. With a whip of her head, she bares her teeth and looks back to me.

"Come with me and you won't end up like Brendon Watts."

His name rings in my ears. All of the other sounds, the beep of the scanners, the faint squeal of wheels, all of it fades away. Cold sweat pops up on the back of my neck, my stomach churning. Through it all, I know one thing for absolute certain: I'm screwed.

I DON'T MEANDER around the store to lollygag or burn time in hopes she'll lose interest, which in retrospect is probably what I should have done. Instead I aim to get the hell out of dodge as fast as possible. I don't even check out, bananas be damned. I make straight for the parking lot, keys in hand, bringing me to a dark and empty parking lot. It isn't until I'm faced with it that I consciously realize the peopled supermarket would've been a better place to work out whatever the hell this is. I kick myself.

"You shouldn't ignore me," she insists, right on my heels. Her teeth remain out, something primal as she flicks her gaze about the gravel lot. "Listen to me!"

I pull my phone from my butt pocket to call my sister, hoping it'll put this chick off whatever designs she has. It's not until she punches me in the mouth that I fully comprehend the gravity of my situation.

My head snaps back as white explodes across my vision. My teeth scream down to the root. She tears the keys from my hand and seizes the neck of my shirt, then shoves me against a car door as the locks pop open. My gut sinks straight to my ass as I realize her intentions.

Is the car a metallic grey? Blue? I'll need to describe it to the police—if I ever get to them—but my head swims with pulsing white noise and dizzying darkness. Why did I not buy pepper spray? I know that my work doesn't allow weapons and that I could have been fired for having one on my person, which horrified me at the time—but being dead seems a far worse alternative. My world tilts sideways as she hurls me into the car and pushes past me, climbing over to the driver's seat. She locks the doors.

"Get down," she says.

I want to explode at her in rage, but my voice comes out more like an indignant squirrel's, high pitched and furious. "Are you ins—"

"Down!"

She shoves my head towards the mud-caked floorboards, my muscles straining against her. Something near the nape of my neck gives a sharp twang and I clap a hand over it, then look up just in time to see and hear a screaming bullet ricochet off the hood of the car.

My heart leaps into my throat. *She was telling the truth.* About some of it? All of it? Or is it a ruse to make me trust her?

She slams her foot on the gas and the tires screech under us, spewing up loose asphalt as we tear out of the parking lot in an arc. After a quick glance over her shoulder, she reaches behind her and into her waistband. The distinct boxiness of the oiled metal shines even in the dark. A lump rises in my throat. I'm a Texan, and if anybody on Earth knows what a gun looks like—regardless of whether or not they use one—, it's a Texan. One protest too loud, one scene too noticeable for her liking and soon it'll be my name in the obituaries.

She throws back the hammer.

"Oh my god!" Panic floods me, drowns me. I hold my hands up in front of my face and shrink into the corner, pressing against the door. Like it'll do me any good. "Oh my god, you—"

"Quiet!" She flashes a glare my way, looking for all the world as if she wants nothing to do with me. "Keep your head down and stay there. Give me your phone."

My hands quiver. I'd hoped she was an amateur at this sort of thing, but no such luck. Regardless, I'm not about to fork over my last remaining life-line. Whatever insanity she's trying to drag me into, I'm not going to take it whimpering and compliant. I eye the gun in her hand, the other one resting firm on the steering wheel. She catches my gaze and shakes her head.

"Good to see your gears turning, but not a smart move. Trust me."

As if she's given me any reason to, but for now I shove that aside and begin wondering about her end-game. Stalk guy, abscond with said guy in grocery store, and then…what? It's a question I'm not sure I want the answer to. She shakes her head in exasperation, long locks roiling like black asps, then shoves her hand in my pocket. My neck turns an angry red at the invasion of space—not that that appears sacred to her—as I stammer like an idiot. She pulls my phone out of my pocket, then opens her window and chucks it onto the road.

"Hey!" I watch the plastic and glass shatter into a thousand pieces under other speeding vehicles. It quickly disappears behind us, now no more than useless scrap.

"You'll thank me later."

"Like hell I will!"

With yet another glance into each side mirror, she jerks the car onto a frontage road and then the highway, me slamming my head into the window with each careen. A new surge of panic flushes through me as I realize I haven't put on my seatbelt—and with my luck this evening, I could very well go flying through the windshield. I fasten the seatbelt across my torso, but don't remind her to. If she wants to die, so be it. The speedometer needle soars, miles of streetlights and neon signs off the freeway streaking past us like comets. How have we not gotten pulled over yet? There aren't many cars on the road, and those I do see are too far away to signal for help. A realization sinks into me, like poison seeping into a well.

I'm being abducted. And no one is coming.

My sister and I are distant, talking only when she's over at the house. My family won't be home for another month, thousands of miles away. My bosses might notice my absence, but they see people quit without notice all the time. It could take weeks before anyone thinks to ask where I am, at which point I could be buried in some roadside ditch. My head begins swimming, the air pulling out of my lungs, my heart collapsing in on itself, pulse splitting. I can't breathe, already a dead man walking. Already in Brendon Watts' shoes.

I'd planned my life so carefully and here I am now, at the hands of likely the last face I'll ever scorch into my brain, having never really lived at all. Something like anger or shame sets my eyes stinging. How much of my life did I sacrifice in trying to gain some measure of stability? Of predictability?

And now, in spite of all of that, to be faced with death in the one way I never predicted.

No. I can't think like that. Once I do, I'm as good as dead. Think, *think*, there has to be some way for me to escape, some way to defend myself. Jumping out of the car at the speed we're going would be suicide, but wouldn't it be better to at least have a fighting chance than be someone's docile kill? My hand edges towards the door handle.

"It's locked," she says as if reading my mind. "And a stupid idea."

"You thinking I'd go down easy is a stup—"

"I told you exactly what I was doing!" Her voice raises, eyes as fiery as a smith's forge. "Those people that shot at us in the parking lot? Who do you think they are, your friends?"

"It could've been police or something! Someone trying to help me for all y—"

She snorts. "They weren't police, I can guarantee you that much. Those are the people who killed Brendon Watts. And now they want you."

My heart—my poor, out-of-breath heart—continues to pound against my ribs and beat my other organs into oblivion. She'd said as much before, at least I think so, but not in as many words.

"Why? What did I do? I didn't even know Brendon."

She falls silent. Whatever irritation and urgency was on her face before folds back, then she straightens, facing dead ahead and not looking at me. But behind it all, I think I see her shoulders curl in by a hair. Shame? Regret? Or is she just cold?

"It's—It has nothing to do with Brendon," she says. "It's because of me."

"Because you what? Did you get him involved with a bad crowd, or did he owe—"

"Nothing like that." She shakes her head. "He was supposed to help me with something and these people, they found out. And they didn't want him to help me. So they killed him."

Her gaze remains fixed. Wisps of hair frame her jaw, like wrought iron framing a portrait of resolve. I go mute and stare at her—before a spark of outrage ignites in my chest.

"Let me get this straight." My teeth clench so hard I half-worry they'll crack, but I keep talking. "You knew Brendon Watts."

"Correct."

"You needed his help."

"Correct."

"And because of that, these people, whoever they are, killed him."

"Again, correct."

The spark explodes into a flame. "Then why are *you* getting *me* involved? I haven't agreed to help you with anything. I don't even know if I can! God, like I would at this point! Your 'logic'—" I throw up emphatic air quotes "—says that they want to kill anyone who helps you, but you've plucked me off the face of the earth before I even agree, and now—and now! Now even if I tell them I haven't agreed to help you, they won't believe me!"

She hesitates before answering. "Mostly correct."

"Mostly? Explain to me what part of that was not absolutely spot on." I flash her a disparaging look, but the expression feels foreign to me. I worry I look like a toddler sucking on a lemon for the first time.

"I wasn't going to ask for your help. But by the time I had surveilled you—"

"Stalked."

Her upper lip twitches into the smallest of sneers. Not a fan of my constant interruptions, it seems—but I'm the hostage so I'll interrupt as much as I please. "By the time I'd surveilled you, I'd already made up my mind to seek out someone else. But then these guys showed up, saw that I was watching you, and I guess assumed we'd already cut a deal. I didn't know until I saw them following you."

"And you what? Decided to save me?"

"Isn't that obvious?" She shrugs, as if there's no danger to her in the equation at all. Her voice becomes faint. "I can't have innocent blood on my hands. Not again."

I swallow. I don't want to ask how many there were before Brendon.

3

THE IMMORTAL

The stretch of highway unfurls before us and silence engulfs the cab. All that hangs in the air is a slight hum from the tires speeding over uneven concrete lanes, joined occasionally by the whoosh of a passing car. Their appearance is scattered, but each time we pass one she tightens her grip on the gun. An hour goes by without change. Green exit signs pass us in the tens, maybe hundreds as I fight the exhaustion that threatens to overtake me, kept at bay until now by pure adrenaline. The clock on the dash reads 12:53. Barely two and a half hours since this insanity began.

"Where're we going?" I lean forward and press my palms over my reddening eyes.

"Not sure."

I resist giving an exasperated sigh. "What do you mean 'not sure'? You've been driving this way for ages."

"All I'm trying to do for now is put distance between us and the people who want you dead. Any complaints with that?" She flicks her gaze towards me, but this time there's a glint in her eyes I hadn't seen before. I remain quiet. "I'll take that as a no."

"What's your name?" I ask.

She purses her lips in a reversion back to her hardass self.

"Oh, come on. After everything you've put me through, I deserve at least that."

A moment of silence, but finally she says, "Corinna. Corinna Floros."

"Well, Corinna, it's—I mean, I wish I could say it's nice to meet you, but—"

"No, I understand. Can't imagine this is your idea of a fun evening."

"What kind of name is Corinna? Not to be rude, I've just never heard it before."

"Macedonian."

"Is that like Greek?"

"No, Macedonian."

"They're basically the same thing though."

She half-laughs, more of a breathy bark, and her eyes glitter like topaz. "Not if you ask the Greeks. You?"

"Eugene."

"God, I'm so sorry."

"About time you said something like that."

"Sorry for your name, not for the fact that I'm saving your ass."

I ignore the jab. "Saving my ass from a situation you put me into."

"Still, saving it."

After another glance in the empty rearview mirror, she pulls off the highway and onto a ramshackle asphalt road that spits up black crumbs as we drive. Corinna heads us into a motel parking lot almost entirely devoid of cars, the one sign in the lot flickering an infected yellow. On the other side of the lot is a desolate strip mall that looks more haunted-house than center-of-commerce, and a couple men loiter under the sheltered walkway, passing a thin, lighted object between them. In the back is a rusted dumpster, and a few very happy raccoons duck behind it as our headlights pass over them.

"Why're we stopping?" I ask.

The car jerks to a halt as she puts it in park, then leans over the console to grab a vinyl duffle bag so worn that it's become shiny.

"C'mon." Corinna throws open her door. "We're getting a room."

My eyes widen and my heart leaps into my mouth again—but this time for a different reason. "A room? But why do—"

"You're tired, aren't you? If you're going to be any use, you need to be on your A-game. Which as of right now, you definitely aren't."

"Of any *use*?" I spit.

"Unless you can think of a different way out of the mess we're in, I don't see many other options." She slams the door shut and, though I can only hear her faintly through the glass, asks, "Are you coming or what?"

I follow.

CORINNA JAMS the duct-taped keycard into its slot and herds me inside, never letting me out of her sights by even a hair. With the door chained and the deadbolt flipped, she then points to the far corner of the motel room, one of the few places the blue and orange flecked carpet isn't worn through, and tells me to stay there until she's done with…well, whatever it is she's doing. I go to the corner and slump down against the wall, trying to make myself as unnoticeable as possible.

From the duffle bag she pulls out a tapered wooden block, gathers up the hair dryer from the bathroom and grabs some towels. She wraps the dryer cord from the bathroom handle to the main door, the bathroom door keeping the other from opening by more than a crack. The wooden block she jams under the entryway, flat edge first to keep anyone from forcing their way in, and the towels line what minuscule crack remained under the door, that open space all that had connected me to the free world.

Some part of my brain worries that, if there's a fire, we'd lose precious seconds undoing her security measures in an attempt to escape—but the other part of me is too tired to care. A fire is the least of my worries right now.

Corinna gets up and brushes carpet lint from her pants. "How do you sleep?"

"What?" I ask, too disoriented to string her words together.

"Not a hard question, Gigi."

"*Gigi?*" I fumble for a stronger retort but come up empty. I've been called a lot of names before, but this is a new one.

"How do you sleep?"

"Far more important, do *not* call me Gigi—"

"On your back? In the fetal position?"

"I—" Already another skirmish I know I'm going to lose. I crinkle my eyes shut and rub my brows. "On my stomach. Arms under my head."

"Perfect. Anything you need to do before you go to sleep?"

"What, are you setting curfew?"

"Something like that. You need your rest and babysitting all night isn't my idea of fun." She loosens her boot laces and pulls them off to show the silhouette of trim, muscled calves beneath. "So yes, it's your bedtime."

Unbelievable. I watch as she rummages through her bag and pulls out something that slithers over her palms: rope. Icy shards prickle in my gut.

"For tonight I'll be tying one of your wrists to the bed." Before I have the chance to protest, she continues. "Don't get any weird ideas. I can't have you sneaking off to god-knows-where in the middle of the night. For now, it's non-negotiable. Are we good?"

"What do you expect me to say? Yes?"

"So we're good?"

'No' is what I want to say, but I'm getting better at figuring out which battles to pick with her. "One condition, and then I'll cooperate."

"You're not in much of a bargaining position." She turns the rope over in her callused hands and a chill slips down my spine. I don't have to fear her—if she wanted to kill me, she would've done it already—but that doesn't mean she isn't dangerous.

"No, but me cooperating will make life easier for you, won't it?"

She sweeps her gaze over me. There's something inhuman in the gesture, something old and animal as she weighs the options. The buzzing lamp behind her outlines her form, her musculature powerful yet feminine. Even in the murky light her skin is the warm brown of hazelnuts. I meet her eyes. Still staring, still unreadable. I swallow down the golf ball that's found its way up my throat.

"Fine." She tilts her head to the side. "One condition."

"Tell me why you needed Brendon Watts' help and what I'm getting into."

She shakes her head with a laugh, then looks at me with mirth still shining on her face. Crouching down, Corinna levels her gaze with mine. "I'm trying to find a way to die."

A stillness comes over me. I feel like I've just seen a bird break its wing or watched a rabbit run under speeding tires—before my sympathies reach the end of their leash. She has a gun. She has rope and god knows what else. People are after her. She has an abundance of ways to die right at her fingertips.

"Is that some sort of joke?" I ask.

"No, though I'm sure it sounds like one."

"Don't lie to me." I feel my patience wear thin again.

"Afraid I'm telling the truth. The hard part in achieving this is because I can't die." She shrugs with a sigh. "Because I'm immortal."

A ringing fills my ears, drowning out whatever other words she has for me. She's not just dangerous, she's *crazy*. Corinna snaps her fingers in front of my nose.

"Are you listening?"

I nod—well perhaps 'nod' isn't the correct word. I violently shake my head up and down, because here's the thing about crazy people. They don't know they're crazy. Everyone sometimes wonders if they're sane, but not so much with people living in their own realities. It's not their fault, they didn't ask to be afflicted with a chemical imbalance or instability, but I'm not in the mood to indulge any bleeding-heart sentiments at the moment.

"What do you, uh, what do you need me for then?" I ask. *Voice steady, stay calm.*

"Don't worry, I know you probably don't believe me. But I appreciate you playing along." She unclips the hair and lets it tumble to the small of her back, a wave of diving ravens. "I need to retrieve a very specific object called a domukardi, a box that my heart is in. The domukardi can only be opened by a mortal, which is why I initially sought out Brendon."

"What made you pick him?"

"Nothing." She leans a shoulder up against the wall. "Any mortal would've done."

Good to know that even now my life has stuck to its inescapable pattern: the commonplace, the mundane of this world is the literal decider of my destiny.

"The box has been lost for a long time, but I've been tracing it and think I know where it's headed next. Downside is that it's likely being watched."

"And as for what I'm getting myself into?"

Corinna quirks a thick brow at me as the devil's grin itself comes alive on her mouth. "I'm sure you already know the answer to that."

"Trouble?"

A nod.

Of course. That's all it's been so far.

"Then why were those people shooting at us if you're just trying to die? Why do they care, and why don't they want me to help you?"

"Mm, answering that wasn't part of our agreement. I've upheld my end, now you do yours." She swings the rope from her hand in a lazy circle. "Do whatever you need to, then it's lights out."

I bite down a handful of choice words. "Can I at least grab something to eat?"

"We're not really in the position to go out to dinner."

"I haven't had enough calories today."

"You track that kind of thing?"

I pat my eyes—a habit I've developed in place of rubbing my eyes ever since I learned that you can thin your corneas enough to need a transplant.

"Yes," is all I say.

"Sorry." She shrugs. I get the feeling she's not sorry at all. "You'll have to rough it this evening."

I look to the cheap plastic alarm clock. There's no way I'll get enough rest nor enough calories, nor do any of my nightly routine that I've clung to for ages. It always changed, depending on what I was fixated on at any given time, but the objectives were the same. Protect myself. Stay insulated from any danger, immediate or long term.

Look how well that's worked out.

I grab my face in my hands and give an even sigh, because I'm worried that if I let it go uneven, something in me will crack and spill out and I won't be able to stuff it back in. A numbness spreads through me to my very fingertips. I've been so stupid. Caring about all of the wrong things, fighting things outside of my control, and even now, faced with someone who could very well end me, I'm thinking about *calories?*

I hear Corinna shift and finally look at her. Her forehead is lined in—concern? Probably not, but it looks an awful lot like it.

"I'm going to take a piss," I say. Words more coarse than those I'd normally use, but it's one of the few ways I can give my resentment teeth.

"Of course."

I stand and head to the bathroom. It's hard not to throw a glance over my shoulder, to not check my many blind spots. Not like it'll do any good.

From the moment my shoes squeak against the icy linoleum, everything slows as if my world has been submerged into a bottle of molasses, and a hyper-clear focus crystallizes around me. There has to be a way out of this. I'm a good student—what the hell, this isn't the time for modesty; I'm a *damn* good student—and a decent enough problem solver. There will be a way out. I just have to find it.

But I have to continue to look unthreatening. Insignificant. I flip on the bathroom fan, then drop my pants to take a much needed whiz as I scan the bathroom for something to use. She has a gun and the upper hand physically, so I'll have to catch her by surprise or give her the slip.

Then I see it. Next to the grimy base of the toilet sits a full trash bin that housekeeping must have skipped over. Nestled amongst crushed-up receipts and a condom wrapper and used tissues, there sits a rusted, half-orange-half-silver razor blade. My stomach drops into my butt. Nausea swoops through me, but I swallow it down.

If I'm going to get out of here, I need to get through that rope. And, short of gnawing through it, the blade before me is all I have at my disposal.

Had it been used to cut drugs? Fentanyl can kill you

through skin contact alone—but you don't cut that with a razor, do you? What if someone used it to cut themselves and now there's some kind of infected blood on it? As I stare at the razor, the hundred things that could be contaminating it dance through my mind, a parade of possible ailments and deaths.

But poison is before me either way, so it's time to pick which I would rather take.

Biting down on my free hand clenched into a fist, trying to keep my retching back, I pluck the blade from the trash between my forefinger and thumb and hold it away from me like a roach.

"You alright?" Corinna asked.

"Fine!" I say a bit too fast, then sit on the toilet. What with the bathroom door propped open, Corinna could walk in at any minute, a chance I'm not willing to gamble with. Might as well try to look as normal as possible.

Swallowing down the gag rising in my throat, I cup the blade in my palm. I curl and uncurl my hand, but there's no way for me to keep the sharp edges from touching my skin. I bite my lip with a moan. Corinna probably thinks my strained noises are for some other bathroom-related reason. Fine by me. As I move to stash the blade in my pocket, I almost wrap it in toilet paper, but even the smallest thing out of place could tip her off. Could it cut me through my jeans, though?

There was a time when I thought my paranoia would help keep me alive, not hinder me like this. I'll be damned if today is the day it does me in. No, today I live. Today I begin to lift this damned yoke off my neck.

I stash the blade in my pocket, splash a handful of metallicy water over my face, rub it dry on my collar, and head back out.

"Survived giving birth?" she asks from the corner of the room, flipping through one of the local newspapers as I flop onto the bed. What is she looking for, yard sale ads?

"I've survived you, haven't I?" Somehow my exhaustion has yet to take all the wit from me.

"You ready to get some shut eye?" She stands and walks over to where I am.

I reluctantly nod and roll my eyes, trying to look like I've accepted the situation, like I don't already have an escape plan ready to burst into fruition. I lay down. She arches a brow at me.

"There's no way someone like you sleeps with their shoes on," she says.

"What's that supposed to mean?"

"You're going to tell me I'm wrong?" When I don't answer, her eyes tighten. "What, do you have plans to go somewhere?"

I swallow. But, in the interest of lessening any of her suspicions, I kick off my shoes and socks before laying back down. Corinna wraps the cord around my wrist and loops it thrice, not loose enough for me to shimmy out of but with enough slack that I can tell she's not trying to be an asshole. A small consolation. The slickness of the rope catches me by surprise. I'd expected something rough, itchy, but this feels more akin to braided hair. There's a tug on my wrist as she fastens me to the bed frame.

"This knot can only be untied with two hands, so don't bother. You just rest, refuel your tank, and we'll be back on the move tomorrow."

"Doing what?"

"Deciding our next move. Now hush." Corinna perches herself on the edge of the bed facing the door and picks up her newspaper again, pistol in her lap like it's a teacup Pomeranian.

That's my cue. I turn my head on the pillow so that I can see her, arms cushioned against my cheek, and close my eyes. Ten minutes later, a reasonable amount of time to fall asleep in, I fake a light snore that rumbles throughout my chest.

Fifteen minutes more of pretending and stomping down my growing nerves. Every so often I peer out from between my lashes to see if she's grown at all drowsy. Little luck, but at least she's moved off the bed and is wedged back into the corner, elbow propped up on her duffle bag. This time it's a National Geographic in her hands—or at least I think so. It's hard to tell in the dimness, plus my lashes obscure most of what I can see. Whatever light there is now is what's managed to slip through the drooping curtains covering the window to the parking lot.

The window. She's rigged the door like some next-level booby trap, but the window was her slip up. The last part of my plan solidified, I set to work. With a free hand already down by my side, I slowly reach into my pocket and grab the razor blade, careful to only touch the flat sides. It's tiny between my fingers, barely bigger than half a stick of gum. I'm still disgusted by the mere thought of where this thing has been, but simultaneously reassured to have it at all. I tighten my hold.

Letting out a jarring snore for good measure, I pretend to readjust and bring my arm up by my head, hand under the pillow. I look to Corinna again. Her head leans back against the wall, eyes shut and, if I'm not mistaken, her shoulders lilt ever so softly in rhythm with her breathing. Asleep, or at the very least dozing.

I feel for the rope and wiggle the blade out from between my fingers with caution. A slashed wrist won't do me any good. I angle the edge downwards and begin to saw at my bonds. Back and forth, back and—no, readjust so it doesn't slip, okay, then forth, then finally I feel the satisfying crackle of fibers giving way. I jiggle my wrist and it moves without restriction. *Freedom.* For the first time in too long, I feel actual tears of joy.

But I'm not out of these bizarre woods yet. I double-check that Corinna is sleeping before slowly raising myself off the mattress. The coils squeal. I bite down on my lip and taste blood, but she doesn't stir. I tiptoe to the window and shimmy through the curtains, trying to keep as much of the parking lot's flickering light out as possible. Ever so careful, I peel back the window latch, pressing down hard to keep it from issuing that signature tinny pop, then slide the window open. The cool bite of nighttime air caresses my palm as I stick my hand out.

"Not a smart move, Eugene," I hear Corinna say, voice flat and calm behind me.

I don't stop to think. Immediately I dive out the window, planting face-first into a sun-bleached flower bed, and scramble to my feet. *Go, go, go.* I might not be the strongest person in the state—let's be honest, not even the motel—but more often than not the antelope outruns the lion. Gritting my teeth against the shrieking voice in my head, I force my bare feet to run into the parking lot, even as the asphalt glitters with broken glass.

I glance over my shoulder to see Corinna following close behind, face set with agitation and exhaustion all at once. What I don't see is her pointing any sort of weapon my way. It's nice I can at least be reassured that, true to her word, she doesn't intend to kill me for now. I veer around the adjacent strip mall, its siding plastered with 'help wanted' and 'for sale' signs. The vaguely sticky ground brings a new wave of bile searing into the back of my throat.

A hand yanks me to the side, but not from the direction I expect. My skull smacks against the exposed brick and yet more stars appear in the spangled sky. I try to blink them away.

"A bit late for a jog, ain't it?" My mugger's breath smells of acrid smoke and ineffective mints, and he leans in to tower over me. The fist curled around my shirtfront has to be the size of a cantaloupe. "Pockets. Turn 'em out, now."

Cursing whatever god or demon sees to my luck, I do as

asked. I've pushed myself out of one mud slick just to slide directly into another. My hands hardly reach my jeans before Corinna rounds the corner, and my new friend's face quirks up in a study of folds and ingrown beard hairs.

"Turn around and get ba—"

"How many times are we going to do this?" It takes me a second to process that she's talking to me, not even registering my current situation.

"You're crazy," I seethe. Being surrounded by danger on all fronts gives me some pluck, I guess. "You're *clinically insane*, not immortal."

He spits towards her. "You looking for a problem?"

"Let him go and we won't have one." She continues to stride forward undeterred, no fear, no hesitation—nothing but measured reassurance. But anyone with half a brain knows how this is going to end. He's a full two heads taller, so there's little chance he'll find her imposing enough to obey. Corinna comes to a halt, feet shoulder width apart with one a bit ahead of the other, and while I might not be sure what exactly that means, I know it means something.

"Get lost, bitch."

He swats a hand in her direction, a mistake I see unfold in slow motion. Her front knee bends, her bare back heel lifts off the gritty asphalt. Corinna lunges for him and he spins towards her, hand going for his pocket. A cruel metal glints in the scant light—a knife. Before I can shout a warning, he swings down and plunges the blade towards her chest. It hits hilt deep, knifepoint buried between her ribs. Cold adrenaline roils through me and I feel acid in my throat. A heartbeat passes. Another. She flicks her eyes up at him, still standing, not staggering to her bloody end, and claps her hand atop his as the air crackles with the heat of her fury.

A millisecond later he's face down on the pavement, her hands at his forearm and shoulder to grind him into the trash-strewn, dust-choked ground. The blade still sticks out from

Death of an Immortal

her chest like a garish Halloween prop, but she pays it no mind.

"A wrenched arm in exchange for a stab. Hardly seems fair, huh?" She digs her heel into the back of his ribs and he screams out, voice echoing off the building but with no one around to care. "Try to come after me and I'll make us even."

She releases him with a final jab. He curls his arm towards himself with a whimper, eyes wide and the side of his cheek gashed a tender pink by the paving. Corinna rips the knife from her chest with a *schlup*, wipes its dark red sheen on the thigh of her pants, then cuts her gaze down to slits. "Run."

He scrambles off the ground, but I don't see where he disappears to from there. I can't. My heart beats into my very teeth, reverberating through every inch of my body down to the tips of my hair. It's not possible. But she's still standing, alive and well even after being stabbed in the heart. I saw the blade go in firsthand.

"Get back inside," she says—no, she *commands*. Authoritative. Not someone to be crossed, and yet she's saved my life. Twice, if I'm to believe her. "Now."

SHE SLAMS THE WINDOW SHUT. I stand in the corner, too rattled to even quiver or wipe the grime off my feet. Corinna's back stays to me, her shoulders hunched over. Heat rises in my throat and I try to swallow it down. My breaths grow shallow and the room threatens to spin. She turns to face me, this time with a vindicated fire. Not daring to so much as breathe, I look up at her.

And then she starts to peel off her shirt.

I throw my hands up in front of me and my cheeks turn hot. What am I, some maiden guarding my honor? "W-Wait! I—"

My voice catches in my throat as she tosses her shirt at my

feet. Her wet shirt, stained with a dab of something warm. Warm and sticky and reeking of iron. I draw my foot back and it comes away with a spot of red. I look to see her standing in a thin-strapped bra, but more important is what I don't see. The gash from mere minutes ago stitches itself together before my eyes, as if pulled back together by some invisible healer's hand, the blood staunched down to no more than a few beads.

"Believe me now?" she asks.

"You should've died," I stammer. I rub my eyes as if somehow that'll set the world back into order, as if she'll somehow drop dead in accordance with natural law, but still she stands. I point at her wound, now little more than a paper cut. "It's… It's fixing itself."

"Can I take that as a yes?"

My throat tightens, at a loss for words. She pulls at the underside of her bra, and my muteness breaks. "Why is your response to get progressively more naked?"

"Come here." She motions me over, bra still thankfully on. She pulls up the underside to expose the lower quarter of her breast and my eyes dart towards the ceiling. My lower abdomen—and perhaps a bit lower than that—experiences a confused flush of heat. "Don't be such a Puritan. Look. Damn it, Eugene, *look*."

I cave in and hesitantly lower my eyes, then a gut-heavy pang of shock spikes through me. A scar at least six inches long and with ragged, shiny edges stretches along her ribcage. Whatever caused this, it's easy to see the cut ran deep. Deep enough to kill.

"From where they took out my heart. Cracked open my rib cage, cut my heart out, and made me what I am now. Made me immortal."

My fingers stretch towards the wound. I stop. She grabs my fingers and presses them against the smooth surface, slick as marble.

Death of an Immortal

"How's that possible?" I ask, unable to keep the horrified wonder from my voice.

"It's a long story." She turns away from me and heads into the bathroom, then reemerges with a damp washcloth to wipe the drops of crusted blood from her torso. "Was long thought impossible. Still is. But a rather clever Persian alchemist and his master were determined enough to crack its secrets—or some of them, anyhow."

She tosses the cloth aside and rummages through her duffle bag before slipping into an identical shirt. Faint pink light begins to slice through the curtains. Morning already. I drop my head into my hands and rub my eyes. *She was telling the truth*. What does that mean for me?

Whoever is after us—me—no longer seems like the figment of a lunatic's imagination. The peril I'm in is suddenly very real. And if it is real, then I need her help getting out of it. Whatever lies before me is dangerous, yes, but I'm out of options. All she needs is for me to tag along and steal an object, one that's rightfully hers by the sound of it, open it, and I'll be rid of this ordeal. If that's the price I have to pay to put all this behind me, so be it.

That, and I'm still half-stunned from seeing her shrug off a should-have-been-fatal stab as if it were a mere slap. To say my confidence in her has risen would be an understatement, even if I still have some reservations, but the fact of the matter is clear: my chances are better with her. At least until this is all over.

"I believe you," I say.

She turns to me with raised brows, unlaced boots in hand. Her eyes rake over me, skeptical, before softening. "I appreciate that."

"And I'm willing to help you."

"Well, makes my life easier." A smile quirks up at the corner of her mouth, yet it holds the brilliance of a star. She tosses her bag over her shoulder with a rattling clang. Not sure I want to know what else is in there. "Ready?"

I pick her jacket up off the floor and hand it to her. Our eyes meet, linking in a way words can't, and this close I see no lenses in her eyes that could've turned them so gold. A side effect of her immortality, perhaps.

Finally, I nod.

"Yeah. I'm ready."

4

BREATH OF AIR

I CHEW ON A BLUEBERRY MUFFIN, its texture like dense styrofoam, and wash it down with a questionable carton of milk. The inked expiration date is smudged down the side, but it smells fine. Fine for lukewarm milk, at least, but I need to catch up on my calories and calcium and protein deficits from yesterday. Corinna sits in the driver's seat and bites into a red delicious, those too-red, waxy apples, then makes a face suggesting it doesn't live up to its name. She wipes her mouth with the newspaper in her hand. The gun still rests in her lap.

I stretch out in the back seat and prop my elbows up on the middle console. The insides of my head feel jittery, and not just from my sugar-laden breakfast. Despite me trying to ignore it, I know why my focus is fraying. My medicine. It's early in the day, so it's not too bad yet, but I can only miss so many doses before I'm more or less useless. The situation with Corinna isn't going to go away—I've promised her that and intend to keep my word—but neither is this. I clutch my stomach and sigh.

"That muffin threatening to make another appearance?" She throws me one of the many bananas she's stashed on the floorboards. "Go with fruit. Much less disappointing in the long run."

"No, it's not the muffin. I will take that though." I peel back the banana and bite into it, trying to focus on my rhythmic breathing and chewing. *Breathe in, out. Breathe in—* "I have to go back to my house."

She snorts. "Lame escape attempt."

"No, I mean I have medicine I need to get if I'm going to help you. And I do want to help you, given everything."

Her eyes soften. "Thank you. It—that means a lot to me." Then a shrug. "Not that you have much of a choice, but still. So, to a drugstore?"

"It's a prescription. It'll just take me two minutes to swing in the house and grab it. Then we can be on our way."

Corinna's mouth drops open, brow creased as if I've somehow offended her. "That's two hours the other way!"

"At least we're still in Texas."

"Because this is a huge state! It's bigger than all of France, for god's sakes!"

"Look, I know it's not convenient, but I'm…" The words stick in my mouth like peanut butter, difficult to get out. "Without it, I'll just slow us down."

"Have your doctor call it in to a pharmacy near us."

"Oh." I blink. "I didn't know they would do that."

She hands me her brick-like burner phone, and I stare at it. While the number was programmed into my old phone, it wasn't one of those I'd exactly dedicated time to memorizing.

"Just call information," Corinna says as if she'd read my mind. My expression must look vacant, because she snatches the phone from my hand and punches in the directory's dial code. She puts the phone to her ear and looks at me. "What's your doctor's office called?"

I give her the name and she repeats it in an artificially clear voice to the automated entity on the other end. After a pause, Corinna digs a pen out of the console's cup holder and scribbles a number onto her hand. She hangs up, then puts in the number and hands the phone over to me.

"Carson Medical Clinic," an uninterested voice drawls from the receiver.

"Hello," I stammer. Phone conversations should be the last thing that gets my anxieties riled up right now, but still my voice wavers. "I need to refill a prescription."

"Date of birth."

"February 26, 1995."

I hear the clicking of her keyboard, and then a sigh. "It's been over a year since your last physical, sir. We can't refill any medications without a current one on file."

"It's kind of urgent." I swallow and squeeze my eyes shut even as my words falter. I'm not one to argue with staff, but I at least have to try.

"Would you like to schedule an appointment?"

"Uh," I sigh, "sure."

"Our next availability is August 13th. Is there a time you'd prefer?"

I choke back a pathetic sound, half like a squawk, at the date. That's over 3 weeks from now.

"So much for that." Corinna snatches the phone from my hand and hangs up, lip curling and brow furrowing. I catch her mutter something about red tape. "On a scale from one to ten, tell me how much you need these pills. Really, genuinely need them."

I chew on the inside of my cheek and stare ahead at the stringy clouds gliding along the horizon. She has the stronger will between the two of us, but I'm not going to let her sway me on this. "Ten."

"Be serious, Eugene."

"I am."

"Nothing could be *that* important. Not unless you were going to keel over without it."

I sense the question in her tone, but I don't budge. She has her secrets and I have mine. I sit there, arms folded across my chest, and stay silent.

"Listen," she growls, "all of this rides on you staying alive, so I need you to cooperate."

"You might find this hard to believe, but I'm pretty invested in staying alive too."

We exchange tight glares. While I don't exactly cut an intimidating figure, I fight to keep my sights locked against hers.

She pinches the bridge of her nose with a groan, and finally her shoulders fall. "Good thing for you, we have some leads that take us back down south anyhow. But for future reference, let me know about things like this ahead of time."

"Yeah, of course. Next time I'm being abducted, I'll stop to ask if I can swing by my house for personal belongings first."

"I don't need your sass this early in the morning, Gigi."

"That has to stop."

"Then stop being sassy." She leans her chair back with a squeal of its hinges and stares upwards. "Problem is, Lycus's men might already have your house under surveillance."

"What kind of a name is Lycus?"

"An old one, and the name of the man who wants you dead. The people we've had to put up with this far have just been his hired guns. Doubt we'll see Lycus in the flesh any time soon."

I can't help but notice the slight snarl that catches in her chest. Perhaps they have more history between them than this ordeal alone. "Do you know him?"

Corinna laughs without mirth. "Oh, I know him, and in more ways than one. But he's not pertinent right now. You are."

"You said I might be under surveillance?"

"Likely, but I can't say for sure. Are you sure you can't just—"

"I need it," I say, a bit sharper than necessary, but I don't care. So long as she gets that this isn't a topic I'll be transparent about. "Without it, you might as well find yourself someone else."

An exasperated groan escapes her as she grinds her palms against her eyes. "Fine. Fine, we'll go back for it. But when we get there, you follow my instructions to a T. Just in case. Deal?"

I nod, extending my hand to her. She looks me up and down without trying to cover her irritation.

"This is Texas," I say. "A deal's not a deal without shaking on it."

After a moment, an unexpected laugh escapes her. "Old fashioned. I like it."

She clasps my hand and gives it a firm shake. Entwined with mine, I feel thick calluses padding the ridges beneath her knuckles and the planes of her palm. Definitely not a newcomer to fighting. Is that what she's been doing in the many years she's been alive?

"Then back south we go. I know most of the main roads, but you'll have to guide me once we get closer in. We're taking a few pit stops along the way."

"Pit stops?" I shimmy into the front passenger seat and toss the banana peel into a grocery-bag-turned-trash-bin. "It's a two hour drive. Pretty sure I can hold it."

"One, you seem delicate as a dandelion, so I'm not inclined to believe that. Two, we're not taking bathroom stops. We're going shopping."

I stare at her for a long moment, expecting to hear 'sike' or its equivalent. Her face remains deadpan flat. After a long minute, something akin to a staring contest, I give in. "What, you want to add a little color to your wardrobe?"

"You need less recognizable clothes—the Chicken Bucket shirt is cute but sticks out like, well, like a chicken in a bucket, plus it reeks of fry oil—, we both need at least one nice outfit so we can blend in to some places we might scout, and we need food. More food, outside of the muffin variety."

I sniff a handful of my shirt and crinkle my nose. Saying it merely reeks of fry oil is kind. Sweat and the scent of rotting garbage from last night's alleyway have melded into a truly horrifying olfactory experience. Whatever embarrassment I feel, I try to keep my face from betraying me. "Can we pick up some deodorant too?"

"Whatever your heart desires."

She throws the car into reverse and makes for the other side of town. After fastening my seatbelt, I reach for my pocket before stopping myself. Were this a run-of-the-mill errand, I'd search for the nearest store on my phone—except that she'd chucked it under the merciless wheels of highway-goers. I slump back into my seat.

"You'll survive without your phone. Pinky promise."

"Okay, how do you do that? Know what people are thinking?"

"Read people long enough and you get fluent in it. Plus I figure you still haven't forgiven me for destroying your phone."

"I haven't, but it's not that I *need* it. I just want to let my family know I'm okay, in case they're trying to get a hold of me."

"I'm sure Spain has more than enough to keep them distracted."

I feel my eyes widen. "How long have you been following me again?"

"Just since the night I saw you at the coffee shop. I got into your email, that's all."

"Oh, *that's* all. Good," I huff in mock-relief, hands thrown up in the air.

"Who're you worried is going to come looking for you?"

I look out the window at the scraggly, dust-choked countryside, mouth set in a firm line. One of my most painful realizations last night had been that no one would come looking for me, not for a few weeks at least. Were my parents home, they would, of course, but realizing that I don't have any friends, any significant other concerned for me... It stung. Stings.

"No one. No one at all."

Even to my own ears, it sounds pathetic. In a way though, I'm not sure how much I care about that anymore.

We come to a halt at a four way stop and Corinna puts a hand on my shoulder. Her eyes don't meet mine, as if a single touch is the most open she can bear to be with me. The gesture alone brings me up short. She continues to stare ahead, but something heavy rests in her gaze, something ageless and infinitely sorrowful.

"I know what that's like," she says after a beat. "I'm sorry."

Her grip tightens before she lets go, then we continue on through the intersection, no more words between us. That hollow darkness retreats, prodded by whatever ray of light her hand carried. Despite myself, I let a smile slip.

We drive on, and I drum my fingers against my thigh. Normally when my nerves chomp at the bit like this, I go down some useless digital rabbit hole to occupy my mind, clicking from one link to the next until the feeling subsides. I never thought of that as a luxury, but regardless, it's one more thing I'll have to do without for now. Instead I focus on my breathing, the expanding and contracting of my ribcage. After a while, my rapid heartbeat returns to normal.

We roll into the parking lot of a decrepit strip mall, asphalt crumbling like wafers and balled up trash collecting in the corners, and I see a white dollar store sign. Well, it was once white. Probably. The passing tanker trucks and dust storms have filled its cracks with brown dust, turning the whole thing a murky color.

"Wouldn't a bigger store be better?" I ask as we step out of the car. "We could get everything at once then."

She tosses a light windbreaker on and throws up the hood, hair tucked into the collar. "The exact opposite, actually. The smaller the place, the less it pops up on Lycus's radar. We can only stay on the outskirts for so long, but let's at least try to keep a streak going while we can."

We walk inside and head towards the food aisle. *The food aisle?* I didn't think dollar stores had those—or, I hoped they didn't. What edible food can we even get for that cheap?

"Stop looking so beside yourself." Corinna squats down to inspect one of the lower shelves of boxed nutrition bars, then drags her finger over their glossy packaging. "Pick a few things you'll eat and we can get on our way."

I pick up a box of blue-colored, berry-flavored toaster pastries and wrinkle my nose. I can only imagine the potential stomachache I hold in my hand.

"Those are surprisingly good," she says as she picks out a sealed medley of nuts and dried fruit. "Awful for you, but it's incredible what they can do to food nowadays."

"People shouldn't *do* anything to food."

"So you eat all your food raw, then?"

I shoot her a withering look.

"Hey, I've eaten my fair share of disgusting things throughout the years—I don't just mean dry meatloaf—and the modern world has finally given me berry-flavored pastries? It could be a lot worse."

"What's the worst thing you've ever eaten?" I ask. As immature as it is, I can't quell my curiosity.

"I've seen enough people die of hunger to not be picky."

A weight plops into my stomach. That ends that line of questioning.

As I paw through the boxes of cereal bars, a card-sized notepad pokes into the corner of my vision. It looks like an inventory list has been scrawled onto it and promptly lost back here in the shelving, its owner none the wiser. None the wiser...

Corinna crouches down at the end of the aisle, basket in hand. While I don't have my phone, there's nothing to say I can't leave a note for whoever might come to my house looking for me. I've agreed to help Corinna and I'll stick by that, but who knows how long I'll be gone? It might not be how she wants things to go, but she'll survive my small rebellions. I grab two boxes of honey-nut bars and slide the notepad into my butt pocket.

We check out and I do my best to keep her immersed in conversation—a blatant distraction, but for all she knows it's because I got more food than necessary. After hauling everything into the car, we stop by two more locales, the last one a big box store with its red-bullseye luring us to the parking lot. How do these places always seem to crop up in the middle of nowhere? As we approach, I roll out my sore neck and stretch my aching back, done no favors by our escapade.

The smell of hot pretzels curls around my nose the second we pass through the sliding glass doors. My head snaps towards their glistening rack by my left, chunks of snow-white salt dotting the top of decadently soft brown crust. Even my ever-increasing exhaustion is second priority next to those.

"We have food in the car." Corinna shoves a plastic basket at me.

I do my best to keep from letting out a sigh and to ignore the saliva pooling in my mouth. Though as I look around, I see the relative wonders the store has to offer. In here, it's a microcosm. In here, I can control things, no matter how small. I breathe a bit easier and walk on the right side of the aisles, just as order dictates—though Corinna doesn't, bobbing around anyone in her path. I get multiple pumps of free hand sanitizer from the dispensers throughout the store until it smells like I've dipped my hands in vodka. It brings me a strange comfort.

We make for the toiletry aisle and Corinna chucks in a few small items. A thumb-sized tube of toothpaste. Blue, waxy floss. A tiny black pot of some cream I've never heard of. I neatly reorganize them in the basket.

"Now's your chance to stock up," she says, rummaging through the clearance bins. "I already snagged you a toothbrush from the hotel plus shampoo and soap, so the rest of it's up to you."

"I can just grab it from my house."

Corinna straightens and wheels around to face me, eyes a mix between confusion and ire. I blink. Apparently that wasn't the right thing for me to say.

"Are you trying to get killed? Or do you just feel bad for Lycus's men and want to make their jobs easier?"

I throw my hands up. "Look, we're already going to be there. Might as well—"

"What, might as well screw up everything we've done up to this point?" Her gaze pierces through me, and I see my own reflection shining back. Young. Naive. Barely clinging to a shallow impression of stability. With a sigh, she stops and closes her eyes, forcing out level breaths. "I don't mean to get angry. You have to understand though, the more time we spend at your house, the more danger we're in. We need to be careful. I'm sorry, but no extra risks, okay?"

"Yeah." I hesitate, a bit taken aback by her apology. "I get it. No worries."

She nods in thanks, anything to keep us from having to say niceties aloud, and I stack a handful of travel sized items into the basket. I didn't even stop to check what they were. I just want to show her that I understand. I get why she's concerned, and it is for my safety after all. For a professional —well, I have no idea what kind of professional she is, but still—to put up with a novice like me must be tiring. Her mouth twitches upwards.

"Now," she says, heading to the far side of the store, "onto clothing."

"You planning to attend any fancy parties?" I say.

"We both are, actually. More of a private exhibition than a party, but same attire."

"Uh, what?" I can't imagine wine and cheese being how she breaks up the tension in her life, but it wouldn't be the first surprise I've had.

"I have a lead on where my domukardi is. After some tracking, I think I've found an exhibition that might be what we've been waiting for. Well, what I've been waiting for. We'll need to blend in as best we can."

Before I know it we've walked into the maze of the women's clothing department, an array of cuts and colors engulfing us. Corinna heads to the back wall and returns with a few dresses slung over her arm, some fabrics shimmery and gold, others a dark matte. There are other differences, sure, but as someone who's never put myself in more than jeans and a t-shirt, I can't put a name to them.

"I'll pick mine out first, then we find you something to match. Deal?"

"Sure, no problem. You go do your thing." My butt doesn't even reach the waiting bench before she yanks me up.

"Aren't you going to help me?" she asks.

My cheeks flush. "Uh, with what?"

"Picking out what I'm going to wear."

"Why would you need help with that? You're a grown woman—well, half grown." I survey her short stature and tuck away an impish grin. For once I get to make the barbs, if only to cover my embarrassment. One look at her face tells me she's going to exact vengeance for that. Still, worth it.

"Just come with me." She grabs my shirtfront and drags me into the changing room hall. Beige particleboard lines us on each side, soul-sucking under the florescent lights, and she finds an open stall before pointing a finger at my chest.

"Stay."

I don't have a chance to protest at being ordered around before she slips inside and latches the door behind her. Perhaps it's time to accept the dynamic. Memories of being towed around with Moira and my mom flood my mind's eye, entire afternoons filled with piles of cheap fabric and deafening shoppers. I rest my head against the wall and sigh, staring at the carpet flecked with suspiciously vibrant stains. Don't want to know. Under the sliver of the door frame, I see Corinna's bare ankles as she shucks her upper garments—*all* of them—to the floor. My eyes shoot up to the ceiling, a sudden interest in the boxy light fixtures. Despite everything around me, the sheer absurdity of the situation I find myself in, I'm calmer than I have been in a long time. Now that my anxiety and paranoia actually have something to latch onto, it's almost as if they've slunk into the shadows to let my more rational brain do the heavy lifting. At least, I hope it's my rational brain.

"I want honest feedback, alright? No reason to make ourselves look like idiots." She steps out of the changing room and my heart stutters in my chest. "Now of course when we're headed to the event I'll be done-up for it, and I'll likely be in heels, but we're focused just on the clothes for now."

It's the dark one I'd glimpsed at earlier, the one that leaves her shoulders and legs up to the mid-thigh bare. When she turns so I can get a full view, hair swinging around her, my gaze doesn't know where to go. What kind of input does she expect out of me? Not the kind I could give, the kind most women would slap me for. I could say that the fabric hugs her from waist to hips, or that its cloudy shade of purple compliments her hair, but even thinking about those things warms my stomach.

Death of an Immortal

I shrug instead. A guy answer. A measured answer. "It's fine, but, uh, maybe something a bit longer? It sounds like a fancy deal. The thing we're going to, I mean."

Corinna's gaze flicks over me, up and down, assessing in the strangest of ways before she goes back into the changing room. "Good call."

I hear the plastic rattle of hangers as she rummages through her collection, like a magpie surrounded by shiny collectibles. She murmurs to herself but I can't make out the words. Something about the dresses that I don't see, the ones that don't pass her inspection. It feels like an hour—an hour in waiting-room time, so likely five minutes in actual time—before she comes out again. When she does, the lull of the ocean beats in my ears.

A pearly fabric hangs from her shoulders to brush the ground, its form loosely knit to her curves with a shimmering undertone of gold. Gilded thread brings together the drapes of cloth, and one of her tanned shoulders is left bare to show the sweep of her collarbone. She's like the gold-dusted fringe of the Milky Way.

"Better?" she asks.

I'm mute. I don't dare say a word—I can't. It'd be near sacrilege. This is the first time she's felt ancient or other to me, looking down at me from some timeless perch. Swallowing, I nod.

"Good, I thought so too."

Her casual air does nothing to remind me of normalcy. Somehow, it highlights her strangeness even more. When she turns to change into her normal clothing, I see the swooping back that leaves her shoulder blades uncovered. Bone moves beneath her skin like rippling sandstone, then the door shuts behind her. It takes more than a moment for my heart to climb down out of my throat. I loose a breath I didn't know I was holding.

A few clattering hangers later, she reemerges and then

we're off to the men's section, where she tosses a pack of solid T-shirts my way and sizes me up for a few button downs. After going with the smaller size then grabbing a pair of black slacks, we wait in the checkout line that's somehow stretched long despite the nonexistent size of this town. 'Village' is a better word. That, plus there are twelve registers in sight yet only two are in use.

Once we reach the front Corinna pays in cash, sliding the crumpled bills across the divide then tossing the flimsy plastic bag over her shoulder. We're almost to the entrance—the sky has turned a milky gray outside—when she veers left, straight towards the scent of sizzling, buttered bread. My brows arch up but I don't object. Hell, I run that way so fast I nearly trip.

"Really?" I ask. I don't care if I sound like a five-year old on his birthday. Anyone who doesn't understand has clearly never tasted these before.

She ignores me and orders two standard issue pretzels, complete with glistening butter and fat pearls of salt. A grin splits my face.

"Who says one's for you?" she says as she takes them from the cashier. My heart feigns seizing until I see her lips twitch. She's *joking?* "Relax, I'm not that cruel. Have at it."

I don't stop to admire the glazed brown crust or chunky flakes of sea salt before the entire thing is in my stomach. I don't stop to even think why she's...but, wait, why *is* she doing this? I pause from licking my fingers—a disgusting habit, and it doesn't help that my hands taste like industrial cleaner—to look at her. There's still that flicker of amusement, but also something more. She returns my gaze, chin tilted up despite the weight in her eyes. A minute passes between us, standing, staring, not saying a word. I see the remorse there, the guilt clear from her earlier words. *I'm sorry I dragged you into all this.*

But I don't need any more apologies, not from someone as

proud as her. It's like seeing a hawk plead with a field mouse. Unnatural. That, plus I don't need the tang of apology muting my pretzel's salty sweetness. Instead, I rip a piece of fluffy bread from hers with a grin.

Consider us even.

She shoves my shoulder—and, good god, she *laughs*—as the natural order falls back into place.

5

THE STAR-SCRAPER

The thief's ink still stained her palms and thumbs, stubborn even against sweat. It'd be another week before the black mess disappeared. Corinna grabbed a handful of wheat stalks and sheared the base with a rusty cutlass, hoping at least the rough handle would do something to make the ink fade. Either way, it wasn't her first time getting caught stealing, but it'd sure be her last if she had anything to say about it.

Dust had choked the life from most of the crops that year, leaving the yields light and her family's stomachs lighter. Word in the marketplace was that the whole region suffered the same, but at least her family was far out enough to make them a rare target for raids. Not that it didn't happen. Not that she blamed them or could say she was any better. Rarely was she caught stealing food from the market, but when she did, her sly, darting steps evaded reprimand. Even if she did get ink splattered on her from time to time. The disappointment on her mother's face was the only hard part—outrunning bazaar authorities or dodging whatever punches they threw was easy enough, fun even, once her older brothers and sisters taught her how to not get hit.

Wheat tossed into the wicker basket around her arm,

Corinna rested her sickle atop the meager pile and made her way home, thatched roof extensions sprawling off from its sides. A brood of russet hens pecked at the ground outside, spearing emerald beetles and lacquered grasshoppers on their beaks. At least they were able to find a meal. She shooed past them and walked under one of the mud-and-reed eaves, the shade instantly cooling her sweaty brow.

"Dinner when Pa and your siblings come back," her mother said, tending a crusted pot bubbling with bright orange eggs and tubers.

Thick smoke curled about the rounded bottom and sparks popped against it. *If there were such a thing as magic,* Corinna thought, *it would be that sound.* Her ten-year-old stomach gurgled at the sight of the frothing bubbles, the egg yolks giving a mouth-watering glaze to the onions and mashed acorns.

It was a small portion though, not nearly enough for six people. Her mother's cheeks had become sunken in recent weeks, but everyone's had. She wasn't sure if her fear of starvation was a legitimate worry—it wouldn't be the first time a family member was lost to nature's cruelty—or paranoia. Still, the crop failures this year had given them little to work with, and for already-poor farmers that could be a death sentence. One couldn't survive on raw wheat alone, and the hens wouldn't continue to lay forever.

From the purpling horizon emerged three silhouettes tugging along a cart—but the numbers did not add up. Not three, but four people had left earlier that morning. Corinna squinted against the dying light as something turned in her stomach. In the cart laid a person, his head just barely bobbing up. She tugged at the patched hem of her mother's skirts.

"Unless you're going to give me a hand, don't be hanging from my neck for attention." She gave a handful of thyme a rough chop.

"I think somebody got hurt," Corinna said, tugging again and pointing westwards.

Her mother's head whipped around and scanned the horizon, then she pulled the clay pot from the fire and grabbed Corinna's hand as they paced up the hills. It was silent as they trudged up and over, their breaths ragged as they fought for what air was left in the barren heat. The figures of her family grew clearer as they approached, and she saw that it was her eldest brother Peithon lying in the cart, his leg swollen, puce, and bent at an odd angle, him clutching around it in agony but not touching the wound itself. Seeing him writhe, seeing pain-induced sweat dampen him, it unsettled something in Corinna's chest.

She'd seen death before. She'd helped her mother wring their chickens' necks and gut the birds, she could remember when her baby brother wasn't strong enough to make it through the first year of life, but this was different. This felt more like an omen, a thing foreboding what was to come. With crops already sparse, a mouth unable to work—nonetheless get about—would be yet another challenge. One that, even then, she doubted her family was ready to face.

With one look at Peithon's leg, her mother's eyes grew as unreadable as the long-absent thunderheads. Usually she was a talkative woman. She chatted with strangers, haggled at markets, and mouthed off about whatever had irritated her that day. But now, nothing.

Her mother and eldest sister navigated him towards the house, not a word between them. And in the space of a moment, Corinna knew deadly change was on the horizon.

∼

CORINNA COULD REMEMBER the exact day her life's path was altered, thrown off course into eternity, and she wasn't even the one who'd cast the die. It was her father. Dad. Pa. She

Death of an Immortal

wished she could say she'd had a choice in her fate, but she didn't. Suspected most people didn't.

It had started, like everything else in times of famine, from a place of desperation. Her father stole in order to put food on the table, but he didn't steal the food itself. That might've been a more palatable crime, more forgivable in the eyes of the law—though any hope of mercy was quixotic at best. No, he didn't target the common man, the market vendors who were almost as hard pressed as he was. Instead he went after the wealthy. Pocketed their wares, snatched whatever rings were left unattended—anything he could sell for sustenance. A loaf of bread provided a day's meal, but a lapis brooch fetched far more.

The whole household knew, of course. How could they not, when Pa came home with loaves of crusty bread, sacks of lentils, and, one day, even a cherished block of goat cheese? She saw the shame in her mother's eyes, but the family ate of it anyway. Famine wasn't the time to cling to lofty ideals.

If only he hadn't gotten caught.

Out collecting the hens' skinny teal eggs together, it was her mother's frozen gaze Corinna followed when her father ran over the hill. Men on horseback, cruel bits in the animals' frothing mouths, followed at his heels—though they could have easily overrun him. But these wolves knew to follow a hare back to its nest. Their short woolen cloaks billowed in the flapping wind, snapping around their frames and cutting them from the hazy sky. Sure enough, she saw that damning ink on her father's hands, like a dark cancer dripping over his skin.

Her mother grabbed her by the shoulders and whipped her around.

"Hide in the crops until me or your siblings come for you." Though her mother's nails dug into her skin, Corinna could still feel the tremor in her fingers. "If it reaches nightfall and no one's come for you, run."

She shoved her towards the fields, no kiss goodbye, no clutching her to her bosom. Corinna hesitated with a look over her shoulder, and her mother smashed one of the eggs at her feet.

"Do as I say!"

It would be years until she realized her mother's severity was out of love, to keep her away for her daughter's own safety. This wasn't a world where women could be both soft-hearted and safe.

Blood and logic rushed out of her head, and deep-seated animal instinct seized hold. She ran, the wheat stalks whipping across her forearms and the growing din ringing in her ears.

Pounding hooves and raspy shouts joined the pleading, then the screaming. The tall grasses obscured her vision, and Corinna crouched further down in them. A weight in her gut said this wasn't something she'd want to see. That, and she didn't want to be scolded by her mother once everything was over.

A crackling noise roared to life as smoke began burning her eyes, and the screaming grew to a fever pitch. She had heard that scream before. Through it was pulled the same thread she'd heard in the cries of goats and fowl when her mother held them down to slit their throats, but where their pleas were foreign to her, she knew these voices too well. Her heart hammered into her throat, her focus sharpening to a pinpoint and her body flattening out like a rabbit trying to stay hidden. She was no viper. Not yet.

Hot tears spilled down over her cheeks and chin, nose running and shoulders heaving, yet still she didn't make a sound. Hand clamped over her mouth, she wouldn't ruin what refuge her mother had given her.

She wished she could say she'd done something. Wished she could say she'd grabbed an axe, a hoe, a trowel, anything, and slammed it into the men's kneecaps to rip them from their saddles. But she was young, still a child with an unblackened heart and no well of rage to draw from. Today, that well would be dug.

How long she stayed there, she didn't know. Her father's voice was the first to go, cut off in a gurgle. Her sisters' cries disappeared into the distance. She could no longer hear her mother. Her brother had screamed in what sounded like a charge at the mens' arrival, which would've left him hobbling on his broken leg only to be cut down. Corinna, had remained in the center of the field, biding what time she had left.

Blood dripped down her trembling lower lip, bitten hard to keep her from weeping aloud. But now the men were gone, and the fire consuming her home had died into sputtering embers. At long last, Corinna stood on knocking knees and parted the wheat to scan the area. It was clear. Both of the wealthy merchant's hired strongarms and of surviving family. As she stepped out of the crops, it felt like stepping out of the womb. Leaving refuge and safety, never to go back, entering into a newly changed world. At the other side of the hut she saw the broken bodies of her mother, her father, her brother, and the one sister not taken captive. The other two were nowhere to be seen or heard, long since gone. Corinna's eyes glazed over their mortal wounds, unable to comprehend it, unable to process the carnage surrounding her. Flies and beetles were already converging upon them, the wetness of freshly spilled blood calling to them like a dinner bell. She vomited up what little was in her stomach. The thatched roof and lean-tos were now no more than splinters, ash, and crumbling mudbrick. The chickens and goats had fled. Patches of maroon stained the dried grass and chalky soil.

A disconnect formed between her eyes and brain, and into an unthinking trance she fell. The world was cold, she knew that. People died, she knew that. Such basic facts were all she could process for now, the only thing she had the capacity to do. Perhaps she should lay down next to them. Curl under her mother's outstretched arm and let the bugs have her.

But then their deaths would be for nothing. Her father's thieving, getting caught. . . It would all be for nothing were at least one person not able to walk away. To survive.

Should she go after her two sisters? While her chances of catching up to them were slim, even though their fates were sealed, at least then she could say she'd done something.

But for what? To ease her guilt in surviving, just to die or face the same unknowable torment as her sisters? Her mother's limp form lay stretched out as if she'd tried to lead her attackers away from the crops—the crops where Corinna had hidden. An unnameable despair weighed in her stomach. She wouldn't waste the chance her mother's life had bought.

Corinna took one last look at her family, then to the dead horizon, and walked on.

6

RETURN FIRE

THE NOTION that white guys can get into all sorts of stuff without anyone batting an eye is something I've heard more than once, but it wasn't until just recently that I believed it—nor flexed it to my advantage. I've spent these past few hours running around abandoned parking lots, buying a strange assortment of items at deliberately spaced out stores, paying solely in cash while looking over my shoulder every two minutes, avoiding security cameras—the whole nine yards. No one has given me so much as one sideways look. I'm grateful that the concept seems to hold true.

But we're not in the middle-of-nowhere anymore. An hour ago we hit I-35—the lifeblood highway stretching from Duluth, Minnesota all the way down to the Mexican border—and have been headed south since. The monotonous scenery of cattle fields, cracked concrete, and adult stores aside, I'm eager to check my errand off our to-do list.

My leg bounces up and down as I exhale a sharp breath. The strip malls and fast food joints and mega-outlets punctuating the flat, dusty landscape are like sores on my eyes, the infrastructure that stitches them together a crumbled disgrace. I stop caring about my spine health long enough to let my posture slip, and hunch over to rest my head against the passenger door. I'll do some orthopedic stretches later to even things out. My hair bounces with the ridges of the road. In my lap is the notepad I'd snuck earlier, angled just-so to keep Corinna from seeing what I'm up to. She doesn't seem to care. Ever since the early morning hours, she's been absorbed in the road.

My pencil bobs with every rotation of our flying tires. Graphite smudges the paper and shadows the side of my hand. Careful, secretive, I scratch out a letter to my sister. If anyone would try to look for me first, it'd be her. Even with grad school, she still makes a point to come by the house once every week or two, if only to use our cable and complain about her thesis. Mom and Dad on the other hand, blissfully roaming about Spain, won't be home for another three weeks.

"Poetry?" Corinna asks as she scans me from the corner of her eye. "Smut doodles?"

"What?" I raise the notepad closer to my chest. "No, why'd you—"

"Must be something embarrassing or else you wouldn't hide it." She shrugs and turns back to the road.

She pries no further. A win for me, finally. She's always so hyper-vigilant, which I suppose she has to be given her background—whatever it is. I wonder what it was that made her this way, and how it all started. The huge scar along her rib cage leaves my queasy stomach twisting with each imagined scenario. She underwent that, and willingly, from the sound of it. I try not to picture the many other, equally horrific things she's endured.

Already Corinna is talking over our plans for how to get into my house while raising the fewest potential flags or alarms, and it's all I can do to stay awake as she goes on. It'll be fine. When haven't things gone smoothly for me? An inward chuckle. *Right.* All the same, I trust her. Talk about a bizarre change.

I nod off as the road lulls me to sleep.

I ROLL up to the curb and put the car in park. In the rearview mirror I can't even see Corinna crouched in the back under a ratty tarp, pretending as if she's not even there. Not to fool me, obviously—she may think I'm dim-witted in comparison to her, but not *that* dim-witted. No, she's still convinced someone could be watching us amongst the shadows of this quiet suburban tract, peeking through blinds and slinking between fences. If they're really after her, us, it'll draw less attention if it looks like we've split up.

Her nerves had been palpable the whole last hour of our drive, Corinna chewing her lip so hard that it'd threatened to bleed. Call me clueless, but my anxieties had yet to bubble up. At first. Sure, I had stressed about the number of handles I'd touched today with all their pathogen-saturated glory, stressed about if such prolonged sitting would up my risk of deep vein thrombosis, and so on, but something as commonplace as going home just wasn't scary. The only thing on my mind at all was that Corinna had us wait until nightfall to make our move. Which made for nearly two days without my medication, a fact that still turns my stomach, but something I can soon remedy.

Cicadas whir in the sticky night air weighed down by barbecue smoke, and moths cluster in ill-defined gangs under street lamps. I take the keys from the ignition and pause for a heartbeat.

"Quick in and out. Meds then straight back to the car, nothing else." Corinna's voice is muffled from where she's hidden, but its low-throated tension isn't. "Three minutes tops."

I nod then step out. My house, my neighborhood—all familiar turf. I'd notice if something was out of place, but at this point I think she enjoys getting worked up. My chest warms as I see my home, a one story with faded red brick, its yellow lawn resisting death, and walk across the crunchy grass. The lock sticks on the first try, but finally I get it open. Despite that I haven't been home in days, it's still cooler inside than out. It chills my sweat. The collection of family pictures is the first thing to greet me, arranged in clusters around the living-room walls. Familiarity calls for me to soak it all in, the collections of thrifted furniture and brightly colored bookshelves, the piles of mail and the shoes dumped at the entryway, but a moment could turn into a minute, and a minute into, God forbid, *two* minutes. Corinna would have my ass for that.

I go into the bathroom and dig through the drawers, pushing past the first aid kit and toilet paper and health magazine articles until I find my blue-capped bottle. My fingers close tight around it. *It's here. I have it, and it's here.* Without taking a single pill, already relief begins to ease into my shoulders. I shove it into the depths of my jean pocket for safe keeping. While checking every half-second to ensure it's actually there, I walk back to the kitchen. Now at the linoleum countertops, I pull out the note I'd written for my sister and smooth out the wrinkles. I glance over it.

Moira, if you're reading this you probably came by to check on me. My phone's busted, but a friend invited me to Dallas with him. Said I needed more spontaneity in my life, and I guess I agree. Should be home—

The floorboards creak. My stomach leaps into my mouth and for the first time, something stronger than mere anxiety runs through my blood. It could just be the wind—but no. The weight of eyes begins to press against me, squeezes me between its fingers, an unseen boa constrictor around my ribs.

I need to get back to the car. What was I thinking blowing off Corinna's warnings?

I look up. By the back door stands a man in a crisp suit, and an eerie silence covers him like a second skin. Time slows and, at the cross-section where my conscious mind meets survival instinct, in that microsecond I grab what information I can. Face clean-shaven, sandy hair shorn. Scarred neck and sun-aged skin. Ex-military? Lean body. Face void of emotion, of humanity, and in his hand is a gun. As he brings it level with my chest, my heart doesn't even have the chance to stutter.

A hand yanks me backwards and hurls me behind the counter. In Corinna's other hand, a raised .45. That one I can recognize, if only for its destructive capacity. Without hesitation she rips the trigger back once, twice. My teeth shake in my skull. The stench of gun smoke clogs the air like firework residue, burning my nostrils. My ears ring yet all I can hear is my own pounding blood, and in my panic all I can see are still-frame snapshots of her wrath. Oh, but it's there. It's there.

Gunpowder hanging in the air and clinging to her white-knuckled fingers. A tiny supernova as it explodes from the barrel with each shot. The hungry eyes of the lion as she bears down on her prey. She says something to me, I see her mouth move, but my ears still ring with deafness.

I shake my head and yell back, "What?"

She grabs my hand and hauls me up, gun still trained towards the back door. I stand to see that my intruder has vanished—for now. Corinna grabs my earlobe and yanks it down to her mouth.

"Don't get a single step behind me," she hollers. "Follow everything I say without hesitation, and *stay down*."

I nod. She paces to the front door, stopping to check around each corner, before we hit the front lawn. I stay hunched over, hands up by my ears in a defensive posture.

"We don't have any cover outside, so make straight for the car. Got it?"

I shake my head, the fray of nervous energy like a whirlpool in my gut. Corinna snaps a new magazine in, and, without taking so much as a second breath, flings open the door and tears across the lawn. My legs move on their own, reptilian brain taking over as I stay at her heels, her the clear alpha between us. No sooner than we climb into the car do the lights of a van threaten to blind us, and a gunshot rings out. A staccato beat rips through my chest, screaming in my ears.

"DOWN!"

Corinna pushes my head below the dashboard and with her free hand swerves us one-hundred-eighty degrees to put the van at our tail. Smoke erupts up under our tires then fades, leaving the charred tang of rubber in my throat. How has no one called the cops yet? Could I be lucky enough for them to start a manhunt?

From the corner of my eye, I see Corinna grab another handgun—hell if I could name it, save that it's boxy and looks forged of death—from a cubby under the wheel. She rolls down the window as our pursuers begin to gain on us. The rumble of their vehicle grows louder, an impending cataclysm.

"Steer," she says. I have less than a moment to process it.

Oh god.

She releases the wheel as my hands snap across the center console, and her gun trains on the encroaching van, now almost parallel to us. Her shot pierces the air, followed by another round, another. Return fire, equally earsplitting. It's all I can do to keep us going straight, deafened into a useless shock. Some people can perform under pressure, and I'd always thought myself one of them. Not anymore. Not now that I've seen Corinna. Never again will I make the mistake of thinking myself equal to someone like her.

Sparks fly up behind us with the pop of rubber. The van swerves and falls fast into the darkness, tire shot out, and Corinna seizes the wheel from me with a glance in the rearview mirror.

"Tell me where the nearest car lot is." Her voice is filled with an intensity I know not to challenge, but I can't give the answer she needs.

"I don't kn—"

"*Think*, Eugene!"

My internal alarm bells warn me that somehow we're still not out of the woods. "Uh, north off 620 and Harper? There should be an old lot there, I think. Not many people."

The next fifteen minutes pass in an adrenaline-drunk blur. We drive to a patch of land overtaken by weeds where rusted pickups, sedans, and motorbikes stretch out in rows, their paint chipped and tires near bald. Corinna turns the lights off, jumps out, and picks a white minivan with a dented bumper. We switch the plates on our new ride, move our gear over, and wipe down our prints as much as possible. Door open, she then pops a screwdriver into the steering column, fiddles with a bundle of wires, and once the engine sputters to life we're back on the road. The car sounds like a rattling tray of nails as it goes. I try not to think about the condition of the tires, about the noisy engine nor when this thing was last inspected.

I don't utter a single word. Not when she demands our bags, not when she tells me to get something she calls a wire-stripper, '*and quickly, dammit*'. Not even once. Corinna is fuming. I'd put us in danger, I know that and stand by my choice, but good god. Seeing the magnitude of her ire sews my lips shut.

We drive for hours. I don't even bother to check the clock, but we stopped at two gas stations along the way so it had to be quite the distance. Already I see signs for Fort Worth, a three hour drive north of where I live. Despite the length of our trip, the fire in her gaze hasn't faded. Not even the endless road quenched that, though I'd hoped it would.

We repeat the same motions from last night. Pull into a hotel, get a room, move our goods, and rig all the entrances for added security, even the window—except this time I have the perk of not being held against my will.

As Corinna finishes jamming the last wooden block under the door, she remains crouched, not a word between us. It's the silence that grates on my nerves the worst, that calm before the storm. But I dig my heels in. This is a storm I'll fight, if only just this once.

Back still facing me, she stands and curls then slackens her fingers, curls then slackens, as if she can't decide to throw a punch or slap me open-handed. She speaks softly, yet her words come out like venom.

"What could've *possibly* been important enough to make you put everything at stake?"

The pill bottle in my jeans weighs heavy, but I try to ignore it. *Deep breaths.* "I don't have to answer that."

She wheels around. "You damn well do."

"Why? So you can yell at me more? You agreed to go back, and we'd talked about the risks—"

"Don't you dare talk to me about risk. I might've agreed to it, but you're the one who lingered back there."

"As if those ten seconds did anything." I force my knees to remain steady and stare back into the eyes of the hurricane. A burn seeps through my chest. She would never understand.

"One second can change everything. Ten seconds sure as hell does." She steps closer.

"Those people were already at my house. All of that would've happened regardless—"

"What was so important, Eugene?" Another step, almost enough for my uneven breath to ruffle her hair.

She would never get it, never empathize. She judges me enough as is. This would only make her look down on me and my weakness further. Provide more fodder for her jabs. My eyes begin to blur, or maybe it's my head. I can't tell anymore.

"I don't have to ans—"

"Eugene."

"I'm not going to—"

"*What was it?*"

"SSRIs!" I crack. "Antidepressants! Happy?"

Corinna's stance slackens. Something new colors her face, but I don't care to decipher the type of disgust it must be.

"Like you'd get it anyhow," I say as my voice lowers, cheeks flooded with heat. I turn to stomp off—to where in our tiny suite, I don't know. Crisp night air and a walk would help, but her security precautions won't even let me try. "Go ahead. Yell all you want."

She grabs my wrist and spins me around, other hand on my shoulder. The touch sears my skin. Those golden eyes cut through me, down to a vulnerable core I don't want to acknowledge.

"Why didn't you tell me that?" she asks. The lack of judgement in her voice shocks me. Or maybe she's just saving it for later.

"It's—" I huff and look away, unable to meet her gaze. "It's personal."

Her hand remains planted, its heat threatening to burn through the fabric of my shirt. A moment passes. "Try me."

I sigh and throw my head back to study the popcorn-textured ceilings. She won't understand, but I can't bring myself to care. Let her laugh. "Life's... rigid. But chaotic. And no matter what I do or try or plan or think, I can't control it. I can't get away from it. So without, uh, some help," I fish the bottle out of my pocket and shake it, "I just shut down. So there. Say whatever you want."

We stand there for a long while, the *tick, tick* of the plastic clock singing like a metronome in the air between us and stretching out the seconds. Silence enfolds us. And then, she breaks it, voice quieter, softer than I've ever heard.

"If there's anyone who could ever understand, it's me."

I look up, raise my eyebrows at her with a sliver of a withering glare. I can't help my wariness. How weak we mere humans must be in the eyes of an immortal. "Why should I believe that?"

"Life is hard, Eugene, and a long one is no easier. I have known and lost more than most ever would in a hundred lifetimes. My entire family is gone. My friends have passed many times over. I've watched war tear apart lives, nations. I've killed people. What I mean to say is, we might be from different times and places, but I understand. Even if you don't want me to. Even if you think I can't, as if you're unworthy or something. You're not. None of this gets rid of what you're feeling, I know, but," she sighs, "hopefully you get what I'm saying."

I lower my head as she raises hers, eyes meeting.

"Not everyone needs medicine," I say.

"And not everyone is immortal. We don't get to choose the body we're given."

"I don't have a reason to be like this. Nothing *made* me this way. It just happened."

"Comets have no reason to fall. But they do."

I shift on my feet as the air turns quiet.

"I understand," she says. "It was worth it to go back."

For a long moment we stand there, trying to decipher what unknown enigmas hide behind the other's gaze. I can't tell. From the moment I saw her, I had the feeling she was something Other, but that could've been any guy's reaction to seeing a beautiful woman. And still, the feeling persists—as do her looks, but it's more than that. I can't read any deeper past her golden surface. What do my eyes show her? My naivety? The crushing weight of my self-imposed structure?

That in a corner of my mind I'm checking my pulse against my fluid intake for the day?

Corinna straightens and lets go of me. In its wake is left an ache where her touch was, and the feeling leaves me sick.

"It's getting late." She chucks her shoes off to rub her feet, sock lint sticking to her soles. "We should get some rest. God only knows what tomorrow will bring."

I clear my throat and roll out my shoulders, trying to brush off whatever that moment was. After I shuffle to the bathroom, nighttime fatigue setting in, I tend to my evening rituals: four minutes of brushing my teeth, then scrubbing my face, taking my vitals, then stretching—extra stretching, given the amount of time I'd spent sitting today—atop an unfolded towel to prevent coming in contact with too many germs. I've seen enough news segments to distrust the cleaning standards of a place like this. Corinna walks in and chucks her used face towel in the hamper, then does a double take in my direction as her brows shoot up. I glance up at her from my forward fold position, forehead almost touching my knobby knees.

"You know what, I'm not even going to ask."

I right myself, cheeks pink, then change into the t-shirt and sweatpants we bought earlier. Finally, respite. This never-ending stress can't be good for my cortisol levels. I don't know how she manages. At last I crawl into bed, the hotel blanket somehow scratchy yet comforting all at once, smelling of overpowering detergent yet musty.

"You gonna tie me up?" I ask, remembering the previous night. Was it only last night?

"Are you into that?" She casts me a devious smirk as she unbinds her hair for the evening.

I'm surprised I don't vaporize on the spot. For all intents and purposes, I might as well have.

Myself sputtering and red-faced, I see the mirth flash across her face.

"Do you *like* doing this?" I stutter.

"You make it too easy. But no, I know you're not gonna make a break for it." Corinna rubs the back of her head, a strangely hesitant gesture for her. "Sorry I did that in the first place."

"I get it. Didn't like it, but I get it." I bury my head under the pillow and huff out a breath. How dare she be so reasonable and spirited this late.

The weight on the mattress shifts. I unsuccessfully try to swallow the lump in my throat, but what am I going to ask her to do, sleep on the floor? There's nothing inherently weird about resting near another person. At least that's what I try telling myself. I'd slept near my sister and parents when I was young, but that was it. I never even went to sleepovers as a kid. I was almost as socially anxious and withdrawn as a child as I am now. I'd never given much thought to what it would be like to lay down next to someone not of my own blood.

The lamp flicks off and plunges us into darkness, and Corinna curls up on her side as her breathing becomes a steady lullaby. Despite myself, a strange intimacy bleeds into the space between us, and as she gives into slumber I almost feel the weight of millennia—however impossible—lift off her shoulders.

7

THE DEVIL'S BARGAIN

Corinna rubbed at where the corded sandals chaffed her ankles raw. They were too tight, and she was growing too fast despite the scarce times. Before her home burned down and her parents were mere memories, Ma had started twisting cord and tanning hide to fit her growing children with larger shoes. She never finished. Making matters worse, Corinna had only been in the city a week and already her stomach was aching with hunger. No confidence to steal bread with, no reserve of energy to even make an escape doable. Corinna bent down and loosened her sandals in the narrow alleyway reeking of urine and rat droppings. At least the sun no longer cooked the smell into a putrid steam. Back against the wall, she slid down and looked past the shingles at the thin strip of night.

The stars burned into the sky above her, flaring into the black. Stars, her one comfort here. A thankfully portable one at that.

If she closed her eyes and thought hard, she could still hear her father tell her about them.

"They connect us," he'd said. "They've been up there since the beginning of the world. We change, they don't. We die, they don't. The stars you and I look at are the same ones people looked at thousands of years ago, and they will thousands of years after. Like something immortal."

"That's not what mom said. Mom says stars are where dead people's spirits live." She'd always been an argumentative child, even when she only meant well. But after an entire brood of children, her parents had learned how to manage her.

"They can be that too, Cor." He scooped her into his burly, sun-browned arms. "Spirits connect us too, right? And are immortal, yeah? All you need to do is look up, and even if you don't see them, you'll know they're there. Most importantly, just like what's in here," he pointed to his chest, "the stars guide us home."

But she didn't have a home to be guided back to now.

Corinna tore her gaze away, stomach gurgling as its empty acids tried to chew what wasn't there. The scent of flat, buttery bread was thin in the air, but still detectable and more than enough to make her mouth water. Following her nose, she weaved through the streets until the smell grew, until it was as if her nose was pressed into the dough itself. A bakery sat at the intersection of two lopsided roads, one big enough for drawn carts, the other only wide enough for two or three people shoulder to shoulder. Out from the open window curled that heavenly scent. Her saliva pooled.

Pillows of soft, cushiony bread dusted with flour sat in rows atop a stone slab. Even uncooked, she could only imagine what they'd be like. Maybe the taste would be even richer that way. The baker turned to see her staring inside, and he snatched up a broad wooden spoon from the countertop.

"Away, street thing!" His voice shattered the dawn air, threatening to cut into her. "Scat!"

Corinna jumped back and stumbled over her feet, hands waving out for balance at her sides, before running away with

Death of an Immortal

tears bubbling in her eyes. *Stupid!* Her hunger was making her absolutely stupid! Who simply walks up and stares at what they want to take, unmoving? Today's market would be her next chance. But even then, would her mind be clear enough? Would she be fast enough or have the energy to get away?

Vendors began pouring into the city as the sun revealed itself, and they laid out their wares under colorfully dyed tarps, fuschias and desaturated greens. As if by some cruel gods joke, from the look of things it seemed crops were beginning to regain their lost vigor. If only such fortune had come a week earlier. Apricots and dried lamb and sacks of ground wheat came to line the walkways with myriad other things, and potential buyers crowded whatever space the goods hadn't taken up. Corinna's eye settled on a burlap bag of glossy plums, and so as long as she could outrun the seller, she'd have enough to eat for days. Morally it did not sit well with her, but starvation was putting her at a greater risk than she could tolerate. Better to take someone else's fruit than allow buzzards to take her flesh.

She shoved down her distracting hunger, tensed her legs to keep her knees from knocking, looked for when the vendor's back turned—and *now*. Edging around the crowd of bodies, Corinna came upon the stand and reached towards the bag.

A meaty palm clamped around her wrist.

"What d'you think you're up to?" Small, olive-pit eyes stared her down, a mouthful of rotted teeth just below. He shook her by the arm, so hard she felt it would wrench out of its socket. "Well?"

"I—" Corinna stammered. She'd only navigated emptier town stalls before, never something this large. Heat burned her cheeks. Why did she think she could pull this off? With what little fire remained, she dug her heels into the dirt and pulled against the peddler's grip. He let go with a scoff.

Before he could spare a single curse, a shattering *pop pop pop!* and confused shouts went up behind her. The bazaar thrown into chaos, heads turned every which way in alarm, a hand the size of her own seized hers and pulled her along, racing away with the bag of plums in tow. A mop of hacked black hair curled behind him, a boy roughly her age. By the time the vendor realized what happened, his protests were already fading into the din as they sped off, as fast as their thin legs could carry them. Her rescuer scissored between alleyways, ducked behind moving carts, then released her wrist to grab hold of a low-hanging eve and hoist himself up, plums and all. His skinny body showed hardly any muscle, but what was there was lean. The street-hungry, pick-pocket sort of lean. The black silhouette before her cut away the harsh sun and offered a hand. Around his wrist was looped a thin leather string. She clambered up after him.

Panting and with sweat dribbling on her upper lip, down the divot of her spine, she collapsed onto the tile roof—and jumped right back up with a yelp.

"It's hot. That'll wake you up real fast," the boy said. He squatted with the bag of shining plums at his feet bound in too-small sandals. Like hers.

"G-give me the bag," she demanded, though even to herself it sounded pathetic.

"Got spark, huh? Keep ahold of that, or else the streets will tear it right outta you." He chucked a lusciously mauve plum her way, its glossy skin catching in the light. "Lycus. And you?"

Within a breath of the fruit hitting her palms, she'd already devoured half of it, pausing only when her teeth bit the woody stone. She swallowed and came up for air. "Corinna."

"Easy now, don't spend it all in one place." He fished another plum out for himself. "You only have half a bag to work with."

She bit her tongue. Half a bag. Half would last her a little over a day, two if she bent her hunger into submission. Even so, he was the only reason she'd gotten anything to eat at all. He was lucky she wasn't the greedy sort, justified or not. Mirroring his squatted position, she took another plum in hand.

"What was that back there? In the marketplace?"

"I'm good with a slingshot. Which makes these pits pretty handy." He picked up the fruit stone she'd cast aside and held it back out to her. "Everything you can carry now, you hold onto. You'll find a use for it, believe you me."

Corinna took it from his dusty palm and balanced it in her own. A dead seed, waiting to grow. Out of its element, but full of as much potential as it'd ever had.

She could easily use it to bash him over the head. Not that she would. It would be too daring a move. Something told her he saw the thought flicker in her eyes too clearly for her to try and find that darker well inside her—the same one she'd failed to find mere days ago, when she'd lain in the fields and listened to her family's wails.

"Why'd you help me?"

Lycus shrugged his sun-darkened shoulders. "You didn't ask anyone in the market for handouts. You saw what you needed and decided to take it. That kind of nerve is good. Useful." He stood, the sun etching gold around his form, and looked down at her with dark eyes almost as muddy as hers. "Few people last long on their own out here."

"You seem fine."

"I'm not most people."

Corinna scoffed, a dry bark as harsh as the roiling heat. It wasn't a noise she was used to hearing from herself. "So you're the exception."

Something told her that he thought as much. Still, he stretched his open hand down to her, and the searing brightness behind him made her eyes water. A moment passed.

Corinna pushed herself up and stared at him head-on. Could she trust this boy? What more did she have to lose from sticking with another urchin? Going it alone had gotten her starved and nearly apprehended, with hardly an ember of spark left. But now that spark flickered.

She took his hand.

THE YEARS SERVED THEM WELL. Though poverty was an ever-present phantom clinging to the hems of their tunics, and every few years a famine would force them to confront their bones, through their work Corinna and Lycus found a place to rest their heads, a fire and crude hearth to cook beside, and enough hope to dream of something bigger. It was all she could have asked for. All anyone in her circumstance could.

'Work' was a term they defined loosely. Pickpocketing wealthy merchants in the posh cities' bazaar districts, swindling fools with fake riches, putting their services up for hire, even stealing a prized ox or two for back-alley auctions. Sometimes Corinna looked to the sky and wondered what her mother would think, but at least she was alive to worry. She had made something of the chance she'd been given, and that had to be enough. The guilt that tugged at her over the years tapered off, and Lycus's penchant for pocketing shiny things always dragged her into his ploys regardless. Not to mention that it kept their stomachs full—something guilt wouldn't do.

It bought them a woolen, heavenly warm blanket for when the winters whipped in. It bought medicine when she'd fallen ill from an open gash, courtesy of a pursuing marketplace guard. It bought the plums Lycus still gave her these eight years later, a lifetime away from when they first met. It bought them enough time and quiet to try to build their lives into something decent, something more. At long last they were able to breathe, if only to pause. It had to be enough.

"I've watched his patrol's posts. Should be no more than five of them rotating tonight." Fingertips dipped in charcoal powder, Lycus pressed down on a map of the estate to leave behind five black dots. It had been crudely copied onto a fragment on some animal's pelvis bone, but papyrus and even wax tablets were too expensive for them to procure. "No guards inside, so once we're in, we're good and clear."

"Except that he has three dogs," Corinna rebutted, brows drawn and unimpressed.

"Dogs that are away with his sons boar hunting."

"And—what?" She opened her mouth to second guess him then stopped short. "How do you know that?"

He dusted off his hands with a smile lingering on his thin lips. How he loved letting her dangle. "Every tip is yours for the taking, so long as you know the person's pressure points."

A sigh and a nod of her head. There was little doubt his information was correct. She wasn't as slippery as Lycus, didn't have his same mastery of words that would spin miracles out of nothing more than air and melody of voice. Half of the time, she was convinced she would catch jewels spilling out of his mouth or honey drizzling from between his teeth. While his physical skills were nothing to scoff at, it was the sly tongue that set him apart. There was an undeniable oily slick to him, and though she couldn't taste it when they kissed, she knew it was there to stay. But it wasn't fair to blame him for that. Neither of them would have survived the streets this long without it.

Corinna chewed on her lip. "Are you sure there won't be more security inside? The satraps and their families have gotten restless lately, what with how hard the princeling has been pushing their borders."

"It's a good thing our mark isn't a satrap then. A nephew, sure, but a distant one at that, and besides, his uncle is no longer in office. The lot of them are over-glorified has-beens.

Persian or not, Philip is probably glad to have his nephew's taxes."

"Alexander now. Or have you already forgotten all of his dear father's wailers?"

When the Macedonian king, Philip the Second, was assassinated by his own guard, the cries from within the city had shaken the very earth. How one could slay their own monarch, the person who'd given them everything, was a cold and savage mystery to Corinna.

"Pfft, paid wailers. If only Alexander had shelled out for a lesson or two in crocodile tears." Lycus half-laughed and rolled his eyes, then sat beside her on the reed mat. "The new *princeling* as you call him is probably jumping at his chance to direct the throne."

"Which is why we should be careful. He'll have his eye set on anyone and anything Persian within his borders to solidify his control, to make people realize he means business. People like the satrap *and* his family, extended or not." She jabbed him in the ribs with the hilt of the dagger she was sharpening. A plain thing, but effective all the same.

Putting that sugared tongue to use, he brushed off her bunt and rested his chin on her shoulder, hands on her hips. Though she never cared for it when he used his persuasive forces on her, a smile crept to her lips all the same. Heat flushed into her cheeks.

"Let's say His Illustrious Argead-descended, Most-High Alexander himself walked in on us," Lycus said. "Our job is to trash the place—something the prince'd probably buy us a skin of wine for. Who knows, he might even be the one paying for this." Lycus kissed her collarbone with a graze of teeth. "Don't get worked up over an easy deal. "

And so she relaxed. He'd never steered her wrong before, and his confidence was hard to argue with. Though she'd certainly tried.

She would forever wonder how differently things would have turned out if only she'd argued a little harder.

THE HEAVY MUDBRICK walls of the estate inflamed her heart with jealousy. How must it feel to claim a chunk of the earth for yourself, to return to it each night and know it was truly *yours*? But tonight the satrap's darling nephew would host others on his land, if unknowingly. Tonight Corinna would see yet again how the upper echelon lived, and imagine a world in which the luxury of a home was her own.

Though their task was a nonviolent, non-thieving one—a rarity for their line of work—still they armed themselves in the event of being caught unawares. The knife girded around her thigh, two at her belt alongside a couple coin-purses—one filled with powdered mustard seeds, the other with crushed glass—and a short coil of rope around her shoulder would serve them well enough. Lycus bore a similar arsenal as well. She gestured to him from across the rooftop tiles. According to Lycus's surveillance, there was a gap in the guard's rotation, a blind spot just wide enough for them to slither in before the next person arrived. The watchman should disappear around the corner any moment now. So long as they were quiet, they'd be in the clear.

He nodded. Together they padded across the roof, staying low until they were within jumping distance to the estate's western walls by the wash house. After all, who would think to guard their dirty laundry? She scanned the area and sure enough, there he was: one guard, tired, uninterested in his work and eager to depart. He glanced at the stars for the time, and Corinna did as well. *Shift change.*

His sigh of relief echoed in the empty air and he disappeared around the corner—not bothering to wait for his relief, just as Lycus had seen him do again and again all those nights before. They edged close to the eaves, backed up a few steps, then jumped in unison for the wash house's slanted roof. She landed softly, but spat a curse under her breath at the roof's angle and its glazed tile. It must've been a fresh glaze, judging by the smoothness of it. It was a blessing that one of the seasonal rainstorms hadn't swept through, or else both of them would have slid right off and eaten dirt. Lycus looked to be struggling as much as she was, brow twisted in telltale irritation.

Both eased along the shingles, muscling down to then plop onto the private grounds blanketed with grass. *Grass.* She ran her hands through it. Wide swathes of it stretched between the main house and its outlying buildings. What moron left arable land to spare and didn't at least grow something edible on it?

They crept around the perimeter and stuck to the wall's overhanging shadow, despite the lack of interior security. No one expected for anyone to get past those walls, jagged glass glued to the top edge. She and Lycus had made that mistake before elsewhere, and it was one they didn't intend to repeat.

With a glance in both directions, they snuck into the main house. Pale gossamer curtains billowed at the entryways, pushed by the night air and more than enough to cover them from the outside looking in. That, plus the dogs being gone? And the slacking guards? It would be a cinch, an easy night's work for tantalizing pay.

How stupid she'd been to not read the signs, not taste the peril hanging like smoke.

Lycus slinked between the fluttering curtains and she followed behind. The inside was dim, but not impossible to see in. Moonlight pooled in the courtyard atrium, bright as bleached bone. Corinna rolled her shoulders and flexed her fists. Lycus's map in mind's eye, she paced to the bedchamber wing and drew out her pouch of crushed glass, then scattered it at the doors' threshold. Her partner was ripping hanging ferns from their hammered copper pots when she rounded the corner, him not even bothering to keep his smile hidden. He reveled in the destruction of it. Always had. Corinna wasn't sure what that said about his character, but he'd be wreaking the same havoc with or without this job. At least they were getting paid.

She approached the purple tapestries dyed with crushed shellfish, and pulled a knife from her hip. She sighed. These bits of cloth had traversed all the way up the coast from Tyre, that famed city of sweet-smelling incense and vibrant color. Yet another place she yearned to go, and another she'd likely never see. Places she knew existed but didn't have the words for, places with wonders outside of her imaginings.

Corinna pushed the thought away. A slash, and one of the hangings came unraveled from its pegs to land with a soft *thump*. She wouldn't hack it to ribbons though, not for now. Purple fabric was worth its weight in gold, but they didn't take from any of the places they defaced. It wasn't a moral hesitation—Lycus did love shiny things after all—but rather a precaution. The moment anything got traced back to them, it was time to hightail it out to a new city and start over. Again. They'd learned that lesson. But cutting it down was as far as she'd go. She couldn't bear to see such a thing of beauty turned to rags.

"The kitchen now?" Lycus walked up alongside her, picking dirt from under his stubby fingernails.

She nodded. Time to ruin the spices. Fling them into the wind, grind them into the dirt, and chuck them into the waterways. It was admittedly her favorite part—though again, such a waste. All the same, there was nothing quite like breathing in a lungful of crushed cinnamon dust or tasting the zing of saffron in the air. With such flavors at their disposal, she could only imagine the foods these plutocrats fixed. Or their servants, rather.

Lycus moved towards the fallen tapestries with knife

raised before she grabbed his arm to stop him. He scoffed. "Really?"

"The sun rises in three hours and we have far more to do." She waved a hand at him. "Leave it."

"A wise move," came a deep voice from over her shoulder. "One of those hangings alone costs more than vandals like you could make in an entire lifetime."

Corinna whirled around, cloak snapping behind her. From the shadows of the entry hall she could just make out the figure of a man, broad and towering. He was cloaked as they were, so clearly not a member of the house. She was just beginning to wonder if their contractor had hired multiple parties when he drew a cutlass from the folds of his mantle. Lycus spun around as another strongarm emerged from the courtyard. The lemon-sized rock rising in her throat did nothing to help sharpen her focus or clear her mind.

"We'll leave," she said. She and Lycus put their backs up against one another to keep a set of eyes in all directions. "We won't do anything more."

"You think we answer to some Persian?" the first man laughed, as if the very idea was ridiculous. Clearly not a fan of Persians, but then what was a nationalist doing in one's home?

"We'll work something out," Lycus said. "Take whatever you want. No difference to us who goes through his pockets."

A third man pushed past the curtains and stepped up onto the lip of one of the windows, his hair close-cropped and a wiry black, looking like every other Macedonian man save his scar trailing from brow to jaw. A scar she'd avoided making eye-contact with when he'd hired them a week ago. "It isn't him we came for."

A set up.

Corinna wasn't going to wait to find out why he'd chosen to go through all that trouble. She darted right, past the formerly tapestry-adorned wall in the only direction left open, Lycus hot in her wake.

Pulse down, breathing even, pace your thoughts. Remind herself though she might, her internal alarm bells still had a way of working their magic. Should she wake the house to cause confusion and panic for her pursuers as well? No, that'd just increase the odds she and Lycus would get caught, no matter by whose hand. She looped through one of the labyrinthine halls and out a window into the courtyard, splashing into the small tiled pool. Lycus followed after, and both crouched behind one of the myrtle bushes.

"We'll only get out either by going right through the front or by scaling back up onto the wash house," Lycus said.

"The guards are with us," said the scarred man as he landed in the pond. "Do not for a second believe their ineptitude was anything other than bait."

Corinna hissed a colorful phrase at him. Of course. Too often guards sold their allegiance to the highest bid—and she remembered with a twinge of regret that this particular bid had been too good to pass up. The estate's security too lax. Now she knew why. Fool, she'd been an utter *fool*. Now it would cost them both.

They hated putting up fights when they didn't have to, both her *and* Lycus, as it wasted energy and precious seconds, but when they had to…Glancing at one another, they nodded. Corinna stood and unlooped the rope from around her shoulder.

Their pursuer charged forward with a raised knife, and she cracked the rope out like a whip as Lycus ran behind him and grabbed the end of it. Pulled taut, they swung and swept his legs from under him. His skull gave a resounding *crack* as it hit the pool tiles, and she saw red blossom into the water as they turned to run. The other strongarms' curses trailed behind them as they broke onto the lawn between the main house and the wall, but they were fast upon them. One yanked her back by the cloak and she spun, flinging her pouch of crushed glass at his eyes. He screamed, ground the fine powder deeper with every rub and blink.

The now likely-concussed man emerged from the courtyard, sopping wet and face baleful beyond measure. Upon seeing another of his men down, he drew a bone whistle from the front of his tunic and blew. It screamed a piercing note. If the household wasn't already awake, they would be now.

The front gate swung open to allow the estate's three guardsmen in before sealing shut with a thud. Corinna's heart threatened to pound up and out of her throat—but she steeled herself anyway. She drew her blade.

Two of the guards charged, striking out with blunt-ended spears. She and Lycus twisted away. *Blunt ended?* Why not bring proper spears if they knew they were in for a fight? Strange as it was, she didn't have time to puzzle it out.

Again Corinna hurled the end of the rope to her partner, this time spinning around to slam their attackers together. They went down with a grunt, but another set was upon them in no time. She flung crushed mustard towards their eyes, but they'd learned from their comrade's mistakes, hands up and guarding. A swear escaped her.

She and Lycus slashed out at them, doing their best to cover one another—but there were too many.

Corinna sliced and punched and spent whatever glass she had left and took their feet from under them wherever she could, but it wasn't enough. Lycus's breathing quickly became just as ragged as hers. They wouldn't last much longer.

Their concussed attacker kicked Lycus's legs from under him at the knee. Right as he went down with a yelp, she grit her teeth and scooped up a large handful of mustard powder, shoved it into her mouth. The burning was incredible, an hellfire searing her nostrils and throat with each breath, clotting

Death of an Immortal

her eyes with tears, but she held her mouth firm as she was struck down from behind. Chains lashed around her wrists.

A hand twisted through her hair and hauled her to her feet as she smelled the rank scent of the man behind her, reeking of onion and cumin. He turned her around to face him, a snarl painted on his face. This close, she could see the burst vessels in his eyes, the grit creased in the folds of his face.

"There we go, pretty thing, now just—"

Corinna hocked a mouthful of spice-laced spit at his eyes to land square on his cornea, and she kicked his footing from under him. He howled in pain, both hands clamped over his eyes—but the other guardsmen stepped in. They slammed against her ribs and forced her to the ground, one of them pinning her with his boot-clad foot as another cinched bindings to her ankles.

Corinna writhed and tore and pulled, pulled, pulled. It made no difference. There was no way out. She and Lycus were outstripped. Ice crystallized in her gut despite the sticky night air.

The wire-haired man crouched before her—though remained slightly angled away lest she pull another trick out of thin air. Good. Let him fear her. At least she had that to pride herself in.

"You can only pull that eye gimmick so many times," he said.

"I'll stop pulling it when you stop falling for it."

Corinna got a swift kick to the back for that.

"Keep off her!" Lycus barked, though he wasn't in any position to argue either.

The man turned and raked his gaze over him as if getting a proper look for the first time. "Quite the team, aren't you?"

Lycus's teeth glinted in the starlight. Three men held him fast, and by the looks of it, his bindings were just as secure. Protest though he might, he and Corinna had lost. But what did these people want? Why go through such trouble? And why not kill them now?

A wagon with an open back rolled through the main gate, drawn by a ruddy chestnut mare. Corinna blinked. Still it was there, tail swishing and hooves stomping with impatience. It wasn't every day she saw a horse doing something as mundane as cart-hauling. That was usually left to oxen or other beasts of burden, for the cost to keep and maintain a horse was astronomical, only to be afforded by someone... She swallowed.

Only by someone with deep pockets, and likely even deeper influence. She and Lycus exchanged a glance.

What had they gotten themselves into?

RISING light rimmed the closed shutters in a bluish gold, but it was no match for the oil lamps left blazing atop the desk and affixed to the wrought sconces. On any other day, Corinna would've been taking stock of her surroundings to see what she could poach or what information she could glean, but the cluster of nerves in her stomach wreaked too much havoc for her to think straight.

She and Lycus had been held here—wherever *here* was—for a while now. Ten minutes, two hours, she couldn't tell how long it'd been. Everything had bled together in a blur of dread. The only detail she noted was that they had been transported into one of the more posh districts of town, into the tidier administrative center. Riff-raff like her usually stuck to the outer rings.

The guards had loosened their hold, but she and Lycus knew better than to fight back. Not now. If they were outmaneuvered at the estate, they would face the same fate here. With the new slack in his chains, Lycus instead reached for her hand and gripped it tight. That perhaps made her feel worst of all. He was never the affectionate sort, but if he felt there might be something worse awaiting them... Corinna couldn't stomach the thought.

"I'm so sorry." His voice threatened to break, eyes growing moist. "I was the one who said we should take this job. Never thought—I didn't mean to put us in harm's way."

"It was a choice we made together." She squeezed his hand back.

Lycus drew in an even breath, nodded as his gaze steeled. "Right. Together."

The study door banged open. Guardsmen snapped to attention as their long-awaited captor made himself known, his short chlamys cloak roiling behind him. A military cloak. He walked to the front to survey them like goats at auction, then leaned back as he chewed on the musty smelling herb pocketed in his cheek.

"Word is that you put up a good fight." His eyes flicked over their wounds, and then his mens'.

Why would their jailer share just how badly his charges had been beaten before subduing their targets? Was it to humiliate them so they'd train harder? Corinna kept her mouth shut. There's a chance this was bait, too.

"You were ambushed and still worked as a team under pressure," he continued. "You kept your head clear enough to think resourcefully, were even willing to inflict pain on yourself in the name of reaching your goal."

"And?" Lycus dared to ask.

"Much needed qualities nowadays. The two of you could do a lot of good with that."

"Because we're so obviously interested in charity."

The man backhanded Lycus across the jowls. Lycus stumbled backward, only to be pushed forward by one of the guards. Corinna's muscles tensed, yearning to do *something*, but her hands were tied. Quite literally.

"No formal training and hardly a proper weapon on you.

One can only imagine what you lot would be capable of given actual instruction."

Lycus bit on his lip to staunch the dribbling blood, and him and Corinna furrowed their brows at one another. He looked just as out of his depth as she felt.

"Why catch us?" Corinna asked. "There are much bigger people for hire out there. Whole rings you could bring in and—"

"This isn't about your," he paused to find a more delicate phrase, "extralegal work. This is about the work you can do for your people. Your land."

Macedon, kingdom of the Argeads and brother to the city-states of Greece, the land where she was born and where she would likely die. Corinna had no allegiance to any particular tract of dirt, but what she heard was that he had no plans to make them into slaves. No plans to execute them. Her interests were piqued even higher at the possibility of him using their talents for work. Work meant regular wages. Wages meant steady food and a place to sleep. A way to climb that elusive ladder usually reserved for those within the bounds of society. Could that one day be theirs? A home, a hearth, a family to have forever?

Throat dry, she swallowed and—in case this was a dream—tried not to wake up. "What did you have in mind?"

He looked them over appraisingly and drew up to full height with a roll of his shoulders. "You agree to become wards of the state, train under its command, and, provided you endure your ordeal, will become employed in our military services in a year and a half's time."

"For who?" Corinna struggled to keep the wind from leaving her, to keep her knees from buckling. In what world did the Crown want or need petty criminals under its thumb? This was the same lot who pursued people like her and Lycus at every turn, who announced wanted notices in forum squares and sentenced their collaborators to public lashings. "Who asked for this?"

"It is of no concern to you."

"Damn straight it is," Lycus jabbed back. "There's someone's dirty work you want taken care of, and you think you're gonna leave us holding the bill. There's gotta be some reason you're not picking from your own conscripts, am I right?"

"You should be groveling at our feet to make something out of your wretched selves." When his eyes met theirs again they were filled with a wicked fire. "Or would you rather pay the price for your crimes?"

Lycus snapped his mouth shut and looked to her, face unguarded for once.

They understood the bargain now. *Do as we say or be jailed. Maybe hanged.* Most of their crimes were small ones with only the occasional noble or bureaucrat on the receiving end, and they had settled scores on behalf of others just as much as they'd created them. She wouldn't put it past those types to be spiteful nor to have men like this in their pockets.

But more than that, she didn't care whose 'dirty work' it was. They already did those things for complete strangers. Lycus might object, but he was always obstinate in the face of authority. He would cut down the sun itself if he stood to benefit.

Yet an entirely different vision swam before her eyes: a chance to claim her place in the sun. To walk without looking over her shoulder. To live honorably, so that when those stars looked down on her they'd see someone to be proud of.

She was upon the words before she took so much as another breath. "You've got yourself a deal."

And the devil smiled.

8

RUSTED RICHES

Why is there so much porn on hotel TVs? I'd already rubbed down everything from the remote to the door handles with disinfecting wipes, but the overabundance of X-rated material leaves me feeling like the room still isn't clean. Sure, I've tried to watch that stuff once or twice, tried to get into it, but it's only ever made me uncomfortable. Is it like the mini-bar, where they try to bait you with overly-expensive things they think you can't resist? And who's falling for it often enough for them to make a profit? My only hope is that by the time I reach my fat and balding fifties, I won't have become desperate enough to keep channels like these in business. I flip through the TV guide for something a bit more enriching as I chew through reheated pancakes, courtesy of this morning's breakfast buffet.

Exhausted as I was, I hadn't woken up today until almost twelve in the afternoon and still can hardly force myself to get moving. Thankfully Corinna doesn't want me to. All she's told me to do is just what I'm doing right now: nothing. She's relegated herself to toil under the glaring fluorescents of the hotel's business lounge most of the day, sifting through leads online while I sit here and try to stay out of trouble. So far I'm doing a bang up job of it. I've taken my medicine, done some jumping jacks and pushups to compensate for my sedentary morning, and have yet to let my anxieties wind me up too much.

How exactly she's searching for this domukardi I have no idea, but I'm guessing she's found something to go off of at this point or else she'd have given up by now. Well, I'm not sure she's the type to throw in the towel, but I haven't heard any computers come shattering out of a window, so same difference. I remember her mentioning something about a museum event, but little else. Must be enough of a lead for her.

All I wish is that I could leave the room to get more food, *real* food not saturated with simple carbs and sugars, but I listen to her order to stay out of sight. After yesterday, I'm sure as hell not going to ignore her warnings.

A lilting, three-beat knock raps against the door as our prearranged signal. I swing my feet off the bed and undo her fifteen-hundred layers of added security before she throws the door open. Victory glitters in her eyes.

"Got it." Though she says the words aloud, I have a feeling it's mostly for herself to bolster any fading confidence. Corinna fastens everything back into place with a piece of paper clutched in hand.

"Found a lead?"

"A hell of a lead."

She goes to the desk in the corner then smoothes the page out over its particle board surface. On it is printed a museum's landing page, and in thick red marker is circled one exhibit singled out from the rest. *Metallurgical Works of the Near East.* Below the slim modern font is what looks to be an ornate water pitcher with a greenish patina crusted around the detailing, a testament to its age. The description beneath it reads '*Step into the past and behold works from Near Eastern metallurgists of the Late Bronze, Classical, and Early Iron Age, demonstrating lasting form and elegance'* before trailing off into ellipses, punctuated with a 'Click to read more' hyperlink. My brow creases as I look to the picture, back to the description, and back yet again.

"I thought you said it was like a box."

"The picture isn't what I'm looking for. That's just an item in the collection."

"But you're sure it's there?"

"I'm not certain, but last I checked it was in the southern US, and this is far more than I've had to go on in a long time. Even if the domukardi itself isn't there, I could at least pick some of the curators' brains and see if they can tell me anything useful."

Her stare lingers a moment longer on the crumpled paper, as if the sheet itself might grant her wish. A death wish. Something I haven't thought much about, and as I watch the intense yearning paint her face, I'm not sure I want to start.

"When and where are we going?" I ask.

Snapping out of whatever thoughts spin in her head, Corinna tucks the paper into her pocket and sets to rummaging through our bags. "Dallas, tomorrow evening. There'll be some hoity-toity fundraising event going on at the Heritage Museum where this is, so in case it's there we need to be able to lift it."

"Lift it?" I almost exclaim.

"What, did you think I'd ask if the museum could just loan it out?"

"That's—What if we get caught?"

"I used to steal things for a living. Trust me, we won't get caught. In order to blend in though, you'll have to look presentable, outfit and all. And I mean a *nice* outfit, the one we picked out for you. Deal?"

I sputter. There hadn't been much *'we'* about it, but it's hardly the topic at the forefront of my mind. "Security has probably changed quite a bit over the years."

"Deal?"

"Look, if we get caught—"

"If we get caught, you get to go home and I'll find a way out like I always do. I'm the one risking my ass."

I hesitate, but her unwavering confidence wins out.

"As long as you're certain." The shock of what she said now past me, a nagging question pushes me to peek at the paper hanging out of her pocket, and my mind tries to cobble together what puzzle pieces of information I have. "The description said Late Bronze and Early Iron Age, didn't it?"

"Also Classical, but yes. Seems they'll all be from around that time."

"And you think the box your heart is in will be with that?"

"Like I said, I can't know for certain until we go there, but from everything I know it should be. Hopefully." She turns to me. "Why?"

I count backwards through the years in my head, willing my long-since unused AP World History knowledge back to me. (I'd gotten a four on the exam, which was respectable, even though my nerves had me vomiting both before and after the test.) There was the Stone Age back when humanity was no more than newborns beating on rocks and discovering what plants to eat, the Bronze Age when we began to group into city-states for agriculture and thought war was a neat idea, and then in the Iron Age we became even fatter and deadlier. Where the Bronze and Iron intersect is a bit fuzzy in my memory, but the Classical Age isn't. Thankfully American schooling focuses on Greco-Roman societies more than most, and those brief 200 years of democracy, philosophy, literature, and war were no exception. But even with that knowledge, it doesn't make her information any easier to process.

"Those time periods were all thousands of years ago," I say. I can't help the dismissive, disbelieving tone in my voice, nor the shock. "There's no way, I mean, how would your box get mixed up with something so old?"

She shifts and lowers the shimmering, pale gold dress before her. A pause.

I know that the past is real. I know that it happened and shaped our world. And yet, I can't help but feel detached from it. After all, who looks at a museum artifact and can imagine the one who formed it, the hands of the servants and slaves who polished it, the nobles' eyes that appraised it? Who can see them as something other than a picture in a textbook or a scene in a Hollywood production? Yes, those ancient years existed. To *know* them is something else.

Words form in my throat, yet I can't even begin to conceptualize their significance.

"You never told me. How old *are* you?"

Corinna sighs and slings the dress across the desk chair, scratching the back of her head. "I don't remember the exact number anymore. It was a long time ago. Very long."

"As in—"

"As in Classical-Age long. I don't know the actual year, but I was born around the time Philip of Macedon was in power, Alexander's father."

"Alexander?"

"Yes, *that* Alexander."

The air whooshes out of my chest.

Alexander the Great.

An oddly specific detail, but it places her firmly in history nonetheless. My jaw hangs slack, I feel my eyes bulge from my skull, but I can't help it. That has to be… No, that can't be right. I recalculate the total in my head, but the answer stays the same. Two-thousand and four hundred years old, give or take a few decades. The number's incomprehensible. Impossible.

"You—I mean," I stumble over the words. Whenever I was little, after every night of reading stories, I wished so desperately to hop in a time machine and see the world as it once

Death of an Immortal

was, as it was made into what it now is. Corinna had that experience as her own. "You must've seen so much."

She barks out a laugh and goes back to putting together her outfit. "That much is for sure."

"Like what?" I lean forward. I can't stop myself. She's seen history. She *is* history. Almost the whole span of western civilization, of nations and empires and conquest and more.

"I was born in Macedon, so I got to visit nearby Rome for a time."

"What else?"

She shifts from one foot to the other, and I can almost see the map materialize in her eyes. "I went all over. The Białowieża woodlands back before even the Tsars hunted there and Haridwar on the Ganges during the Kumbh Mela festival. The Yakutian tundras as reindeer ran across it. Villages settled in the Yangshuo mountainsides as millet and tobacco came into season. I've seen it all." Her face goes distant, as if reliving the many lifetimes and wonders she's witnessed. In my anticipation, I almost miss the undercurrent of a shadow there. "Including the wars."

Her gaze doesn't refocus, doesn't show any sign of letting light creep back in before I notice it. I rub my neck, unsure whether to back off the subject or let her talk about it, provided she wants to. My silence could be just as awkward for her.

"Is that why—what I mean to say is, did you—"

"I did." She nods. "I fought in a lot of wars. Too many. But I suppose that's what brings me to where I am now."

"To being a good fighter?"

"That." Corinna takes a leveling breath. "But more."

Oh.

Too much carnage. Too much light lost. Too much of whatever it is she's seen that's left her like this. I'd like to think I understand, but I don't. I can't imagine anyone else who does nor how lonely that reality must be. Yet I've known people who've wanted out. I've been that person more than once, and even if I don't know what it is to have lived as she has, I know the script.

"You don't have to, you know," I say. "I know you've lost a lot, but there's—"

"You have no concept of what I've lost, Eugene." Her eyes turn hard.

"I don't, but that doesn't mean you have to do this. Hell, there have been times when even I wanted out but I'm glad I didn't act on them, and I know—"

"I'll be charitable and let you assume you understand. But if you do, it's only in theory." She tosses her hair back and squares her shoulders, that indomitable spirit filling her once again, and lays a scar-flecked hand over her absent heart. "You don't understand where it counts."

"Suicide isn't the answer, Corinna. It never—"

"Don't start this," she warns.

But in the silence that rises between us, I dare it. If just to lift the sentiment from my chest.

"I'd thought about killing myself, once." I've never admitted it so plainly to myself, not out loud. Certainly not to others. "I didn't think I'd ever see a day when I wasn't so anxious that I couldn't breathe, when I didn't lie in bed at night worrying about every little thing that could ruin my life. As if I wasn't the one already doing that." Despite the tension thick in the air, I snort with a half-laugh. "Then things got better, and they keep getting better, bit by bit. Sometimes I back-slide or whatever, but still. I'm doing better."

I turn my sights up from the carpet and to her. Corinna's expression has softened, but only by a hair. She sighs, crossing her arms.

"I appreciate your honesty," she says. "It's admirable, but my point remains."

"But *why*?"

"Because our reasons aren't similar in the least! This isn't

Death of an Immortal

me trying to cut my time short! I may look young, Eugene, but I'm not. I haven't been for far, far too long. I'm a crone who will not die, a spirit who cannot find rest. A star left burning." She shakes her head and straightens. "Do not treat me as a mortal when I'm not one."

Whatever rebuttal I have comes up short, which would usually be good. It would mean the issue is resolved, the talking point over. But I don't want it to be.

"For me, this is a reset to the natural order." She uncrosses her arms and turns back to her clothing. "All things must end, both for every war and every warrior."

I divert my eyes, as if it will shield me from seeing her point. She's had her time, an incomprehensibly long amount at that, and now simply wishes it to end. Nothing morbid about it, just a statement of fact. Or so I try believing. An old woman ready to sleep, a sun ready to blaze out.

Retiring the topic for now, I pick up a glossy paper menu propped up on the bedside.

"If tomorrow's going to be as busy as you say, we should eat." I hold it out to her, my olive branch. "Room service?"

Corinna's shoulders drop a fraction, the tension evaporating as she realizes I'm done bothering her. She nods. "Order me a burger?"

I can't keep back the smile that cracks past my lips. So typical. Some things satisfy everyone.

Twenty minutes later and the sun begins to scrape low behind the horizon on its descent, a Persephone taking the world's vitality with her. We both sit in the worn sweats we'd gotten from a thrift store, on the bed with sloppily-made entrees in our laps, TV blaring whatever 90s comedy the local stations can pick up. I slurp the burrito juice that drips over my fingers as Corinna almost inhales her burger in one fell swoop. The only times we stop for air is to burst out in laughter. At least comedy doesn't pretend to be anything it's not.

It's not until ten at night that we wind down, later than

we'd hoped since we plan to leave at 5 AM. Clothes laid out, bags ready, and alarms set, Corinna flips out the lights as I bury myself under the stuffy comforter. As soon as I feel her drop beside me—something I'm still unsure how to feel about— the warmth of her weight sets my heart at ease and I drop into sleep.

~

I JOLT AWAKE. Five already? The alarm-clock radio buzzes like a squawking parrot, and sure enough it reads '5:00' in backlit numerals.

Already Corinna is up and getting ready, or I presume as much from the sound of splashing water coming from under the bathroom door. I haul myself up and punch the off button, then cradle my head on my knees and spend two, maybe three minutes debating if I should just crawl back under the covers. Corinna comes out with a towel slung across her shoulders, cushioning her damp, glistening hair.

"Morning, Rapunzel." The toothbrush clenched between her teeth garbles her words.

"Don't you mean Sleeping Beauty?"

She shrugs. "I'm not a princess trivia buff."

"I'm not—" I rub my eyes with the palms of my hands. "Morning, I guess. Why're you already up?"

"It might only take you ten minutes to get ready, but us ladies aren't so lucky. Not if we want to blend in, at least." She dumps a bag of makeup out on the desk and sits at the awful damask chair. "Shower, pass that burrito, get dressed and do whatever else you need to, then we'll head out."

Grumble under my breath though I may, I've gotten used to her rattling off orders. I nod and turn to what she's laid out for me for this evening. Black slacks and, good god, is that a tan button down? Beige? I can't imagine a more bland color. I pinch at the fabric, as if that will somehow scare it into changing hues.

"Are you seriously going to make me wear this?"

"You'll look handsome as ever."

I open my mouth to protest.

"And you'll like it."

No room for argument, then. I look over the ensemble she put together, half hesitant but also half appreciative. At least I've been spared the torture of high heels, and the shirt doesn't look *too* hideous. I fold it into our bag. Regardless of how I feel about it, wrinkles won't help. I strip down in the bathroom, give myself a quick wash, then dress in jeans and a tee.

"All set?" Corinna pops her head in the door and I start right as I zip my pants. She raises a brow. "This is going to take some pluck, you know that right?"

I wave her away and dab toothpaste onto my brush. "I'm aware."

Scrubbing at my teeth, I look her up and down. Her outfit is more akin to casual streetwear than the golden, pearly dress she set out, though I suppose it makes sense for her to look as unextraordinary as possible for the first part of the day. A thin blue cardigan, a T-shirt, and jeans sure fit the bill. Such a commonplace look clashes with my mental image of her, but I'd venture a guess that she's donned plenty of period clothing before. I spit foam into the sink then sling one of our bags over my shoulder, but she grabs my arm before I reach the door.

"Hold on." She reaches up and combs back my hair with her fingers, a gooey blue substance coating each one. It smells of minty wax. I stare at her chin, unsure where else to look. After a minute of arranging and with my hair no longer sweeping along my forehead, Corinna gives me an assessing look and nods. "Better."

She lets go. A rush of warmth stays behind where her

hand was. I clear my throat as we both make for the door, bags in tow and prepared to execute god-only-knows whatever plan.

"You ready?" she asks.

"Yeah." As if I'm going to back out now. "I am."

To my surprise—and though I'm still wondering how to dissuade her from her ultimate goal—I mean it. I am ready. Ready for whatever lays ahead. Ready to do anything other than sit and wait and worry.

We step out the door.

AFTER MUCH RESISTING, Corinna finally let me drive for once. Only after a pathetic amount of pleading on my part, but it felt nice to do something other than doze in the passenger's seat with that queasy road-trip feeling somewhere between hungry yet nauseous, tired yet restless.

An hour and a half has passed at this point. Flat dusty land begins to be punctuated by the occasional building, then tattooed by rail lines, and soon the landscape gives way to manicured suburbs and strip malls. Dallas proper wouldn't be too far off. As soon as we see its glinting skyscrapers outline the horizon, Corinna edges me out of the driver's seat.

"Defensive driving," she says. "In case the guys from yesterday find us again."

The justification falls flat on my ears—I think she just has a thing with control—but I don't argue. She looks tense enough as is. Not that I can blame her.

We drive into the heart of the city without another word spared, flying over the concrete boughs that crisscross the roads beneath, and I shield my eyes from the glare that flashes off the glossy towers. Things here certainly aren't as understated as in Austin. Our unofficial mantra is that, if the decor doesn't look like it would fit on a kombucha-drinking, thrift-bin-diving pseudo-hipster's mood board, it's a no-go. The glitz of this city by comparison is unnerving, albeit pleasing to look at.

After sitting through a half hour of traffic, we pull into the garage attached to a massive limestone building and park on the ground floor. I can't help but notice we're near one of the exits, likely in the event we need to make another quick getaway. Here's hoping it doesn't come to that.

Corinna yanks the keys from the ignition.

"Ready?" I'm surprised to hear my own voice, me asking her. That's new.

She nods and takes a deep breath. She pulls a huge purse loaded with everything we need—one of those monstrosities you could fit a small child into—from the back seat, then we both step out of the car. I barely catch the shimmer of her dress stuffed deep within the bag, hidden partly under the clutch wallet and makeup, all part of her ruse. Save the kohl etched around her eyes, I doubt she wears anything on a regular basis. If I look close enough, I can even see a few faint acne scars from however long ago. It's a brief walk before we enter the alabaster building I saw a moment ago, its front paneled with rose-toned etchings.

We make it past the doors without riling any suspicions. Not that we're acting suspicious, but the feeling that anything could go wrong at any moment nags at me. Yet, no bag searches. No metal detectors or scanners. The museum building looks old, with the security to go with it. Perhaps that means the protections around the domukardi are just as lax. Hopefully our smooth sailing is a good omen for the rest of our day. A woman with box-braids and a kind face greets us at the front counter, and we secure our general admission tickets.

"Thanks." I wave at the cashier when Corinna snatches me by the elbow and suddenly drags me away. A bit taken aback, I yank out of her grip. "What, what's your deal?"

"There." She points to a wall-mounted sign just ahead of us, and I swear I detect the slightest hint of a tremor in her hand. There in crisp font, like a lighthouse on a darkened sea, reads *Metallurgical Works of the Near East.* I look back at her to see how wide her eyes have become, her hand still up and shaking.

"Deep breaths, okay?" I squeeze her shoulders, unsure what else to do. I've never seen her as anything other than a portrait of fury or confidence, not...this. "We don't want to draw attention to ourselves, right?"

To my infinite surprise, she listens. Still distant, but at least I get a nod from her.

"Calm and steady," I say.

Again she nods. "Calm and steady."

Corinna pushes her shoulders back and heaves out a breath from her nostrils. She walks forward and I follow. Up the floating staircase, through the maze of halls, and finally we come to where the signs have led us, to a single open room. Its size is intimate, and the dim lighting catches the swelling curves and edges of copper embellishments, bronze bowls, golden edging. The lacquered cedar floors seem to scent the room, as if trying to drag us back in time to Cyprus, to Lebanon or further.

"It's here."

When I turn my head I see her tight-laced control threatening to break free, her gaze pinned straight ahead. Corinna walks forwards, myself at her elbow all the while, and at last I see what we're here for. A hammered metal box with a thick wrought top sits upon a pedestal, underlit by a golden glow from the glass panel beneath. A patinated knob with three numbered clasps upon it seals the box, a thick crust of amber rust around its locked lip. Her domukardi.

"It's," she mutters, "it's—"

Old, I think. I knew it'd be old since that's the whole point, but to see something so ancient and think of the

Death of an Immortal

hands it's kissed, the lands it's traversed... That's an entirely different beast. A beast I'm not sure I can confront just yet.

Corinna bends forward, head bowed, shoulders tense. Her knuckles turn white as piano keys as she grips the bannister separating her from the domukardi. A rattling rises from between her ribs, and she shudders.

"Hey." I put my hand on her back, but lightly. Will touch help? Comfort? Or has she become a bomb and the slightest brush of a fingertip will set her off? My palm rests there for a second, then two. Her shoulders draw away from her jaw a tad. A good sign. I clear my throat. "Let's go sit down."

She shakes her head and takes a moment to regain her voice, sights still in an unbroken line to the box. "I'm staying right here."

"You're sure this is it?"

"Without a doubt."

"Okay, that's good, but let's at least go to that bench over there, alright?" Emotional as she is, I need to find her some relief from herself sooner versus later—to say nothing about us potentially drawing the attention of museum staff. I've seen her raging and I've seen her paint a calm facade, but not whatever this is. I can't let it crack me. "You can still see the box from there. It won't go any—"

"You don't understand." Corinna wheels around to me, the first time she's looked my way since entering this room. A few black locks of her hair gently hit my cheek. "I let this out of my sights once, just *once*, Eugene, and I've been looking for it ever since. It's torn me apart. I can't make that mistake again. It's—"

"It's fine, I promise. It's not going anywhere this time." Nothing grants me any power over such a guarantee, she and I both know that—and yet she takes a small, doll-sized step back from the railing. I swallow. Before she loses her nerve any further, I take her hand and give it a gentle tug. It's considerably rougher than mine, as if that's somehow a surprise, but I don't mind.

She lets me lead her over to a bench with a shiny copper finish, its fresh polish at odds with the pieces on display around us. We sit. Sure enough her eyes go straight back to the domukardi. I pull a half-crushed water bottle from her purse.

"Drink." I hold it out to her, and her eyebrows quirk up with a sidelong look. Frustrated, I sigh. "Look, I don't—You seem upset, and I don't know what else to do for you right now, so just drink it, okay? You'll feel better. *I'll* feel better."

Her gaze scrapes over me for a second longer than I can take, and I look away. Corinna swipes the bottle from me, takes a long, desert-quenching sip, then wipes a stray drop of water away with the back of her hand.

"I don't mean to freak you out," she says. "After all this time and everything I've gone through to get here, this is huge for me."

I shift in my seat though still avoid eye contact. "Have you been looking for it ever since you, well, since you were made like this?"

She shakes her head and leans back. To any passerby she would look for all the world like a brooding college student, but the unnerving fire that runs through her warns otherwise.

"No, not actively. Only the past eighty years or so."

Eighty years. A mere sliver historically speaking, especially given the thousands of years she's been roaming the earth, but still the number hits me like a brick wall. My grandparents were mere infants then.

"I'm just glad it's not at the bottom of the ocean or some other impossible-to-reach place. Say what you will about the modern age, but there's still a lot of places we can't yet go." Corinna drains the last of the water and shoots it into the unnecessarily ornate, wood-paneled bin to our left.

"Better?" I ask.

She shrugs.

"We should walk around or else we might stick out." I put my hands on my knees and force myself up with a grunt. These past few days have taken more out of me than I'd like to admit, even with my regular runs giving my physicality a boost. "Look at the other exhibits instead of being planted in one spot."

"Enjoy yourself, but like I said, I'm staying here."

"Come on, Cor—"

"*Ssh.*" She throws a furtive glance around the room. "Does 'laying low' mean nothing to you?"

I lower my voice to match hers, but press on. "Does it mean anything to *you*? Anyone who's keeping tabs on us will expect you to be right here, exactly where we're standing, and sitting here won't make things any better. It won't sprout legs and run off, alright?"

Corinna opens her mouth to argue before closing it again. Her nose crinkles in frustration. "These things here in this museum, these are bits of people's lives thrown under a spotlight for the world to see. A curio. But to me, that's a part of myself I can't risk losing." The longing in her eyes, the aching rimmed around her irises lances through me, threatens to tear open my chest rib by rib. "And I won't. Not again."

I extend a hand out to her. "After tonight, it's yours. Promise."

Though we both know I have no such control, she begrudgingly takes my hand and I hoist her to her feet, and as we leave the room she gives one last glance over her shoulder to the box. Through the dampness in her eyes, I see something begin to harden as she looks at it. Wheels turning, gears fitting together in her mind. A plan is hatching there. I can tell.

More for my sake than hers, I quicken my steps to draw us away faster.

9

A PLACE IN THE SUN

The sun raked across Corinna's sweating back, warming the bloody gashes lain into her forearms. The drill yard was emptier today than it had been in the previous months, and even more so than the months before that. It seemed whichever higher-up was calling the shots was whittling down his selections to those he deemed fit, separating the chaff from wheat. 'He' could be a 'she', Corinna supposed—after all, there were quite a few women among the conscripts here—but the demographics only served to puzzle her further.

A ragged grunt pulled her back to reality and Corinna looked up in time to see her sparring partner charge. She blocked him at the elbow, hooked her heel behind his, then shoved his weak chest to send him tumbling backwards into the packed, chalky earth. She pinned one foot on his wrist, another atop his opposite elbow.

"Don't be so loud," she said, picking caked blood and dirt free from under her nails. "You signal your attack before you even get close."

Not that it would do him any good. The way recruits were getting cut around here, if he hadn't picked up basic pancrache technique and stealth yet, a request for his removal was already trickling down. His wet eyes told her he knew as much. His partner would be sent packing as well. No one got in around here without either being given a partner or coming in with one, the two expected to function as a complete, seamless unit. It was how the Spartans operated, and it clearly served them well.

She stepped off him and offered a hand up. Arithmetic would be soon, and their lecturer was a grisly, mean old bastard if she'd ever known one. Aside from the physical, their handler seemed to need them educated as well, something Corinna was more than fine with. Not only could she read some basic Greek now, she could write too. Basic and ineloquent words at best, but she could still put reed to parchment and do something other than their repetitive sketching of tactical maps. Brawn wasn't the only asset of value. As she helped her bruised opponent to his feet, she hoped camaraderie would stand for something too.

The yard overseer's whistle bit through the air to signal that it was time for lecture, and a sigh of relief went through the sixty or so of them left. They'd been in drills since before daybreak, and the intense heat of the Macedonian sun was wringing every drop of water their skins had left to give. She slicked sweat from her brow as she trotted up alongside Lycus. He'd put on at least a good ten pounds of muscle since they'd been here, finally filling out from the street child she'd grown up with.

"Got any salve on you?" he asked. His lower lip was split an ugly, purpling red, though the bleeding had been staunched. "Karas knocked me good."

"Don't let her think you'll get her back, or else she'll find some way to ambush you. And no, no salve."

"Damn."

She clapped him on the back as they walked on, yet over her shoulder she couldn't help but see Enyo Karas's snide, predatory gaze at their backs. That woman had something to prove, but Corinna didn't care to get involved with it. *Everyone* here had something to prove. She herself would give anything to stay under their mystery benefactor's employ, be it as a guard or a simple servant, and she knew the same held true for Lycus. Though they could read and write and do math, unless they wanted to serve at a temple or in some scribal position, the likelihood they'd find rest and food and steady wages elsewhere was minute to none—to say nothing of the chance at becoming something more. She might've been content serving a cult of Artemis or Athena, but that would mean being separated from Lycus. A future without him wasn't one she wanted any part of. Transcribing documents, if she ever learned how to write fast enough for it, wasn't for her either. No, it was the promise of *more* that she wanted. Everyone here did.

In the dark of that following night however, she learned firsthand what lengths some were willing to go to.

It was a light sound, so faint and harmless she was surprised she caught it at all. A tinkling snagged her ear and Corinna's eyelids fluttered open to see one of the knock-kneed recruits crouched beside her cot. Crouched, and pouring something into Corinna's water skin.

Corinna shot up and slammed her into the stone wall, its rough-hewn surface biting into the girl's back as she yelped. Before Corinna was able to land more than two blows, their barrack master, a thick-set woman with a brow heavier than any boulder, was peeling her off.

"Explain yourself!" she demanded. She raised her baton between them in warning, and Corinna knew firsthand that she'd use it.

The other seven women in the barracks—female recruits were rare but still very much a reality, merely bedding apart from the men for propriety's sake—set their oil lamps alight and hovered at the edge of their bedrolls, now awake and watching with rapt attention.

Death of an Immortal

"She was putting something in my water!" Corinna jabbed her finger towards the trainee, wide-eyed and quivering, who was curled up where the floor met the wall. The crystalline powder was too familiar a sight for Corinna to gloss over. It spilled from the pouch in the girl's hand, scattered over her sandals and the mouth of the spilled flask. Corinna's jaw tightened, her gaze an icy flame. "Powdered glass. You put—"

She didn't even finish her sentence. Betrayal wasn't a thing she had come to expect here. They were comrades as far as she could tell—but no. No, were she younger and scrawnier and weaker, she wouldn't view them as comrades. They would be competition.

"Treachery from within our own. As you sleep, no less." The barrack master stepped back and gave a weighing look between them, with particular disgust to the girl crumpled on the ground. As she turned to walk away, she gripped Corinna by the shoulder. "Do you know what we do with traitors?"

"I'm sorry, I'm so sorry," the girl wept. She pitched forward to tug at the barrack master's sleeping robes. "My marks—I wasn't going to make the week. They were going to cut me—"

"As they well should." She kicked her off, then repeated, stern authority lacing her voice, "What do we do with traitors, *soldier?*"

There sat the underlying question, the one on which her future sat. *Will you disobey my orders? Or will you do whatever it takes?*

Corinna pushed down the unease that knotted in her stomach, already frothing hot with premature guilt, then shifted her gaze back to the girl small as any lamb, who now looked up at her with watering eyes. Corinna's lips tightened, but she stood firm.

"Everybody pour out your water," Corinna said.

A small comment, but she didn't want to get ahead that

way. Even if it was someone else who'd pay the price, she wouldn't wish a stomachful of glass upon even Enyo. Sights never leaving the girl, she stepped forward and flexed her fingers.

Was this who she would be? Someone who would follow orders blindly, regardless of whether or not she agreed? She could simply haul her out to the steps of the compound and throw her out, let her seek her chances elsewhere.

No. It wasn't an option. Corinna would do anything to stay here, even this. Here was where her livelihood was, her shot at becoming something better. Even if this is what 'better' meant. She wished that her parents' souls, wherever they had departed to, couldn't see her now. Corinna drew back her arm, the first strike of many.

And so the traitor was dealt with.

~

THE YEARS PASSED with brutal work. A toil unending, complete with bloody sparring matches, training on every weapon at their disposal, even instruction in stealth and the darker disciplines of torture and subterfuge. And then, their first time witnessing battle.

That was when the difference was made, when those who weren't cut out for the addled chaos of war were set apart from those who kept their direction, their focus, despite the cries and gore of battle raking at everyone's guts. Nothing could prepare someone for it. No amount of training, no amount of exaggerated, late night tales. As if by some cruel cosmic joke, only bloodshed could prepare a person for even more bloodshed.

Horses were lopped off at the knees and toppled their riders forward, only to crush them underneath their barreling weight. Weeping men lay gurgling blood in the muck, their bladders loosening as they lost function.

Screams, whether of rage or pain, echoed like a symphony of the damned. Fear and instinct had taken control of her as she speared one man after another, and another, and another. Tearing into human flesh was too different from the live pigs they'd practiced on, if only for the agony and light in their eyes.

The next ones were easier. She made it through. At the end of it all, twelve of them remained. Six pairs. The nightmares of her parents being ripped from her life were now replaced by those of battle. She wasn't sure whether to be thankful for it or not.

When Corinna stepped into the hall on commencement night, it had been transformed into something near unrecognizable. Lush, heavy garlands were wrapped about the pillars and tapered candles shimmered like a blanket of stars come to earth. She'd only seen such extravagance through a noble's window or while sneaking through a wealthy merchant's home.

Lycus weaved his way through the crowd of people behind her.

"Fancy guests of honor?" she said, hazarding a guess.

"No one'd come to honor us."

"Well this certainly isn't for our enjoyment."

He shrugged, but she knew he was just as curious as her. "Maybe our mystery patron's someone important after all."

That much she had already assumed. Still, seeing the manifestation of his clout before them made it all the more real.

Her gaze sifted through the crowd only to find the majority of the party-goers to be stiff, bulky men without an ounce of merriment in them. *Guards.* Plainclothes ones, at that. Whoever their patron was, he was an important person indeed. One of them caught her watching them. Corinna stared back, gaze unbroken. How many were genuine attendees, and how many were security in disguise?

Lycus sniffed, then sniffed again. He clasped her hand and dragged her to the right.

"Hey!" she said.

"Don't you smell that?"

As she paused to nose the air, her mouth watered. She sped along with him through the yard. They'd stolen enough feasts to know what one smelled like. Cured and delicately sliced meats, thin as parchment. Waxy honeycomb dripping with gold. Spiced hummus. Buttery flatbreads cooked in bubbling garlic oil. Cardamom stuffed hens. The air wafted full and rich with its aromas; she could pick out the threads of each and every scent. Not like soldiers' gruel in the slightest, though she hadn't turned her nose up at that either.

They approached the dining hall only to find a contingent of leather-armor clad men blocking it off. Beyond them she could see a table, a pressed cloth lain across it and gleaming with the many foods she knew so well, plus a sloshing amphora full of what could only be wine.

"You think it's him?" Lycus tried to peer around the guardsmen.

"Who else?"

From this distance she couldn't make out many details, save that he was younger than her instructors—who themselves looked to be regaling him with stories—that he had a mop of curly flaxen hair, and that he had the build of a man in his prime. She wouldn't be surprised if he was a fighter, too. Corinna craned her neck to see more. If only he wasn't faced away from the hall.

"Move along." One of the guards shooed them off with a flap of his hand.

They grumbled but did as told. If they had one thing beaten into them from their time here, it was obeying orders. It took Lycus a few more knocks than her to learn the lesson. Corinna's disappointment, however, didn't last as she recalled the sight of the table. From the sight of it, their meal was coming to a close. It wouldn't be long until he came out to greet them and make a proper introduction.

One of the junior instructors milling about, apparently not important enough to be invited to the dinner, herded their group of twelve conscripts together and directed them to a back room Corinna had never seen before. It was small, only about ten paces wide along each wall, with a musty smell indicating that it didn't see much use. There were no windows to air it out either. Just stone at all sides. Hummingbirds buzzed in her stomach as Corinna realized what this meant.

They stood at attention. Two years. Two years they had waited to meet this man, this stranger who could somehow afford to fund this venture. The 'who' still nagged at her just as much as the 'why'. But now he sat a mere room away, eating his fill and no doubt being put into a grand mood. Would he install them in the service of his officials? Have them act as spies? Obviously he had some military purpose in mind, which she would be more than amenable to. The benefits that came with the occasional pillage could add up.

She heard the rhythmic stomp of feet from down the hall. Lycus, ever by her side, flitted his eyes towards her and winked. He was just as eager as she was.

Two armed men flanked the door, followed by another two who took either of the opposite walls, then their fair-haired patron came before them. The lot of them remained silent, even her instructors falling still. Corinna looked him dead on.

Her stomach hit the ground as if the earth had been yanked from under her. Lycus went cold at her side. The air felt as if it had left the room. That profile was one she recognized all too well, stamped onto all of the newest *drachmas* since Philip II's death. She averted her gaze forward, hoping, praying he didn't read her as insolent. It couldn't be. No man of his status would lower himself to be in their company. Not him. He—

"They are highly skilled in hand-to-hand combat and weaponry, are adaptable, work with their Cohort effectively, and obey without hesitation." The overseer inclined his head as he finished listing their assets, like they were livestock. In comparison to the man before them, they were. "I do hope they meet your favor, your Majesty."

He circled the twelve of them, as slow and deliberate as a stalking lion, chin held high. Regal. The oil lamps bathed his golden curls, his tanned skin in honeyed light.

"The women?" he asked, looking to the only three in the group. Enyo, Galene, and herself. "Are they fit for this sort of work?"

"Absolutely, your Highness. Just like the Scythian women, they work without issue and form a seamless pair with their Cohort partner."

"And their kin. Any family to speak of?"

"None, your Highness. No previous loyalties, no debts owed, and no relations left to speak of."

That's why they wanted vagrants. Without anyone else laying claim to them, their service would be only to whomever fed them and gave them a place to rest. But that again left her with questions. What on earth were they being molded for?

And why did Alexander III of Macedon need them at all?

10

THE RAVEN AND THE SPARROW

We meander about the museum corridors and anterooms for a solid three hours. The dioramas and main exhibitions are no doubt gorgeous, and I realize how strange it is we came here for a rusted box of all things. Corinna's mind seems to remain elsewhere, brows in a thick knot as she studies the ceiling. Throughout the afternoon she's come to greater attention, but not on par with how she typically is. Something about her is still distant, though not in the dazed sense. Instead, like she's planning something. Still, I feel a strange responsibility to watch out for her, which has distracted me from my usual neuroses around unfamiliar places. I have yet to even find where the fire exits are located.

Thank god this place is big, at least. Evading detection in a museum the size of an apartment would be impossible, even for Corinna. Definitely for me. We stroll through a nondescript hall to the side of the traffic's main flow, lit by blaring fluorescents that tell me it's for maintenance workers and other staff. A few frayed-edged pamphlets are stapled to the wall advertising household services or raffles long-since passed, all of no interest to museum goers. Corinna goes up to one of the doors with a custodial sign hanging above it.

"You peed ten minutes ago, so we should be fine." She draws a screwdriver from her bag then slides it between the frame and the lock.

"How did you—"

The handle pops open to reveal a few buckets, an iron rack stacked with bottles of cleaning detergent, and a variety of wet floor signs. The room itself—more like a closet—couldn't be larger than three desks put together. Corinna snatches me by the shoulder and pulls me inside, then closes the door behind us.

My entire face flushes a hot crimson, and I snap, "What're you—"

"Hush!" she whispers.

Her elbows dig into my chest as she pushes against me in the cramped space, and I step into one of the buckets cluttering the ground.

"Stop, stop moving!"

I do, nearly blinded in the dark and foot still in the bucket.

"Please god, tell me you have a good reason for this," I say.

"What, you think I came here without a plan?"

"Not to be whatever, but it sure seems like it."

She crinkles her nose at me. "We're laying low until the party starts. Soon they're going to start shuffling people out of the museum to get the venue ready, and we don't want to stick out as the people who're hanging back."

"Won't we stick out as the people who're hiding in the closet once a janitor comes by?"

"I jammed the lock. It'll only open for us from the inside, so we stay here until the gala is well under way. We have our clothes and we packed extra food. We'll be fine."

"Yeah," I scoff, "especially with such luxury accommodations."

As my vision begins to adjust to the darkness engulfing us, I see Corinna make a rude gesture in my direction.

Death of an Immortal

"Here." She crouches down to stack the buckets onto the supply rack, the lemony astringent scent clouding around the vibrant bottles, and she takes my foot out of the last one to clear the floor. "Better?"

"Yeah, a whole 'nother two feet of space." Irked though I am, my voice trails off in the blackness. Slivers of hard light stream between the door's ventilation slats to pour across the planes of her face, catching a fragment of a golden iris here, a stretch of jawline there. I clamp my teeth on the inside of my lip and exhale hard. At the very least she seems balanced again, measured in a way that she wasn't earlier.

"Don't be weird."

"I'm not being weird." My gaze suddenly goes to a corner of the ceiling where a ball of spiderwebs have collected dust.

"It's going to be a few hours. Might as well get comfy."

"And how am I suppos—Oh god, don't do that."

Corinna sits on the flecked-tile floor where the dust bunny population would put all other rabbits to shame, and she looks up at me with a raised brow. I think it's raised. It's hard to tell in here.

"What?"

"It's filthy down there!"

"Keep your voice down," she says. "I know you're probably a hypochondriac on top of everything else you've got going, but some dust won't hurt me."

"You're—"

"Unladylike?"

"You being unladylike isn't exactly a surprise at this point." I give up my scolding and lean against the door, sighing. "What's the time?"

"Four forty seven. A little over two hours until the gala starts, but we'll wait until things get going."

"So we're going to be in here for. . ?"

"Three hours."

Normally I would've groaned, but I don't have it in me

anymore. That, plus seeing how Corinna acted back in the metallurgy exhibit, her pained longing for that damned thing…I'll do what she needs of me. Even if it means breathing in the acidic smells and grit of a grubby janitorial closet. And enduring whatever plan she claims to have.

I crouch down on the floor across from her, though I'm not cavalier enough to put my ass to the ground and introduce it to the no-doubt thriving bacteria colonies. I see a faded pink leaflet, thoroughly water-damaged but still intact, poking out behind Corinna's head.

"Pass me that sheet of paper behind you."

She looks over her shoulder and tugs it from the shelf. "This?" She pauses to scan it over. *"Ancient Greece and the Micropenis.* Huh. Have something you need to get validated?"

"Dear lord, just hand it to me." I swipe it from her grasp and begin creasing the paper, folding it over at different angles and tearing off excess tidbits here and there. At the end, I have a thick isosceles triangle the color of old salmon. I hold it steady between my thumb and forefinger, close one eye, and aim it at her. "Make a goalpost."

"A what?"

"A goalpost."

"Why?"

"Paper football. Please tell me you know what paper football is." I flick the tiny projectile and it pops her square on the nose—or would have if she didn't have such adept reflexes.

She snatches it up. Turning it over in her palm, she looks the paper over and scoffs. "You're kidding, right?"

"What, you're too good for fun?"

"I don't get the point of it."

"Of fun?"

"No, this." She chucks the folded paper back at me, and I have just enough time to form a goalpost before it passes between my skinny fingers.

"Ever considered going pro?" I tease. Despite herself, I see the smallest upward quirk of her mouth as she shakes her head.

"Keep your voice down." A pause. She reaches for the paper football. "Give me that."

I don't know how long we go back and forth playing—at such short range, I'm not sure it even counts—exchanging whispered jokes and jabs and anecdotes all the while, but when I see her face lighten, no longer so solemn or fierce or calculating, it's worth it. I don't know why. For what she's dragged me into, I should hate her. For a bit, I did. Not anymore, though. Whatever explanations she put forth shouldn't have been enough, but they were. There's a strange comfort in this new dynamic, one that'll continue for as long as she flashes those brilliant eyes or that quill-sharp wit. For as long as she keeps her end of the bargain in preserving my life, all the while hunting to end her own.

For now, at least.

After what feels like both an eternity and a second, in some dreamlike bubble outside of time, Corinna rummages through her oversized bag. The light of her burner phone's clock washes over her face. As if on cue, the rumblings from down the hall grow louder, rising above the level of mere background noise. Where the scraping of table legs and clanking carts were, now the lilt of classical music meets my ears.

"Just about time." She pops up onto her feet then kicks her shoes off with a heavy clunk against the tile. After digging through the bag again, she tosses me my formalwear before slinging her shimmering dress over her shoulder. Even in this lightless closet it scintillates like crushed glass tossed into the sun.

She turns away from me and pulls her shirt up over her head.

I reflexively jerk back and smack my head against the wall

with a resounding metallic *whoomp,* no room to swivel around in. She gives me that same aggravating grin.

"I know, I know, 'fair maiden'," I snap as I close my eyes. "You don't have to say it every time."

"You don't have to hit the ceiling every time."

"You don't have to keep trying to get naked in front of me!"

She snickers, voice echoing back at me off the tinny cabinets. "Consider it charity."

My movement restricted by the cramped space and surrounding minefield of potentially hazardous, chemical-filled bottles, I can hardly do more than stand there as I hear the rustling fabric of Corinna shimmying into her dress.

"It's safe now, mister chastity."

Unsure whether to believe her, I slowly open an eye to find her telling the truth. She leans over to tug off her pants from underneath. There's never a graceful way to take off pants, even for someone as fluid as her, but I pay the otherwise comical scenario no heed and try to focus my attention elsewhere. Small scars fleck the still-unzipped swatch of her back. Slivers of tight, coruscating flesh.

"Acclimating, are we?" she teases as she at last yanks the bra over her head, careful not to smear her cat-eye makeup.

"I'm not—I—" I falter in exasperation. Someday I'll learn to stop protesting altogether. "You just have, uh, nice shoulder blades."

Corinna half-turns to face me, eyebrow cocked and her mouth quirked up. "Is that code for something else?"

"No!" I feel my face flush as I do my best to avert my eyes. Still, I can't help dragging my gaze over the curve of her lower back, the swell from her waist to hips, or the sleek bones gliding from her shoulder to spine. "Just... shoulder blades."

"Uh-huh." A momentary pause, an assessing silence. "Here, zip me up."

I inch forward and pull the clasp to the top.

"Thanks." She shakes her inky hair out from its clip as it spills over her shoulders, down along the planes of her back. After placing a few pins through her hair, catching the stray wisps tickling her cheeks, she looks like something out of an impressionist painting, all light and vague angles. Even what's tangible is more like some transparent and unseeable *other*, reminding me of when I was a child and thought I could grab onto a rainbow. I never could catch it.

Corinna turns to face me. "Why aren't you dressed yet?"

An obvious question with an obvious answer.

I have no doubt she's more buff than me—while I'm not a twig, the muscle I have is a thin layer at best—and the idea of stripping down in this small of a space with her watching, especially given that she's more attractive by every conventional measure...It's not an enticing idea.

"Uh, some privacy?" I await the snappy remark that'll no doubt follow.

"I mean," her voice falters as she looks about the closet. "I can close my eyes, if you want?"

"Oh." I didn't expect her to return the favor. "Yeah. If you could."

Turning to stone before me, she closes her eyes and waits, and in that moment I become acutely aware of the distance between us. The *lack* of distance, all one and a half feet of it. I've never gotten undressed in front of a girl before, and certainly not a woman. Sure, I'd been shirtless in front of others at the pool and at annual physicals and whenever I'd lounge around the house in my underwear, but the context is too different here to escape my notice. Swallowing down a lump in my throat, I lay my fresh-pressed clothes atop an upturned bucket, then grab the hem of my shirt and pull it over my head. Though I know she's not looking, my pulse doesn't. I button up my new attire, sling the champagne necktie around my shoulders. Only now do I notice that she's matched our outfits to compliment one another, my camel to her gold. Somehow it's an endearing detail—though it means nothing. Just another costume.

I unbutton my pants and let them drop to the floor, not enough bulk on my thighs to keep them up on their own, and dig the toe of my sneaker into my other one to pop them off. Anything to keep me from having to bend over into her space. Standing atop my pile of clothes, I shimmy into black slacks and wiggle my feet into loafers. No fiddling with laces needed, thank god.

"You done yet?" she asks, a hint of a laugh in her tone.

"Yeah, all good." I loop the tie under my collar and finish it off into a standard knot.

She cocks her head, eyes now open and leveled with my neck. "No, too simple for something like this. We want to look like we belong, which is all in the details." She grabs a hold of my tie and pulls me a step closer. The air between us grows still, charged with a certain magnetism—though I'm probably the only one who feels it. "Balthus knot. It's classier."

She smells like oranges and the bare flesh of a cedar tree. I don't even pay attention to the intricate loops Corinna manipulates my tie into, only the slight crease between her brows as she works. Her hands, small yet calloused, are close enough to wrap around my throat—or pull me closer.

"Done." She leans back to survey me. I thank whatever deity is out there that it's dark enough to hide my no-doubt reddened cheeks. "Much better."

I nod at her in lieu of thanks, then swallow whatever this is rising in my throat.

"Here, tuck this into your jacket. We'll need it."

She hands me what looks like a huge canister of hairspray, and I raise my eyebrows. "Are you planning on throwing this at security or something?"

"And if I am?"

"I can't imagine that's your plan."

Death of an Immortal

She shakes her head with a fiendish grin, half-looking like she'll pat my head. "Sweet Eugene, you couldn't imagine my plan even if I drew it out for you in crayons."

I resist rolling my eyes, but tuck the spray can inside my jacket.

Corinna flips open one of those compact mirror things girls always seem to have in their purse and jams it under the door, turning it sideways to see if anyone is coming. Flipping it closed, she grabs our bag.

"All clear."

She opens the door and strides out, looking for all the world like it's normal to be emerging from a maintenance closet in a dazzling gown. I probably look like a cat on the way to the vet. Stressed and wide-eyed. In danger of peeing on the floor if a stranger approaches me.

Corinna stuffs our bag into a trash can.

"Hey!" I whisper.

She waves me off. "Nothing in there is important anyways. Worst case, maintenance assumes someone upgraded their bag. Best case, they don't even notice it."

As we draw nearer to the sound of bubbling laughter and clinking glasses, Corinna stops and grabs in my jacket, taking the hairspray and placing it in the trash.

"We'll come back for it later," she says upon seeing my perplexed face.

She was right: whatever plan she has, I won't be able to guess at it. I keep from second guessing her, at least aloud, and follow as she starts back down the hall.

Almost around the corner and into the party, Corinna stops at the sound of footfalls.

"There's—Oh!" A man with a glass of shallow amber liquid stumbles as he rounds the corner and nearly plows into us, his friend steadying him with a grip on his shoulder.

Corinna jumps back with hands raised in mock surprise.

"Sorry," she says, voice higher than I've ever heard it

before. Somehow she feigns a blush, her darker skin turning a shade of wine as she avoids his gaze. "So sorry. Come on, babe, let's get back to the party."

The gentleman steps aside as we scurry off, our flustered faces no doubt being mistaken for embarrassment at being caught. She turns on the point of her heel—god only knows how in shoes like that—and swings her hand behind her. I know I'm meant to grab it, and so I do. Even with its many calluses it feels like a finch in my palm, warm and fluttering with life. I do my best to ignore it. We enter the throng of the party. The lighting changes from glaring fluorescents into a softer hue as we walk into the main room. It looks as if the air has been drowned in a thick blanket of honey, giving off a waxy amber light, and she loops her hand around my elbow as we make our way into the heart of it all.

"Keep things casual," she tells me at a whisper. "Don't talk to anyone unless you have to, and don't give away any information. Stay with me at all times."

"If we're not going to interact with anyone then what was the point of coming here?"

"Patient, Gigi. Or would you rather I break out the crayons?"

I hold back a disgruntled sigh. While I'm not supposed to draw attention to myself, I certainly don't want anyone to think I look like some young socialite annoyed with his date. If only they knew.

Corinna swipes two flutes of bubbling champagne from a server's platter as he walks by, then hands one to me. "It'll take the edge off. Just don't drink too much. I, on the other hand," she tilts her head back and slams down the full glass in one gulp, then smacks her lips, "have a plan to attend to."

I blink.

Wrist once again linked around my elbow, she gives a breezy laugh that tinkles like a wind chime as we fold into the crowd. If you didn't know her you would think it was genuine, but I can hear the ruse constructed beneath. It's for show, just like everything this evening. Even my tie's fat, ridiculous knot. But if I think it's absurd, I guess that means some would consider it fashionable.

We meander around the open hall packed with guests, jewels hanging from their throats and dripping down their fingers, satin cravats and pressed pocket squares all in place, for a solid slice of the night.

Corinna had taken one glass of libations after the next, and it wasn't until I caught her discreetly dumping one of them into a potted plant that I began to understand her plan. Or at least part of it. Once she was 'tipsy'—or could play the role with the scent of champagne on her breath—she'd fallen into one of the security personnel and, as if by mere sleight of hand, his badge was gone. Not that he was any the wiser.

The word 'gala' had led me to believe this would be a larger ordeal, exciting and swimming with interesting people, when instead it largely turned out to be history buffs with more than a shiny nickel in their pocket, all with the same penchant for gossip and alcohol that the rest of society has. I have to hand it to them though. A museum seems like a much better place to party than some vomit-soaked bar district.

After an hour of wandering between the chattering masses, Corinna's head rests against my nonexistent bicep in a convincing show of fatigue.

"I need a smoke," she says to no one in particular, voice amplified by her faked inebriation.

"What?" I blink. I've never seen her smoke before, but then, we have only been together for a few days. My nose crinkles up. "That's a disgusting habit."

As her lower lip forms a sultry pout and a rakish man of about 55 comes to her side, lighter in hand and eyes salacious, one of her many puzzle pieces falls into place before me.

"I can help there, sweetheart."

"Thank you."

My mouth twists as she flutters her lashes at him.

"He's never any fun," she complains to the man, torso still facing me but craning her head in his direction. He places the plastic lighter in her palm and grazes the pads of his sweaty fingers along hers as he does so. Even if he can't see how she bristles, I do. Her expression however remains pleasant as ever. "I'm going to go take a drag in the bathroom, then I'll be back. Honey, wait for me outside?"

Realizing that I'm 'honey', I nod. "S-sure."

She flashes a sparkling smile at me, then the man at my side. "I'll be back."

With a twirl, she weaves through the crowd and disappears. I follow. When I look over my shoulder expecting to see his hungry eyes trailing after, part of me is relieved to find him staring at a different woman, though one still tastelessly young.

I stand outside the women's bathroom and wait, checking the wall clock and bouncing back and forth on the balls of my feet. The hands tick on. And on. I doubted that she was actually planning on taking a smoke break, but not so much any more.

"Psst," comes a voice from the shadows.

I seize up only to find Corinna around the corner of the bathroom, waving me over. When did she even slip out? Did she ever go in at all? Checking over my shoulder, I then tip toe towards her.

"Smoking kills," I say as I reach her side.

"If it were that easy for me to die, we wouldn't be here, now would we?"

She does have a point.

We walk through the darkened halls and stop by the trash can Corinna stuffed the spray can into, and she reaches the full length of her arm inside, digging deep, to pull it out. I grimace but hold my tongue. Weaving through the halls, we eventually come to a corner of the building. Beneath it is a bench. Corinna grabs the slack in her dress as she gets atop it, then turns to dump the spray canister and lighter in my hands.

A chill skitters down my spine and I bite down on my lip, trying not to think about where this was. *There was no trash in the bin. Just this.* The thought does little to help me swallow my revulsion, though. But then, before this I *did* grab a dirty blade out of the motel trash. This is an upgrade. At the bottom of the spray can, I see something like a sticker begin to pucker up. Whatever this originally was, it's exterior must be a facade for what's really inside.

With those deft fingers of hers, Corinna grabs the vent over the bench and pries its metal cover off.

"Spray can." She holds her hand out expectantly.

I give it to her with a raised brow, and she shakes it.

"Take a few steps back."

I do as she says, looking this way and that in case anyone else passes through. The hiss of the can meets my ears as I see Corinna spray it into the vents. I watch her for a moment, brows knitting together.

"Mercaptan," she says, as if sensing my forming question.

"Am I supposed to know what that is?"

"With how paranoid you are, I assumed you would." She shrugs, but still holds down the nozzle and sprays into the vent. "It's the smell companies add to gas so people can tell if there's a leak."

"Where—Where did you find something like that?"

"Online delivery is a wonder. These past few decades, a whiff of this stuff has proven the most effective way to clear a building. I keep a ready supply of it." A wicked smile paints her face. "We'll be alone soon enough."

My eyes go to the vent—a vent I now realize she kept walking past during our time in the museum today. One of the many she'd looked at. I thought she was just staring up at the ceiling and walls to focus her mind, not that she was puzzling out which vents lead where.

As soon as someone catches the first smell of gas, the gala will erupt into a panic.

Corinna steps down. A quick shake tells her there's still some inside, and she hands it back to me as we head towards the room with the domukardi. We make our way through the corridors, ever cautious to keep an eye out for any additional personnel that may be doing security rounds. At least we don't need to risk going back for our bags, since Corinna threw them away. She wouldn't need her things for long anyway, since—

I stop myself from finishing the thought. My stomach clenches as if I'm going to be sick every time I consider her ultimate goal.

"How long until the place clears out?" I ask.

She shrugs, even though I imagine she has a precise timeline unfolding in her head. It does little to lessen my anxiety. I rub the back of my neck and roll out my shoulders.

"How can you deal with all of this waiting around?"

"That's what most of my life has been. Waiting." She continues forward, yet despite her breezy tone, her eyes look harder now than ever before. "But I've waited long enough."

11

A LAMENT OF HEROES

EMPIRE. That elusive goal, achieved by so very few.

Philip II, father to Alexander and late King of Macedon, had died with that dream still far from reach—but his son was determined to conquer. To succeed. Already he was swinging back to strike the iron.

Corinna supposed that was where they came in, for whatever use they could be over his standard-issue soldiers. She still wasn't sure how, but she wasn't about to complain. The eleven others and herself had sworn an oath of loyalty to Alexander's service either way.

Alexander's legions had been marching for weeks now, baking under the broiling heat of the Anatolian hillsides with jagged mountain peaks swelling on either side of them, as if guarding their lands against these foreign invaders. The mountains however were no comparison to the strait of the Hellespont they'd crossed earlier in their travels, a Herculean labor in and of itself. Thank heavens Alexander was a pious enough man to route his troops past Ilium, where at least he could make sacrifices, pour out libations, and lay out offerings for the gods and goddesses to thank them for their aid in the crossing. Such deities were likely the only reason they'd managed it at all.

While his Highness was welcomed into the halls of Ilium's court, the city couldn't very well accommodate a legion of over thirty-thousand, and left them to raise their tents outside the city walls. Corinna could have bunked in a stable for all she cared; a day's rest would do them all well.

She ruffled her hair as it swung down her back, let loose from its leather thong, then collapsed onto her cot beside Lycus. She flopped over onto her side.

"Long day?" Lycus asked. Despite his swaggering nature, weariness collected in the fine lines around his eyes, around his lips cracked dry from the sun.

"Long week."

She rummaged through her rucksack and pulled out a pot of beeswax and olive oil. Propped up on her elbow, she tugged Lycus to face her and, fingers dipped in the salve, traced along his cupid's bow and full lower lip. After a pause, he flashed his devilish smile and pulled her towards him, fatigue forgotten.

Every Cohort pair had a canvas tent of their own—albeit modestly sized—for bonding's sake, yet another of the Spartan concepts Alexander employed. He'd always pushed for his chosen soldiers to not only be partners, but lovers as well, believing they would fight harder in battle if their beloved's life was at stake. The Spartans themselves, perhaps second-mightiest of all, believed the complement of a primal, sensual bond along with the more strategic kind could enhance fighting coordination beyond measure. True or not, the idea of bedding down with a room full of testosterone-saturated, raucous men didn't do much for Corinna, and she and Lycus had shared the same cot since childhood.

"Feels weird," he said afterwards. He massaged his lips together and spread the salve about, or at least what hadn't come off on Corinna's mouth and skin.

Death of an Immortal

"Since when've you been so picky?"

"No, this. Having time to lay back and do," he grasped for the right words, "do—"

"Do nothing." She nudged him with a smirk, then breathed in the night air tinged with salt from the nearby port. Eyes closed, she melted into the cot with muscles unwinding. The evening wind rustled their tent flaps, a melody she could nearly fall asleep to.

Except their Cohort didn't get tomorrow off for idle revelry, even if the other soldiers did. Tomorrow Alexander was set to pay tribute at the tomb of Achilles, the Cohort responsible for escorting him along the way. Where his regular guards had gone off to, she didn't know, but it wasn't her job to pry. It was her job to obey.

After getting up to scrub herself clean with sand and placing her *xiphos* short sword within arm's reach, she lay down once again and doused the light.

THE TWELVE MEMBERS of the Cohort stood to the side, out of sight and yet with eyes in all directions, as Alexander looped a garland around the stone tomb of Achilles, his beloved Patroclus buried beside him. The earthen heap where his pyre-burnt bones were laid to rest had been enshrined between these chiseled slabs and pillars where the entire company now stood. Hephaestion, the high-ranking commander and lover by Alexander's side, laid a wreath at the base of Patroclus's altar. As Achilles and Patroclus were, so were Alexander and Hephaestion. She supposed the bond between the two heroes of such long-gone days mirrored their own love. Not just love, but respect. A mutual reverence. Corinna kept herself from glancing at Lycus, her own half.

Alexander crouched before the *Iliad*'s esteemed hero and murmured to the sacred dirt with a voice passionate yet sober. Even from this distance, the air was silent enough to let stray words waft her way. Words praising the son of Thetis, prince of the Myrmidons, lionhearted and wild. All characteristics Alexander was familiar with, all things he sought to embody. As far as she could tell, it was what drove him forward.

But something besides adoration of long-passed heroes pushed him on into Persian territory, something boiling just beneath his skin. Before, she could catch the slightest glimmer of his aspirations. A hungry gleam in his eye. An eager note in his voice—then it was gone. Here, standing before the tomb of the greatest hero to have ever lived, she saw his ambition as clearly as if it stood beside him, like a creature in its own right. A swelling desire for the everlasting, for a legacy carved out by his own two hands and larger than that of any mortal. An empire with him upon its throne for time immemorial.

As he bent down to cup the earth around Achilles's burial mound in his war-roughened hands, she glimpsed why her king admired him so. A great warrior, yes, but it was Achilles' choice that defined him. His choice to abandon a quiet life in the arms of safety and instead to live in the briefest flash of glory eternal, even if it meant death. It's not one she felt she would make, but the pursuit of greatness wasn't her aim. It was Alexander's.

She shifted on the balls of her feet to keep her knees from tiring. They'd been here for an hour now, and though she was disciplined enough to remain both still and alert, the stomach was a harder thing to train. It gurgled, begging for some of the buttered flatbreads or roasted peppers they'd passed earlier. Both the king, cavalry commander Hephaestion, and the shorter, brown-skinned man beside him had to be getting hungry by now.

The latter was a newer edition, though others said he'd been here from the beginning, just tucked away in back rooms doing gods-know-what. She'd seen this man and Alexander together a great deal as of late. Certainly there was no romance with him as there was with Hephaestion, but there was something. The man's pointed cap, billowing robe, and trousers gave him away as a Persian, so he would have been too dangerous to keep around unless he had proved his worth. What with the conflict between Macedon and Persia, it was likely he was feeding Alexander information. Here, loyalty to his birthplace would get him a swift knife to the throat and little else.

Dimnos, one of her fellow Cohort members, caught her gaze and shrugged. Seems she wasn't the only one in the dark, not that that was unusual. The Persian spent most of his days in his tent anyhow, scribbling away in a strange script of equations and formulae. Biases getting the better of her, she scoffed inwardly. *An old man of little consequence.*

She turned her gaze away without so much as a second thought.

12

A DARKER HALF

You can hear our breath as it meets the air. An utter stillness hugs the night. After our wandering through the corridors, we've at last returned to where the box lies waiting for us.

A sharp intake of breath snaps me back to attention. Corinna sees it before I do and stops to stare ahead at that thing, so small yet so heavy. There it sits. A crusted patina paints the outside of one edge, and a rare shimmer of bronze that has escaped time's ravages on the other. A few other pieces, a large coiled basin and a lapis encrusted comb, sit upon the dais as well, but they're no more than scrap to her. Corinna puts one foot forward, then the next, and suddenly she's sprinting towards it, having waited long enough. I follow after, and we both stop at the partition.

"Heat sensors. A smart move." With a scornful grin she points to the little black boxes circling each stand, each hardly bigger than a thumb tack and trained on their respective object. "Almost impossible to get around."

She withdraws another spray bottle, this one purple and travel-sized, from her clutch.

"More of that gas smell?" I ask, though I can't imagine how it'd help us here.

Death of an Immortal

"No, this is just hair spray."

Whatever my puzzled face contorts into, I'm sure it looks ridiculous. I swallow. Angled just out of the camera's field of view, Corinna shoots it onto the lenses, coating them in a tacky layer of the spray. I blink, unsure what to make from any of it. She reaches for the box—and I jerk towards her.

"Wait!" I whisper.

She stops, but straightens and sniffs as if insulted. "What, you think I didn't do my homework?"

"The sensors—"

"Don't work. Not if you spray hairspray on the lenses."

"You have to be *sure*."

She snorts. "You act like this is my first modern robbery."

I open then promptly shut my mouth.

She places her hand over mine where it rests on the banister. Her lips tug upwards. "Don't look so grim. You'll be able to go home soon."

But you'll be dead.

I wonder if I should feel bad about helping her do this, but where guilt should be I find only a deeper ache.

"Why—" My voice falters. I already gave my word. "What do you need me to do?"

She swallows. "Once I hand you the domukardi, all I need you to do is open it. The code's in roman numerals. You know those right?"

"I'm not stupid." There's nothing acrid or joking in my tone where I expect there to be. Listlessness meets me instead.

"These days, you have to make sure." She shrugs. "The code is 3-7-1. Then you just lift back the lid and leave the rest to me, okay?"

The word 'yes' sticks in my throat like hot tar.

Don't be selfish. This is her choice, not yours. I nod instead.

My heart thrums into my mouth as I feel my hands begin to quiver. Despite my best efforts, my brain won't fall into autopilot like I so desperately wish it would. How much simpler this would all be if I didn't have to think about the gravity of what I'm doing, didn't have to think at all.

Corinna turns towards the box, then halts. Her hands hover over it, as if it might lash out at her or unleash a bolt of lightning. I see her shoulders tense up towards her ears before she forces them back down. She's not going to let herself be anxious. Not after all this time.

She grasps the domukardi by the bowed handles then turns to me with eyes limned in wet silver, prize clutched to her bosom.

"I can't believe—This is," she says between thin, elated breathes, "the closest I've been to it in—"

The alarm blares, screaming against our eardrums. I crouch down against its whining peals and white bursts of light. Its reverberations beat into my chest and set my teeth chattering. Gratefulness that I hadn't drank at the gala washes through me. If I had, I almost certainly would've pissed myself by now.

"It's fine," Corinna says. Or what I think she says from the movement of her lips. "It's the gas smell. They're evacuating."

Hands clapped over my ears, I nod. So long as this is part of the plan.

"Let's move." Corinna grabs my wrist and tightens her grip on the box. Her fire reignited, intensity alive again, she pulls us ahead. "Come on!"

We tear out of the room and through a corridor in the opposite direction we came, toward the side of the museum. Everyone would be evacuating out the front of the building, so exiting this way should give us a clean getaway.

"Through here!"

I almost bust it face-first as Corinna tugs me towards a maintenance stairwell. Even knowing that the alarm isn't for us, my eyes are clotted with stars from it, pulse screaming through my body—when she pushes through the door and it slams closed behind us. Corinna screeches to a halt in front of me.

Even muffled by the alarm, a slow clap steadily punctuates the night air, ringing out near the flight of stairs below her.

"Almost perfect," comes a voice.

Dread sloshes in my gut. It's then that I see him, a foot resting atop the bottom step. His skin is the same color as Corinna's, his eyes too. A white suit jacket hugs his lean torso, but everything else he's wearing is a heavy black straight down to his polished shoes. For whatever reason, I can't help but feel that I'm looking at a wild thing in human skin—much like Corinna herself. Looped around his shoulder is our bag, unzipped and rummaged through, and a series of glinting rings adorn his scorpion-like, calloused fingers. I feel Corinna tense alongside me. She stares down her nose at him.

"You really thought you could kill me that easily?" he asks.

I stop. Breath halts in my throat and strains in my lungs. *Kill* him? I look at Corinna, but her gaze remains fixed. He sighs when she doesn't respond, and then his sights come to rest on me. His mouth cracks open in a dazzle of gleaming bone.

"I see your whipping boy doesn't know the whole story."

"It's been a while, Lycus," she says, jaw still clenched. As if not wanting his focus anywhere near me.

Lycus. I remember the name. The man who'd sent gunmen after us, who'd killed Brendon Watts—but what if there's more to it than I initially imagined? Has she tied me up into something worse than what I've been led to believe?

"Too long." He takes another step up and she jerks back. Lycus pauses and raises his hands, face smug even as his eyes flick towards the box. Undeterred. Another few steps, halfway to us now. He tosses a gesture of his eyebrow, somehow flirtatious of all things, her way. "Big fan of museums. You always have been, though I was never much the admirer. Like so much else, we just couldn't see eye to eye."

She doesn't say anything. Her silence is perhaps what frightens me most of all.

Lycus continues. "I've made donations to this particular museum for some time. I knew you'd make your way to it eventually, and with this exhibit? Well, that was just something I had to fund. When I saw *this*," he shrugs our bag down onto his elbow, "I knew our paths were finally going to cross again." Another step closer, hands easing down. "It's been too long, sweetheart."

A trap, the two of us damned from the start. But we have the domukardi, and if we can just make it to the exit—

"I see the wheels turning in the boy's head," he says. My blood runs cold as his gaze comes back to rest on me. There's something predatory, slippery about him, a thin veneer of sensuality the only thing that hides the monster within. His eyes scrape over me, disgusted. "This kid's my new replacement? Good god, Cor. My bed is always open, y'know."

"Snakes aren't to be replaced," she spits. "They're to be put down."

So she does want to kill him. For all that she's talked about ending her own life, I'd believed her. Should I have? My head swims, my breath is thin in my chest, but I try to cut through the fog, to focus only on what's pertinent for making it out of this in one living, breathing piece.

"This is yours, if I'm right." He takes a few more steps and leans forward to place the oversized bag at our feet. Hesitant, Corinna hands me the domukardi and lifts it, unzips to see what's inside.

"A dye pack?" She looks up with her mouth caught in a snarl. "How stupid do you think I am?"

His eyes go disconcertingly bright, lit with glee. "Stupid enough to pick it up."

She stills.

Death of an Immortal

"Those things're sensitive these days, and they don't come off easy. Or did you think I'd let you walk through the crowd out front and be on your way? No, the minute you try to run or fight your way out of this, that dye pack explodes on you and that delicious dress to brand you a criminal." His mouth ticks up. "Sound familiar?"

A sudden wave of rage boils off her. "How *dare* you—"

Hoping we might be able to lose him in the maze of halls, I dart behind us and try the door at our backs. It's locked. The lump in my throat hardens. Two suited gunmen, one a deceptively lanky, sallow-skinned man and one a stocky black woman with long box braids, stand at his back. I recognize the latter as our ticket clerk from earlier today. A set-up from before we'd even walked through the front door. Corinna's eyes flick to them as well, but her sights quickly return to Lycus.

"Couldn't see to this yourself?" she mocks, though her voice remains as flat as a pit viper.

"Insurance." He says nothing more, simply continues flashing that damned shark-tooth grin at her. A wave of jealousy coils in my stomach. "*You* taught me that."

"*I* taught you to fight your own battles." Her voice snaps as she grabs me around the middle, hands inside my cheap jacket. My neck almost heats—but I feel where her hands go, to where he can't see. Just inside my waistband, to the two objects stuffed there. "What you taught *me* was that people in life will double-cross you just for the hell of it. Just to make a quick coin."

"You and I remember a very different set of lessons."

"Maybe. But you still never learned the most important one." She leans closer into me. Though Lycus likely reads it as her rubbing his nose into her supposed partner, it's then that I understand the last-ditch plan brewing in her skull. She grabs the lighter and hairspray in one hand. "Never back me into a corner."

In the span of less than half a second, Corinna chucks the duffle bag at him, ink pack exploding through the fabric to stain his pristine jacket. She kicks out in front of us to land squarely in Lycus's chest, toppling him backwards down the stairs, then ignites the lighter in a roaring conflagration before us. His guards crouch to shoot, but she descends upon them before they can let a single bullet fly and forces them to the opposite side of the stairwell until we can get to the lower flight. Lycus just manages to right himself as we pass him at the landing, but he doesn't move for us.

"Come on!" she yells to me, and I close the distance between us.

The can sputters. A faucet running dry, the fire begins to die.

Cursing, Corinna holds it as long as she's able, then chucks it to the side and grabs my wrist in one hand, box in the other. His guards are fast upon us.

We burst through the door at the bottom of the stairs, now on the first floor of the museum. The front entrance is just within view, the city lights a hazy glimmer in the distance, before Corinna veers right behind the reception desk, kicking and toppling over everything that she can in our wake. Fake potted plants, file cabinets, all obstacles that we can only hope will buy us precious seconds in a desperate effort at saving how far we've come.

"Stay down!" she yells, both of us crouched as low as we can get at a run.

I don't have to look back to know our pursuers have already drawn their weapons. A gunshot roars against my eardrums.

We race through the corridors and make it to a heavy metal door. Past the thinly criss-crossed wires in the window, I see the parking garage loom, taunting us, beckoning us to safety. *So close.* We could actually make it.

From down the front of her dress, Corinna whips out the

security guard's keycard from earlier and swipes it through the beat-up reader.

"It's automated," she says. I'm not sure if the talking is for her benefit or mine. "It'll close on its own after a few seconds. Thing's weighted. They're not going to be able to follow after us. Not this way, at least."

The commotion behind us as Lycus's hired hands obliterate the debris in their way grows steadily louder, and a heartbeat that we don't have time to waste passes, the reader light blinking, thinking. Dread pounds through my veins as the seconds stretch. If it doesn't open, there's no way I'm surviving this.

It flickers green. Corinna yanks the door open towards us —just as the woman with tight braids runs into the room. Corinna slips through the barely-open door with the box clutched tight to her chest, and I follow, pulse ferociously split, blood pounding into my ears and behind my eyes so hard that I barely register Lycus's guard take hold of me.

Barely register my own scream as the door slams down on my arm.

I turn to look. From the elbow down my arm is trapped against the weighted door, closing, and the guardswoman's hand is clamped around my bicep, a vice, a python trying to drag me to my death. I pull. Her nails dig through the sleeves and into me, clawing at my still-soft skin, but it's nothing compared to the crushing pressure of the door that threatens to crack my bones. She hisses explicatives from the other side as she attempts to reel me back in. The door buzzes in protest.

"Corinna!" I yell.

She whirls around, just now seeing that I've fallen behind, her at least twenty feet ahead of me. And she looks. Domukardi in hand.

I realize something. Something she probably also realizes —no, something she *undoubtedly* realizes. A fact as plain as day.

This box is her mission, the one thing she's been seeking for god-knows how long. Me, I'm a cog. A means to an end. I'm not stupid. Her eyes tell me she knows it too.

Another mortal would serve the same job just as well. She can walk away right now and wipe her hands of me this very night without a single change to her plans, just as Lycus will no doubt be wiping his hands of my blood. It's over.

Somewhere deep in my chest, everything goes cold.

Her eyes blaze into mine, a reminder of her promise. *'Come with me and you won't end up like Brendon Watts'.*

She runs to where I stand struggling to pry the hand off, ignoring the streaming curses and pounding fists on the other side. It won't be long now before they find a keycard or go around through a different exit.

"Move your hand," she whispers.

I do so without hesitation. A feral look poisons Corinna's eyes as she crouches down and snaps her jaws around the woman's hand, digging in her teeth and thrashing her head like a mad dog, blood spurting down her chin and lips. A horrific scream from the other side pierces even the metal door. My assailant lets go, I yank my arm out, and the automatic door slams the rest of the way shut. For a moment I find the wherewithal to look at her, a golden icon, an Athena with blood upon her mouth, before the immediacy of everything rushes back.

I don't have time to admire nor thank her, but my awe remains.

She puts her hand at my back and pushes me forward. "We need to go."

We weave through the parking garage until we find and climb into our van. She pulls the keys from her clutch and the tires screech as she throws it into drive, flinging us about in the cab as the scent of burnt rubber clouds my nostrils. We peel out of the garage onto the main thoroughfare before we can even fasten our seatbelts, and soon we're lost in a sea of cars indistinguishable from our own.

A small internal sigh escapes me. I slide down against the seat with palms to my face and begin to notice just how hard I'm shaking, sweating.

One hand still at the wheel, the domukardi on her lap, Corinna grips my fingers in hers and gives a steadying squeeze. She doesn't breathe a word, as if not wanting to acknowledge that I doubted her for even a second, and I don't either. I should've known better. But now…now I do.

We drive on, luck intact.

13

A SECRET KEPT

Something's changed.

I can't pin down what it is, but I can feel it bleed from both of us. We didn't talk for the whole car ride, didn't heave a single sigh. Nothing. We'd just looked straight ahead, unflinching.

It wasn't focusing on the road that made us this way, and it's not the extravagant decor of the room we now stand in either. Swaths of gossamer peek out from behind the heavy velvet curtains framing the window, and marble meets ruddy wood where the suite opens up to the bedroom. A chandelier catches what light the room grants us and sprays it back in kaleidoscopic patterns on the walls and our skin. Corinna clearly shelled out for this room, but I suppose money's no object when it will soon do her no good. She can't take money where she's going.

Maybe that's what's changed. The finality of it all. Now it's not *if* she finds the domukardi. It's not *if* she gets the chance to kill herself. She can do it right now, at this very moment. All that's left is for her to select the right moment, the perfect second to cast the die. If it is her own life she plans to take, that is.

Death of an Immortal

The damnable box—I can't tear my focus away from it—rests on the queen mattress's downy duvet. I put it under the bed, out of sight for now. How did *this* end up in Texas of all places? How many hands did this thing pass through before it came back to her? Does it really contain Lycus's heart instead of her own? If so, why have I been made to risk all of this to kill an unwilling man? His actions would make sense, were that the case.

I trusted her. I still do. Had she wanted to kill an innocent person, she would've left me behind at the mercy of his hired guns. No, there's something I'm missing, and it's time I learned what threads, what entire tapestries I'm unaware of.

"You never told me," I say. My voice is pitiable, not even a whisper.

"Hm?"

She looks up from where she lounges in one of the overstuffed chairs, a dab of the tiramisu she'd ordered from room-service still on her fork. *Last meal.* I can't help but think it.

"It's not my place, I know that," I say. "But I can't help feeling like there's something I'm missing."

"From the car?"

"No, not— What I mean—" I close my eyes and stop to collect my words, letting them pool in my mouth until they're a dam about to spill over. Looking at her will only make this harder. "I've only known you for a few days, and I know there are parts of your life you don't want to share. You shouldn't have to. And that's fine. But we both know what you want to do and just how close you are." I swallow. "I can't help but feel like you know so much about me, and me — I know nothing about you. Or Lycus."

Realization sinks into Corinna's face, and though I expected to be met with another wall, another defense against anyone drawing too close, I see only a yearning warmth. A touch of the faraway. She looks to the bed and the box stowed underneath it, then back.

"Why do you care?" she asks.

"Why does it matter?"

"Because it's my story to tell."

"I get that," I say, but I continue to press forward. "Really. But I've helped you get this far, and there are some things I still don't know. How did all this happen? Why does Lycus think you want to kill him? Who—"

"Stop." She puts up a hand, then drags it across her face. The kohl around her eyes smudges slightly. After a long moment, she sighs. "You really want to know?"

I nod.

"I can't promise you'll think of me the same."

My laugh surprises even myself. "When we first met, you punched and kidnapped me in a parking lot."

"I *saved* you."

"All I'm saying is that I'm surprised you're worrying about my opinion of you. I'm almost flattered you'd even think about that."

The laugh fades from me as I look at her watching me. Finally a sigh, a gentle rise of her shoulders. Then Corinna, the enigma, the immortal, pads across the floor and folds into one of the plush chairs opposite me. Eyes betraying something more ancient than I can fathom meet my gaze.

She takes my hand in hers, the strong and steady grip of friends. Of companions. I fight to keep my breathing even and mind clear.

"I suppose, if this is in fact the end," she says, "then someone might as well know."

Corinna looks up at me, and begins.

14

THE CURSE'S QUEEN

THE CHURNING waters of the Granicus roiled just below the horizon, a black strip of water waiting, promising power on its opposite bank. Alexander's single goal once he had crossed the Hellespont into Asia minor was to usurp the Persian Achaemenid empire and bring it under his reign, this looming battle his first true chance to prove his mettle against a realm so vast. Macedon was a flea by comparison. The green shrubs that dotted the landscape did nothing to hide the Persian ranks across the water, massive and clad in strange garb. Despite their enemy's size, Alexander's forces couldn't help but scoff. What self-respecting man wore pants? Yet though it was a wonder why warriors would choose such effeminate dress, the empire they belonged to was nothing to mock.

Corinna's steed bounced anxiously under her. Horses had a way of smelling the tension in the air, so she couldn't blame the beast. Even if it was distracting. She strained to hear Alexander and his counsel Parmenion disagreeing on how best to advance.

"It would be a disgrace to the Hellespont should I fear the Granicus," her king said. "Crossing it will be an easy feat, and

I ought not let a mere brook keep me from moving my men forward."

"A mere brook! Your Highness, the Persians—"

"The Persians grow closer to striking while we sit here squabbling. They do not yet know to fear me." Looking out to his troops, his blazing eyes snagged on Corinna, his bronze armor shimmering as sunbeams poured across him. In that moment their eyes connected, she knew he would do it. He would lead them to victory, both here and at the ends of the earth. "But they will learn to."

The Cohort's semi-circle tightened around him. The conference of military generals around him in addition to the alabaster plume springing from his helmet was nothing if not conspicuous. A clearly marked target for the Persians, easy to track and glimpse. But the Cohort was to defend him with every tooth, nail, and bone within them. In Corinna's eyes, he'd given her a second chance of becoming something. Her savior, her champion. In return, she'd give anything he asked. Even if it meant death itself.

Philotas and the cavalry, Amyntas and the archers, Nicanor and the shield-bearers, the ten and a half thousand men swelled up on the hilly plains, ready for whatever may come.

As they neared the muddy banks, the Persian chariots and spearmen gleamed like a scorpion's back, ready to strike from where they sat upon the slopes. Iron spikes jutted out from their wheels' spokes, begging to tear into the knees of man and horse alike. Stillness fell over the hillsides as both armies stared towards one another, separated only by the flow of water. As far as her sights stretched, every man was still as a statue. Even her stallion had gone motionless. The flash of spears, the pin-prick brightness of arrow tips, the glint of forged blades, all omens promising the macabre.

"Remain here," Alexander commanded the Cohort.

He spurred his steed into action and charged down the

length of his front line, shouting praises of bravery and honor with fist raised high to rally the war cries of his men. She could barely make them out, but his words themselves were unimportant. It was *him* that mattered. Given that extra vigor, his force cried out and leapt into action, voices booming across the plains. Alexander shouted orders to his best among them, then charged ahead.

Corinna and the rest of the Cohort galloped to his side, her legs digging into her mount's barrel-thick sides. Before she had time to breathe so much as a single prayer to Athena or Ares or whatever deity could see her through this hell, the ford's water was sloshing upon them. She gripped onto her horse's mane, did her best to let it do the laborious wading while she focused on their position. A sudden hail of javelins blackened the bright canvas above.

"To the sky!" shouted Lycus as he threw up his shield.

Others followed suit—of those who had shields. Not everyone was so lucky.

Bodies splashed into the water with red stains blossoming around them, soon overtaken by the muddying current. She didn't stop to watch death rain upon the frontlines. They were moving forward, foot by costly foot, and Alexander remained alive, filled with verve and fire. It was all that mattered.

Another volley followed, aimed at the lines still on the banks and felling more bodies with each hurl. The Persians' upper angle worked to bear down on them too well, and the detritus cobbling the shore drew ever-closer. The phalanx at Alexander's left charged first, meeting the Persians' blade and bone. She followed as he navigated to the bulge where they'd begun to cut a path onto dry land, Persian soldiers bleeding out at the edges.

"Your back!" She barely had time to react before a Persian soldier snuck up on Enyo's side, and Corinna cut him down without mercy. Battle lines were already jumbling.

Enyo gave a wide-eyed nod in thanks, a rare sight, before continuing to plow forward.

The Persian horses atop the bank's ridge ran down to meet their opposition, chestnut coats rippling with corded muscle. One of the beasts came her way.

As soon as her steed hit dry land, her spear was thrusting and flashing against her opponent's shorter one. With a feint to the right, she impaled the front of his leather armor and pushed through, moving her steed on until she felt a *pop* through the other side. For a moment his face screamed in choking agony, and the next he slumped over to hit the ground. Spear tip facing skyward, she ripped it from his carcass. Blood coated her hand, sticky and warm.

The phalanx, though badly wounded and a good many of its men lying dead in the silt, pressed on to carve a path as it was joined by another assembly from the rear. Crackling punctuated the air as spears shattered in the heat of battle. The Persian's downhill-facing chariots could only barrel into the waters ahead instead of reversing over the incline, damning them to face the incoming onslaught or abandon their vehicles. Some jumped out only to be slashed down, weapons unfit for infantry battle. Cavalry locked tight with cavalry as they pushed against one another, and infantrymen vied for ground with their opponents.

A crack rang in her ears from the direction of her Cohort, and Corinna's breath caught in her throat. Did Lycus's spear fail him? Her heart lifted by a fraction. No, he was just ahead of her, still encircling Alexander with the others and stabbing away. But—Alexander. His spear dangled at his side, useless and freshly fractured. He asked a nearby Cohort member, yet his spear too had failed.

The Persian cavalry drew nearer. She loped to his side and offered her own.

"Your Highness!" she cried.

He took it without hesitation.

She knew, knew it was her duty to serve, and she would give whatever it took, even if this was as far as her parents' sacrifice took her. Still, the acute awareness at her lack of long distance arms left her pulse screaming. She had her sword, but if only there was a more effective way to overwhelm the enemy—

"Have you gone mad?" Lycus roared over the din as he came to her side.

"What choice did I have?" she shot back.

Her world dropped sideways as her mount screamed out.

She just had time to jump and roll to the side to avoid her leg getting crushed beneath, and then looked over her shoulder. A crossbow bolt had ripped through the animal's leg to leave it gasping its death bellows, blood gushing over the rock to meet the rest of the muddled red. Corinna scanned the horizon. There she found a massive gastraphetes, its wielder loading another bolt.

One look to Lycus told her they were thinking the same thing.

She understood why they had been selected as a fighting pair. Inseparable halves to a whole, they knew each other to their very marrow, even when amongst utter chaos such as this.

He reached down to swing her upon his riding blanket, then braced his javelin ahead as she drew her sword. One hand at his back, she steadied herself. Lycus's warhorse dug into the rocky slope and fought up the hill, meeting no pushback in the fray, and the gastraphetes's wielder turned wide-eyed as he scrambled back, bolt still not fully cocked. Foolish, bringing a weapon like that into close quarters. The reload took too long for anything but long-range battle. Still, even a single bolt could be devastating—and therefore must be eliminated.

Lycus cut off the man's retreat as Corinna jumped down. Her opponent whipped out his sidearm, but with Lycus's spear to his back and her blade at his front, he was run through within moments and left to die in an unceremonious heap. The weapon's wooden frame was quickly crushed beneath a racing stallion. Corinna swung back up to sit behind her partner.

Persian forces swelled to their left, pushing them back towards the slope with a roar of clashing bronze and iron, and a wedge of their cavalry began to slice down the plain towards Alexander himself. At its front charged Mithridates, son-in-law to the King of Persia, waiting to bathe his blade in the blood of his challenger.

"To the king, now!" She pointed to where Alexander struggled on the hillside, death's fingers tightening around the scene.

Lycus whirled his steed around. They pushed into the press of bodies slicked with sweat and blood and silt, both man and beast shoving one another for even footing. Corinna watched as Alexander hurled his spear at Mithridates, knocking him from his mount and to the ground with a painful crack, his own men forced to veer their stallions off to keep from trampling him underfoot. A soldier charged Alexander's flank and smacked him across the helmet with a cruel scimitar, taking a chunk of the proud white plume with it.

"*No!*" Corinna pressed the horse on faster.

The Cohort assembled to Alexander's defense, but the crush of soldiers was too dense. Her heart pounded up into her throat. Should they fail here, everything they'd worked so hard for would be dashed in an instant, and a life of poverty would await her once more. If she survived.

A lance collided with Alexander's shining breastplate. The force of it knocked him to the ground, clean off his beloved steed. Corinna swallowed hard. With a squeeze to Lycus's shoulder, she jumped from her horse and raced to her king on foot, just the two of them on the ground among the fray of outer cavalrymen, Corinna squeezing between steeds and carving herself a path.

A few toes crushed and throbbing, blood screaming in her veins, she broke into an opening where yet another Persian raised a scimitar high above the bloodied and dazed Alexander. Her world narrowed. Focused to this one sliver before her. His skyward blade. The tightening grip of the metal hilt against her palm. The flurried beating of her heart.

The Persian's blade sailed down—but before it came even halfway, she slashed out to strike him just below the shoulder then up with a violent twist, lopping his arm off. Blood spurted across the distance as he collapsed in agony, shrieking in a tongue foreign to her. Corinna looked to Alexander, emboldened to see no fear, but a grateful recognition as he righted himself without heed to the puncture at his flank.

Bucephalus, loyal warhorse to Alexander since childhood, tamed by his own hand, cantered to his master's side. The king hoisted himself up for all his men to see, and a rally of exalted cries followed. She could have wept in relief—but now was not the time. She would celebrate only once victory was well and truly theirs.

Lycus's stallion ran up to her side.

"Idiot!" He pulled her up to him with an expression that spoke to equal parts fury and pride.

"Scold me all you want," Corinna said as she laid her head against his back.

They'd made it. Their king had made it, and that was all she needed. She looked down the length of the ford to see the extended cavalry and troops make landfall, now pushing back the Persian forces in vast strides and claiming swathes of land for Macedon. For the empire and king who had given her everything.

Reunited with his steed, Alexander pressed on to brave yet more of the hostilities, and not ten minutes later, a block of Persian forces took to their heels and retreated, the battle clearly lost as the Macedonians claimed the opposing side of the Granicus. Her countrymen cut down entire battalions who crossed their path, and, seeing their brothers' flight, yet more Persians followed.

"Shall we pursue, your Highness?" Parmenion asked.

"I have no interest in cowards," he said, shifting his gaze. "Take the traitors instead."

With a booming command for his Cohort to join the cavalry, the remaining soldiers altered course and encircled straggling Persians as well as Greek mercenaries, traitors to their land for the highest bidder. The phalanx crashed into them from one side and the cavalry from all others, hacking and slashing apart any who remained. Men pleaded for mercy, but they too were cut down, flies before a god. Blood splattered upon her thighs and up to her elbows, staining her sandals and the tunic pleats that peeked out from her armor.

Then, silence. The only souls left breathing on the enemy lines were those Alexander chose to take as prisoner, to do with what he may.

"Royals, too," Lycus observed as they walked, inspecting the dead bodies caked in muck.

Corinna nodded. It seemed whatever divine favor the Persians once had was wavering fast. Her fellows in arms were among the dead as well, but at least success ended up on their side, a prize won by their sacrifice.

Alexander swung down from Bucephalus. All about him was a mix of the many faces of victory—and the cost. While soldiers shone in the afterglow of hard-fought triumph, yet more languished in agony, however dignified and silent, clutching at their wounds.

"How did you earn this, soldier?" Alexander gestured to a raking slash upon an infantryman's left bicep and thigh.

The soldier blinked before snapping to attention. "A duel, sir. Against two Persians at once."

Death of an Immortal

"Good man!" Alexander clapped him on the back, and the soldier's face split into a startled grin. "Be sure to wash and bind it properly. My ranks are made better with men such as yourself in it."

Corinna watched her king file through entire ranks of his soldiers, looking over their wounds and listening to them recount how they'd persevered in the fray of battle. For a commander to treat his subjects as more than mere pawns…it was strange. She and her Cohort had certainly been surprised by the consideration they were paid. Not that it was unappreciated. Here as well, the gratitude on every soldier's face was plain to see. On top of the concern for his own, he then had the enemy's dead buried as well.

Corinna watched as infantrymen piled the bodies into a mass grave, the rest of the Cohort seeing to their arms and allies. Then, none other than Alexander himself trotted to her side.

"Floros," he said. From his mouth, her surname sounded like a lyric. He flashed her a brilliant smile, like the sun itself descending on her.

"Your Majesty."

"I will spend the rest of my reign trying to repay you."

"I'm but a soldier, your Highness." It was a wonder she managed to keep her voice steady.

His eyes softened.

"What I mean is," she swallowed, "it is I who will forever be trying to repay you."

"I admire the modesty, though I do not think you need it. With or without, you and your Cohort shine as true as any star."

Corinna continued to look at him even as her ears rang. Was she hearing him correctly? She dared not tell him to shove off as she might've to Lycus.

"For what you have done here today, Corinna Floros, you will be forever honored."

Whether it was the flush from battle or the heat of the lowering sun—or at the flabbergasting compliment from one so high—her cheeks heated. She almost laughed in disbelief. Clapping her on the shoulder, Alexander then turned back to his men and carried on.

"Corinna." As Lycus rejoined her, his gaze went back and forth between the two of them. "Is everything alright?"

She shook her head. Alexander might have praised her, but that was who he was. It was still him who came out shining, ever a beacon of her hopes. Of the good worth fighting for.

"Yes," she said. "It is."

"What of the living, your Highness?" one of the Companion cavalry asked as she and Lycus reunited with the rest of his forces.

Alexander's face stiffened as he surveyed the plains, all hint of his former warmth gone. He walked over to a Greek mercenary whose wrists had been lashed together. "I want every last one of the bastards bound and sent to Macedon. Perhaps they will glean something of respect in tending the soil of their people."

"The *Greeks* are my people," the fallen soldier hissed, "of which you barbaric lot will never be part."

"This from the man who fights against his own lands." Alexander tilted his head with brows creased in contempt. "I doubt the weight of your opinion is worth much in the eyes of your former brothers."

The soldier said nothing, but bared his teeth and snarled like a caged animal. And as the King of Macedon walked away, Corinna saw in his wake a promise to not only make the Greeks accept him as their own, but for the entire world to hold him high.

Death of an Immortal

THEY CLEARED out one of the nearby temples and set up around its fringes, the cooks and other tradesmen Alexander brought along carrying in baskets of hot bread and amphoras of wine, a line of ants marching along.

He had been good to them before the recent battle at the Granicus, but something had changed. Corinna would catch his gaze lingering among the members of her Cohort, only then to duck away to a more private place with his Persian confidante in tow. It wasn't like his romantic trysts with Hephaestion—say what one may about nobility, but Alexander at the very least was not a man of the flesh. No, this was something else. If only she could puzzle it out.

"Relax. You'll wish you'd saved your strength this evening." Lycus tugged her away from the canvas tent's opening and back to their mats.

Corinna wrinkled her nose. She hated the feeling of being left in the dark, but there wasn't much to do about it. The king was likely just considering how differently his fate might have turned had the Cohort not come to his aid.

"Feel ready for tonight?" she asked.

"For getting hammered, stuffing my stomach, and general debauchery?" Lycus snorted and flopped back onto his mat. "Born ready."

"As always," she laughed.

The symposium was usually sealed off for male attendance only, but there was a suspicion among those invited that this wouldn't be any ordinary drinking party. Aside from herself, Galene, and Enyo being allowed to attend, Corinna couldn't place the stranger nature of it all. Perhaps the hypervigilance of battle had yet to wear off.

Once the evening sun began to throw pink-soaked gold into the hazy clouds, she set to her preparations. By the smell of burnt meat trimmings curling in the air like fatty incense, it seemed the rest of the encampment had begun to cook supper. But, while the others ate, the Cohort's meal would have to wait. She slipped into a cream-colored chiton and fastened her leather belts about herself, then wrapped a saffron palla about her shoulders and pinned it with a half brass, half bone brooch. After she applied a dab of fragrant oil behind her ears, she braided back her hair.

"I never thought burned fat could smell so good," she moaned as the scent wafted throughout the grounds.

"You can manage another few minutes." Lycus brushed whatever invisible dust clung to the front of his shawl.

"Stop preening."

"One of us has to." He cut a grin her way, canines sparkling.

The two of them left the tent arm in arm and made for the limestone complex. The architecture certainly showed how far they'd pushed into Persian territory, and there was something harsh, though not unattractive about the blunt lines and unforgiving stockiness, the burly wooden poles and deep-set reliefs. It looked almost like a wild landscape playing at civilization—though when it came to sneering at wildness, a Macedonian surely had no place.

They reached the building's maw where the aroma of honied pork and cardamom-stuffed chicken and fenugreek rice hit them head-on. Corinna chewed her lip before snapping back to her rehearsed stoicism, yet she could feel the anticipation clench in Lycus's stomach too. One of the court attendants glided to their side and whisked them into the complex. They passed through a long arcade before breaking into the courtyard, low retaining walls and copper pots spilling over with heavy ferns and violet crocus blooms. The high set sconces were lit, and the oil lamps threw glittering light into the darkening sky. On the far pavilion sat a table laden with delicacies. After a look between the two of them, they made for it as quickly as possible—while conscious to maintain at least some of their dignity.

"Glad to see you could join us," said Bakchos, a cluster of

grapes in hand as he leaned against one of the archways. His Cohort partner, Galene, lounged on the steps with a tin cup of sweet barley water.

"Didn't want to look over-eager, though I see some don't mind," Lycus said. For all the times he'd butted heads with others, those in the Cohort rarely seemed to faze him. It was more akin to taunts from a sibling.

"Got to keep up our strength, considering Issus still lies ahead."

"I'm sure you're gathering enough for all twelve of us."

Bakchos clapped him on the back with a laugh, his cheeks the slightest bit ruddy.

Together they mingled into the larger group and plucked what they wished from the table—it was difficult to not run off with the whole thing—to savor every morsel. The greasy glaze of meat fats and honey painted her fingertips, and laughter tinkled throughout the courtyard as the upper caste of military men churned about them.

"What do you bet I've eaten an entire pig so far?" Lycus asked.

"I'd bet a whole pig."

"And yet, hungry I stay."

"Don't be greedy now," she mockingly warned.

He nudged her with his hip and a devilish grin. "But isn't that what you love about me the most?"

Damn the crowdedness of this room, the inability to drag him off into some dark corner where they could be alone. She pushed the flush from her cheeks and squared her shoulders.

"Don't be crude." Despite herself, she continued to survey the room for hidden spots.

"Always the soldier," he sighed, the fire in his muddy eyes cooling.

As Corinna scanned the room, close to giving up, she spotted only three of the Cohort pairs still milling about the room, visible by their yellow mantles. Some of them must have found empty rooms, surely. Come to think of it, Alexander wasn't present either. She swore she had seen him earlier.

"Pardon," came a voice at their back. A manservant inclined his head as they turned to face him. "Your presence is required elsewhere."

Corinna couldn't say the vague orders were anything new. After she and Lycus looked to one another without protest—though she did groan at leaving the banquet table behind—they followed their guide back into the temple complex, trudging up stairs and around corners and down long stretches of dim-lit corridors, until finally they saw the beacon of amber wraps that marked their companions. Standing huddled outside a door, they looked just as perplexed as she was, even if they hid it well. The manservant sent her and Lycus to stand by the others before leaving to fetch the rest of the Cohort.

"A briefing?" she guessed aloud.

A few shrugs, a nod or two. No one on edge, she let her concern recede.

"What else?" said Acteon.

"Can't help but hope another round of food is back there," Nikias joked, the most childlike and innocent among them—if any could be considered such. "Maybe even sweets."

"Leave the kiddie shit behind," Enyo snapped, picking boar meat from between her canines.

"Lay off," Corinna said.

Even in the relative darkness, she could see Enyo roll her eyes.

A spindly shadow moved from under the doorframe, and though the others had taken to chatting amongst themselves, Corinna watched as the figure's silhouette slid into view, then away, then back, then hidden again. The conspiratorial murmur of voices on the other side threatened to creep over her.

Death of an Immortal

Something told her this was no secondary banquet hall.

Corinna leaned against the smoothed wooden door and held up a hand to silence the others. They continued on. Lycus yanked at one of Enyo's thick black braids, and she gave a look to suggest she would've clawed his guts clean out had she not first glimpsed Corinna. Intrigue crossed her face as the hall fell silent.

"Only a moment longer," came the servant's voice from at her back, four more of her comrades in tow.

She turned to scan the corridor. All twelve of them were now accounted for.

"At attention, you all," the manservant advised as he disappeared back down the dark hall, leaving them to face their fate. "You may be surprised who sits behind that door."

Corinna straightened, despite that he was a mere orderly. Anyone who wasn't an officer might as well be a servant, but still the warning set her bones tingling. Were they to be reprimanded? Or found lacking? The door swung open, a slow creak pealing from the rusty hasps.

Beyond the door, Corinna glimpsed the room from over the others' shoulders—then went rigid. Alexander stood firm before them, gaze trained as if daring them to retreat, and in his eyes burned something valiant and proud, something so totally alive and all-consuming that it compelled her to show only reverence. How could they refuse the man who'd given them everything?

The group filed forward into the room, uncertainty swirling about them as a serving boy sealed the door shut, lock and all. High on the walls hung blazing sconces that stung her eyes. She averted her gaze and blinked at the ground for relief, only to see something stranger still. Drawn upon the floor were thick strokes of white chalk in bizarre patterns. Concentric circles, a six pointed star. Other lines had been drawn as if at random, and a curved hand was scrawled in the margins of strange boxes, where sketches of waxing moons and unidentifiable powders and crystals sat near the center. Whatever she'd been expecting, it wasn't this.

At Alexander's side stood the Persian Corinna had seen earlier, a film of chalk on his palms and fingertips and dusting the knees of his navy robe. Heads bent together, the two of them whispered for a moment, the only sound in the room aside from the sputtering oil lamps. Grin sliding across his teeth, Alexander turned his attention to his Cohort.

"At ease," he said.

More simply said than done, especially in the presence of their king. Worse, Corinna couldn't glean anything from his voice. His tone was warm yet tight—but how could it be both?

"I don't believe I have yet had the opportunity to introduce my aide, Roshan." Alexander flitted his fingers towards the man, a person of no obvious polish or charisma.

Roshan gave a slight incline of his head. His Persian femininity—his wearing trousers, his thick brows close to meeting in the middle—aside, there was a perplexing aura about him, something more than what lay at the surface. His scrawl upon the floor showed as much.

"Roshan has been under my employ for some years now, working on a strategy to advance the empire of Macedon, and for you, a gift of my thanks. A chance at something that, for millennia, humanity has only dared imagine."

Alexander stepped back as serving boys hauled hammered bronze boxes forward, six of them in total. A heavy push-in knob at the front sealed its mouth shut, and beneath was a neat row of Roman numerals inscribed on stones. At the sides, broad, coiled handles gleamed in the flickering light. The boys set each down with care before backing away, as if the boxes were asps ready to strike. Roshan stepped forward to each and, inputting a sequence of numbers, opened them one by one. Inside each, thick cloth was wrapped around an enormous, empty glass flask.

Corinna's brows creased. What air could be so worth guarding?

"Roshan, as you may have noted, is not Greek but Persian. You may wonder how one could trust him, but rest assured that he cares not for worldly conquests. Already he has secured our sure victory. He long ago accepted an offer of ours, a binding agreement for his services and their fruits in exchange for the full depth of our resources and protections. His skills lie in Hermetic alchemy."

A new word to her. Not one she'd heard in or outside of her studies. Corinna flicked her eyes towards the man busying himself with the empty jars, white ash piles and quartz. Though she wasn't sure what her commander meant, she'd been right to watch the Persian. If Alexander himself had singled the man out, that must mean he was worth keeping an eye on.

"He has proven his skills to me and mine over the years, and we've long been in discussion about our future plans under my reign," Alexander continued. "Thus, I took Roshan under my purview in pursuit of one of mankind's eternal aims. Eternality itself."

She had to stop herself from jerking back. *A children's tale.* The floor wavered under her. *Impossible stories.* But then, she never thought she would be standing where she was today. There were many things outside her imaginings. Might this not be one more?

No, it was foolish to think as much.

"Yet as heir to the Argead dynasty, I must preserve myself for the sake of my people. I cannot risk my life as a scholar's subject. However, my most loyal, most dear Cohort, who in their risk could extend my life into infinity itself, would surely seize that chance." He turned to survey them. "Would you not?"

Corinna's muscles went rigid. Of course. *Of course.*

Slowly the pieces began to fall into place, scrambled

puzzle tiles no longer. She had wondered before why the Cohort was made up of orphans or the forgotten or street trash—but Alexander hadn't seen worthless people. He'd seen people without attachments. People who, in the event of something going awry, wouldn't be asked after. He couldn't attempt the same thing with a host of aristocrats' children, not without risking a coup if they died during a trial run. However, the vagrants of the world were fair game.

As a leader of war, his skill was in leading men to their bountiful successes—and also their glorious deaths. Now it was her turn.

In the past, his mission was something she'd admired with pride swelling in her chest, with a sense of duty. She still did. From where she stood now though, she was too dumbfounded to decipher the bundle of nerves quivering in her chest. Was this fear, or excitement?

Alexander's words muddled together in her ears and she strained to focus. It was as if a bucketful of blood had been drained from her. By the time he was done, Roshan had laid out the six empty jars, one at each star point and a heavy pewter pot at the center, a short knife and deep ladle resting on the lip. The hollow ringing in her head grew.

Lycus nudged her. She looked at him, his eyes bewildered in what she imagined was a reflection of her own. There she saw the question he dared not ask aloud, yet hoped for all the same.

What if this actually worked?

In that case, Alexander would have suddenly acquired a fighting force for the ages, a legion that would make him undefeatable. A host of immortals, trained to fear no death and to impart it swiftly. And for them, they would have... Gods, it was almost too much to hope for. Impossible to even imagine such fortune.

Roshan opened a wooden chest from the far side of the room and drew out a chicken, its feet roped together with a

Death of an Immortal

sackcloth over its head. Alexander stepped outside the chalk circle to a floor cushion, away from the web cast under his Cohort. Usually Corinna would have looked more closely to read his mood, to try to guess at what he was thinking in that brilliant mind, but she couldn't bring herself to. It was hard enough just to keep her breathing even.

"Stand alongside your partner at a star's apex, and we shall begin. And remove your shoes." Roshan stepped into the circle's center by the cauldron and lay the fowl at his feet. The bird did nothing, already wrought into submission. He waited. "Well?"

They stood there, half frozen despite their racing thoughts. Slowly, Corinna bent down to unfasten the sandals reaching her calves, and the others did the same. With a toe dipped into the water, her movements began to speed up, faster and faster, more eager to reach this potential wonder despite the obvious risk. Soon enough, each pair stood at the point of a star, side by side and a mix of hungry fear upon their faces. Undeterred by the people looking on, Lycus squeezed her hand. It reassured her, yes, but fed her worries of his fate. Of theirs.

Roshan inclined his head to Alexander, and with a swoop of his robes turned back to the center. He picked up a pitcher, poured water forth into the pot, and from drawstring pouches scattered crushed nettle and scrapings of a grayish mold, stinking yellow crystals and delicate flakes of gold, eggshells from a turtle nest and the flesh of a white peach, then with his ladle stirred the medley. From an ox horn he dripped out a silver flash of mercury onto the swirling surface, forming an eternal spiral on the water's face. The chicken squawked aloud as Roshan scooped it up by the feet with dagger in hand, and he sank it hilt deep into the creature's breast. With the cut dragging from under its ribs to the sternum, he set the knife aside and plunged his hand into its organ cavity to tear out the heart. Blood coated his hand to run down his elbow, and the bird flailed, wheezed, and within moments fell silent. Though a gruesome method, every one of them in the room had seen worse on the battlefield. Done worse. Corinna failed to see its significance.

Roshan hurled the chicken heart into the cauldron, and with a rattling gasp the animal began to shriek once again. Corinna's breath stuck in her lungs.

As if granted extra sinew from the air itself, the creature's wound began to stitch over and then, though the chicken still writhed about, it was as if it had never been cut at all.

Roshan dropped it to the floor and it landed with a squawk, then ran to one of the far corners where it paced aimlessly, as unperturbed as any normal bird. The alchemist wiped the blood from his hand and grabbed the ladle. Into each jar he portioned out the cauldron's contents, a gleaming and translucent golden mix.

"Enyo and Myron," he said as he strode towards them, "compatriots in life eternal."

Enyo's eyes narrowed as Roshan again withdrew his blade—though Corinna saw the fearful apprehension as well, seated alongside her pride. Enyo and Myron faced one another as directed.

"Hold him still." Roshan pointed the knife at his ribs.

Knowing what awaited, Corinna could see Myron's heart thrumming desperately even through his thin tunic. Roshan lay his uncalloused hands against Myron's chest and felt down the lateral edge of his ribcage. He drew back, then stabbed.

Myron's piercing scream shook the room and rattled her to her bones, and though horror flooded her eyes, Enyo held him firm. Their connection had never been what Corinna and Lycus's was, but still Corinna could see the horror on the other woman's face. Blood gushed from Myron's side to slick over Roshan's blade and hands, then Roshan speared his hand up into the man's chest as the screams went on and on,

Death of an Immortal

so loud and primal and gut-wrenchingly burning that Myron soon went slack, blacked out either from pain or blood loss. Corinna could hardly bear to watch—but she had to. She had to know.

With a *schlup*, Roshan tore his heart free and Myron crumpled in Enyo's arms, limbs heavy. The air hung full with silent pleas, the entire Cohort begging for Roshan to do his work quickly. The alchemist placed the dripping red muscle into the golden mixture, then with a rattling and rheumy gasp, Myron shot alive as if lightning had struck him square on. His once-dark eyes flashed a brilliant gold. A wave of murmurs rolled throughout the room, and Alexander looked on with no small amount of wonder. But she knew he couldn't risk putting himself until he knew the ritual could go beginning to end without fail, not to mention testing whether a human body could endure the aftermath.

Time seemed to condense down, passing in bursts faster and faster until soon it was Corinna and Lycus who Roshan stood before. She knew it worked. She knew she'd survive this. And yet, the terror remained. A primal part of her cried to run, to fight.

Corinna wrapped one arm around Lycus's right flank and pulled him close, only half to keep him upright.

"You can do this, okay?" she said.

"I know." He bent down to rest his forehead against hers. Hesitation shined clear in his eyes, something she wasn't used to seeing.

"Think about the plums, alright? Remember those?"

He closed his eyes as if picturing them. "I'd never forget. You—"

Roshan drove the knife into him, and Lycus's wails scraped down to her bones, curdling her very marrow. Every fiber of her cried out to beat Roshan away, to preserve what she could of her partner, but she remained still, cradling him to her as the alchemist wormed his hand into Lycus's chest and pulled his heart free. Blood dripped down his elbow. Time stretched on without mercy as his limp body sat in her lap, his mass having dragged her to her knees, the ichor soaking through her clothes like rancid wine. The pool grew beneath them. She had seen carnage before, incredible gore, but this—

From somewhere, she heard a distant *plop*.

Lycus's sputtering gasp broke the silence tearing her apart. The world's tempo returned to order. Corinna barely had the chance to cling to him in relief before Roshan slammed the blade under her ribs and sawed in deep.

She vaguely knew she was screaming, she could feel the voice pealing harsh out of her throat, threatening to grate it raw, felt the hot blood slipping down her side and thigh, but the pain, gods the *pain* was so intense it ripped her from reality to render her little more than a phantom watching the scene below. The veins in her eyes threatened to explode, her nails tearing as they dug into wherever she found purchase.

And then, darkness.

~

Darkness. An unendingly vast expanse, neither cold nor warm, neither suffocating nor drafty, and on the faintest edge of her sights shone pinpricks of brilliant stars, just out of reach. Was it Hades or his Persephone? Perhaps Mot come to claim her? Which god would it be who came for her in these foreign lands? She stretched to arc up towards that light, that deliverance—

Blood spurted from her nostrils. Corinna doubled over, hacking out the iron pooled in her lungs as her cut flesh began to knit over. A glimpse to the center of the room showed her her own heart, nestled right alongside Lycus's in the gold-filled jar. She looked down at herself and, movements fragmented from the shock, moved to touch the wound. The reconstructing flesh tickled her fingertips, but while it was the cut's ragged edges that were healing most rapidly, she felt a tremor throughout her entire body, shaping and reshaping to smooth over whatever flaws it found, whatever improperly healed bones or cuts or deficiencies remained.

Corinna let out a deep breath, then looked to Lycus. He placed a hand just above her collarbone. No pulse. Not even a flutter. She expected to hear the thunder of rushing blood in her ears, her pulse beating up her throat, but nothing remained. He'd done it.

Cohort now and forever changed, Roshan turned back to the cauldron and topped off each jar, then sealed each one shut with bitumen, thriving hearts in the elixir's waters. With a heave, Roshan grasped the lip of his cauldron and threw it onto its side. The remainder of the brew spilled across the floor. Lapping between her toes, it washed away the chalk and herbs and powders. He seized the chicken from the corner of the room, a withered hand wrapped tight around its neck, and splashed through what golden water remained in the vat.

Roshan picked up the chicken's heart, and as it came out of the water the chicken's breath scraped in its throat. In a thick cloud of dust and ash, the fowl burst into the air like soot. Black. Dead. Not a single feather remained.

Corinna swallowed hard.

"So long as your heart remains within the waters of your domukardi, your life remains untouchable. Remove it or break the jar," he knocked the cinders, formerly a living, breathing bird, from his robes and hands, "and you will die. From dust to dust."

For a moment she wondered if her heart would not be safer in her chest, but she dismissed the notion. If she could trust anyone other than Lycus, it was her king. Their hearts would be secure, doubtless to be placed under lock and key by the highest Macedonian command available.

So why did a queasy feeling begin to unspool in her stomach?

Corinna straightened and locked eyes with her partner, then the rest of her Cohort. Her immortal compatriots. All wide-eyed, all with a palpable new vigor on their skins. If they felt as alive as her, as powerful and strong-boned and fang-bearing, putting the twelve of them together on a battlefield would make Alexander's armies a thing of legend. The enormity of this, of the power they'd just been granted... It had to have been exactly what Alexander was hoping for. And in this dream, he had allowed her to take part.

Overwhelmed, Corinna couldn't help but lean against Lycus's now-silent chest and smile.

15

THE STARS USURPED

The hills of Issus ran crimson with rivulets of gore, the sky a somber olive hue as clouds bore down heavy above them. Where the sun had retreated to, she didn't know—perhaps it couldn't bear to witness the raging battle below, the spilt blood. Corinna had since learned how to bathe in it.

In her first clash since being reborn as immortal, it had taken a good few blows, a few of what would otherwise have been deadly encounters, to appreciate the power now singing through her veins. A soldier had cleaved a spear so deep into her shoulder it scraped against the plate of flat bone beneath, and though the agony nearly blinded her, Corinna had whipped around to tear it free, body coursing with adrenaline and her healing rapid. Another had attempted to cut her off at the knee, leaving her leg dangling by a thread that thickened back into a cord. The pain was immense, and though she stumbled, it was quickly whole again, so fast that anyone who blinked would've missed it. Even those who saw it may have doubted their own eyes at the lack of blood—for those without hearts did not bleed.

With no fear or risk of death, the Cohort had sharpened into a lethal machine. What was one more myth of a monster on the battlefield? The gluts of men previously too dangerous to confront directly were now targets to throw their bodies at, going head-on as their limbs regenerated and flesh knitted. Any normal soldier would have fallen long ago. Ruthless, they dogged them at the edges, tearing apart their defenses one man at a time, ceaseless where others would have fallen back.

With blood up to her elbows and high on her cheekbones, she could rest assured that none of it was hers. None of it ever would be again.

After the past few centuries of Achaemenid rule, the Persian empire's subjects welcomed foreign conquerors. Few put up a struggle at all. Some even celebrated their deliverer with feast and festival. Still undefeated, still without a single blot clouding their hard-earned streak, the might of his legions had yet to meet a challenge formidable enough for them. Even if they admittedly had an unfair advantage. But, Corinna wouldn't complain. Some were blessed in life and some were not. Such was the natural order, and this was merely an extension of it.

Issus was a beautiful landscape of sloping hills and crystal sky—at least, it had been. Before the current battle tore apart the land and people on it. Now a veil of smoke drifted in the air and hung in vapors about their ankles, gliding over the corpses and into the gashed earth. Even in her battles at Halicarnassus and Miletus, Phrygia and Cappadocia, none had borne this same degree of devastation. But none had so resisted Alexander, not like Darius had. The enthroned King of Persia, who was desperately trying to maintain a grip on the empire crumbling beneath him. And so he crumbled here as well, turning to flee as his men were cut down one after another. Freezing rain made the river a deadly mire, slippery yet boggish, trapping men and their mounts in the muck. Darius hadn't considered the position of his troops nor heeded the advice of his men, his ego his downfall. For it, over twenty-thousand of his men now lay dead on the marshy field.

Corinna surveyed the landscape with a smirk. *Alexander's war dead looks to be only half that.*

In the stampede to follow their king's retreat, the Persian fools had trampled many of their own men to death, and then scattered like roaches in torchlight. Yet even in the fray, Alexander pushed himself onwards after Darius, leaving almost his entire regiment behind. Lycus, Bakchos, and Galene went on with him, but the others stayed behind. Three immortals and a god-king would have no issue if it came to blows.

The watery light splitting through the storm clouds began to dim, nighttime closing in. Corinna trudged across the mud-caked hills, tending Alexander's wounded and putting the few Persians who still clung to life out of their misery. Horse shit and river grit caked one's breastplate and face, jaw lolling open as he exhaled his death-rattle. To die with such little dignity. Good gods, to die at all, an insignificant worm crawling upon the face of the earth. At least she would never have to face that. A relief. She drove a short sword through his throat.

As nightfall swept upon them, Alexander and the breakaway of her Cohort returned to the battleground. They were empty-handed, yet the all-consuming fire on her king's face remained. He may have lost Darius, but the battle had been his, and now too whatever spoils the Persian king had left behind in his flight. Corinna swung up on Lycus's steed and followed behind their commander, the rest of his soldiers marching close behind.

The Persian encampment was almost wholly abandoned, only the noncombatants such as cooks and servants remaining, darting between tarps to escape their enemy's gaze, a few openly weeping at what they must have assumed was a rapidly approaching death. So fragile. So easily crushed. The rows of tents became larger as they neared the center, a sea of white expanding out in every direction, until they had come upon the pavilion of King Darius III himself. Corinna cocked her head at its obscene luxuriance. It wasn't so much a tent as a palace constructed of starched canvas and wooden rods.

Alexander swung down from Bucephalus and strode between the entry flaps. Corinna nearly ran into him as his legs froze. She ducked her head to peek inside, only to jerk back, shocked by a scene dripping in gold and silver, lapis and lacquered wood, such richness that it threatened to blind her.

"Good gods," Nikias whispered from over her shoulder.

Alexander snapped from his stunned silence and went into the room, top-ranking command and Cohort behind him. The pillows' brocade of silver thread, the intricately carved furniture with aurelian overlay—it was almost gaudy. What king traveled with such opulence? What king needed such constant reminders of his wealth? The lavishness around her was beautiful, no doubt, but the thought of the weak character who required it turned her stomach. As her gaze lingered on the woven purple rug beneath her sandals, she was transported back to a different life, her former existence an entire continent away and many years ago as she stood before that purple tapestry. And to think, this man *stood* on purple fabrics.

The far left wall hanging quivered. A slow whine of metal-on-metal met her ears as Enyo pulled out her short sword and padded across the room, silent as a panther. She tore back the tapestry with her arm raised to strike.

A group of women tumbled to their knees with a cry, faces tear streaked and shoulders trembling up by their ears. From the finely dyed clothes they were wrapped in, the jewels at their throats and wrists and expertly braided hair, it was clear who they were. The royal family—of those who didn't have the chance to flee. Corinna swallowed.

Death of an Immortal

"Please," the eldest begged, reigning back tears as a middle-aged woman tried to push both her and the young women behind her, shielding them. A few soldiers smirked to one another. Corinna's lip twisted. *Lecherous bastards.* "Do not—"

"At ease," Alexander commanded Enyo as he stepped forward. She fell back into the fold. Crouching down to the level of the four women still huddled on the floor, he asked, "Are you the kin of Darius III?"

The youngest girl, still just a child, met his gaze for a moment before hiding behind her mother and grabbing the elderly woman's hand. Corinna knew what the girl was seeing. A mother's back, bracing, prepared to sacrifice for her children. She recalled seeing the same thing herself, albeit a lifetime ago. The girl wiped her runny nose, lower lip quivering.

"You need fear no harm from me or my men," Alexander said. "I make war upon your king for his lands, no more and no less."

They relaxed, if only by a fraction. With a bent knee, easy tone, and undrawn blade, he was far less threatening than they'd likely imagined, him approaching the royal women more as one would a spooked foal than a conquest. If only her family had had the fortune of someone like Alexander to deliver them. A silent moment passed.

The middle-aged woman rose to her feet.

"Rise," she ordered those behind her. She faced Alexander, shoulders now square and strong. Whether legitimate or a farce, Corinna didn't know. "I am Stateira of the House of the Achaemenids, formerly of the House of Ostanes, and wife to Darius III of the Persian empire." Stateira aided the elder woman to her feet with a tug and, despite her cowering state only moments before, a cautious fire settled in her eyes. "I introduce to you the mother of King Darius III, Sisygambis, and my daughters Stateira II and Drypetis."

The younger girls inclined their heads in turn, but their anxieties were still plain to see in their swollen eyes and trembling chins.

"It is my honor to be among the fine ladies of the Persian court." Alexander smiled, blinding as the sun. Even with mud streaked down his face, he was a vision. "I'm sure you are aware that, being property of the Achaemenid empire, you constitute war gains."

They stiffened.

"Yet rest assured that as long as you are under my charge, you and your family will be met with the utmost respect and furnished with everything you would ordinarily receive from your husband."

Their eyes widened all at once, this time in relief. Disbelief. Any other invading army would have likely raped and tormented or even murdered the women remaining at the camp, nonetheless of the royal family. And to be allowed their luxuries?

"So that you may know," he added, "your husband was not slain but rather turned and fled."

Shock flashed across their faces, and even though she didn't understand Aramaic, Corinna could've sworn Sisygambis muttered a few foul words.

"Thus, he will likely bargain for your release in a few weeks' time. I'll negotiate with him when the time comes, but for now please be assured of your safety and comfort here. One of your ladies-in-waiting can collect your evening meals from my chefs once we've completed setting up camp. The women's quarters will be left as they are, though as victor I am to claim all other material spoils."

Stateira inclined her head, the breathlessness of her surprise still apparent. "Your benevolence is appreciated."

Alexander's grin was one of pride, even as Corinna noticed his eyes linger on Stateira II a moment longer. "Royal blood is a sacred thing, to be honored even in times of war."

The women inclined their heads, hands clasped at their bosoms in gratitude.

His charming nature, his golden tongue. Mental fortitude aside, Corinna knew that was how he had been able to take his military this far. He had no troubles in fashioning himself friends, in creating allies out of enemies. She did wonder, however, if that ever allowed any detractors around him to slip into hiding, to prey on his chivalry and lay in waiting. But, she knew without a shadow of doubt that if that day ever came, she would be waiting with eleven others at her side and at the ready to protect the man who had given them everything. Even so, it was a foolish fear.

For who would ever turn against Alexander of Macedon?

MANY WOULD. Too many.

It was a slow change, but one starkly present. The campaigns became harsher, and yet smoother. They had carved out a path through Phoenician lands and into Egypt, liberating the people from their Persian puppeteers, and then looped back around to push Alexander's forces farther east past the flash-points of Gaugamela and Bactria. Years of unending campaigns saw droves of men exit Alexander's employ either from death or disillusionment, and, save the Cohort and commanders, Corinna now looked upon mostly new faces. Even the mortal commanders looked different. Aged. Sun-worn and battle-weary. They'd seen the same upheaval she had, the brutal battles that left bodies stacked on the hillsides. But where the Cohort had cut through the masses like a plow in wet soil, their lives untouchable, those around them weren't always so lucky. The mortal commanders' ill-set fractures and lost limbs and ailments followed them to the grave. Many left before they could suffer such fates.

It made Corinna's throat surge full of ire. Death was just the way of the world. Disillusionment, though? For the man who had given them a purpose and a goal, who had led them with such conviction, they couldn't stomach times of discomfort? Of being humbled? It was unforgivable. Cowardly and soft. Them leaving had been a favor, in a way. Corinna would just as soon cut that rot out of Alexander's ranks herself. At least they had saved her the work.

Persian lands gradually fell into Macedonian control, and Alexander even took a few of their own as his wives. He visited their temples and married his men to their women and adopted too many of their customs to count. He even took to wearing *pants*, of all things. Whatever sense of propriety Corinna had recoiled at that—but she'd bitten her tongue. She would see a great many things change in her fated-to-be-long life. It was something they would all look past.

He had left city after city in his wake bearing his name. In Egypt he'd even presented himself as a god. But again, criticizing him for hubris wasn't her place. Images of mighty godkings had swayed the masses for millennia, and she knew her distaste for it changed nothing.

The Hindu Kush was little better. Corinna wished he'd make different decisions, better decisions, but soldiers never swayed their kings. Nor dared to. Amongst themselves, the men murmured of home, of the way they ached for their wives' goat stew or olive bread, how they would never be the ones to take their sons on their first boar hunt. After the battle against the Apasiacae, vicious and protracted, those same rumblings soon turned to whispers of mutiny. When Alexander ordered the slaughter at Massaga, even after the city's surrender, and his mens' hands were left bloodstained in more ways than one, the forces' whispers turned into tangible threats. The Cohort had turned their spears inward in defense of Alexander.

Death of an Immortal

Blessedly, however, he had stopped moving east. They would at last begin their long trek home.

Or to Macedon, at least. 'Home' was a mere word to Corinna and the rest of her Cohort, moorless as they were. Her and Lycus' home was with Alexander. Even if it was an increasingly distressing one.

Years ago, her deification of Alexander, her unerring loyalty, would have held her back from thinking such treason, but things had changed. Swap out the bandages though he might, the wound remained. And began festering. Corinna had turned a blind eye, had looked away and tried not to care as the king's actions pushed, pushed, pushed his men down.

The rest of his court did not overlook his behavior so easily.

"I will not bow like a street dog!" one of his courtiers had shouted, veins popping from his neck and forehead.

The prostrate bow was a Persian custom, foreign to Alexander's own and utterly demeaning, but the king had begun insisting on it nonetheless. Much to everyone's fury. *A unifier*, he'd called it. All it had unified was his ranks' disdain, which still managed to grow even as they marched west.

"Respect your top of command," Alexander snarled, wearing the wools of the former Achaemenid royals. "Or face the consequences."

The courtier reeled back and spat before the king's feet, then turned on his heel to storm out. At that, warning clenched in Corinna's stomach. Insubordination was not something a man like Alexander would accept. Alexander had killed Cleitus—a friend and a long-time commander—in a drunken rage when he criticized the king's abandonment of Macedonian customs. He'd had his own pages and royal historian tortured to death for a suspected plot, one that ended up being no more than mere rumor. Some poor manservant or stable-boy would likely find this transgressor's corpse behind a supply tent the following morning.

Corinna chewed on her lip and said nothing. None of the Cohort did. They had received their end of the deal, and knew they would face greater change throughout their long lives than cultural customs alone. She saw Roshan lean over to whisper into the king's ear, covert dealings as always, and wondered. For the one secret creation of his that she knew of, she could only imagine there were a hundred more.

The sole aspect she couldn't figure out was why the king had yet to make himself immortal. It was within Roshan's power, after all, and Alexander loathed his own mortality, his frail-natured humanness, and it made him pull away from his Cohort more and more by the day. Valuable as they were, he still kept them as dutiful charges, but he was a mere man before them. Something he could only be too aware of. A product of culture and circumstance and corruption—but with a simple command to Roshan, he could be so much more.

The question raked at the back of her mind, knives over her skull. *So what is staying his hand?*

MOURNING wails shook the walls of Susa. The arduous trek back across the desert had killed many along the way, but the wails were not for them. They were for Alexander's dearest, his most esteemed companion in battle and life. Hephaestion, now dead.

It had been a simple fever, common enough to cure had it been caught in time, but it took his beloved and turned him into a walking shell, then broke him over its knee to leave him vomit-stained and gleaming with sweat.

Alexander didn't eat for days. He had other relations, three wives, sure. But not another Hephaestion. Not another bond as pure and honorable as theirs. Sleep evaded him, even drink evaded him, but madness did not. Corinna watched as

Death of an Immortal

he wrote letters petitioning his favored oracle for Hephaestion to be remembered as a divinity, began planning monuments in his honor. Both morning and night, swollen darkness now ringed his eyes.

"Floros," he said, shaky voice grabbing her attention in a very different way than she was used to.

She looked at him. Though the rest of his men were drinking together in the ancient Babylonian kings' halls, Alexander had secluded himself to the upper terraces of the palace. Thick-trunked palms, sweeping arches, glazed brick ornamented with lapis and gold, none of its splendor was enough to hold his attention. Not enough to so much as snag it. Even as she kept her focus on guarding him—threats against the king only seemed to increase—she was entranced with the city's beauty.

"Your Highness?"

Alexander waved her over as he looked out at the ancient city unfolding beyond the terrace. She came closer.

"It has been difficult, since—" He fought to hold back his tears, unsuccessfully, and diverted his gaze to the side.

Corinna stared at the horizon. *Since Hephaestion's death.* She wanted to comfort him in some way, but it wasn't her place, and her attention would only worsen his feeling of being exposed.

"I require your help."

"Anything, my lord." She meant it. Anything, if it would ease his grief.

"Hephaestion's doctor was neglectful. As Hephaestion drew his last breaths, Glaucias was entertaining himself at the theater." His gaze met hers, those once-fiery eyes that commanded the devotion of legions. No light reached them. "Execute him."

Corinna withheld a swallow. She had known what he was going to ask of her before the words left his trembling mouth, yet she dared not refuse him. Killing wasn't what bothered her. Heads had rolled and bodies had tumbled under her blade, but that he continued to eliminate those within his own ranks... Now was not the time to object on grounds of principle. Not after all he'd given them.

"I will." She inclined her head.

Hand outstretched, he reached up to touch her face. Had she a pulse, it would've stuttered—but she did not rebuff him. There was nothing sensual in the way he touched her. Rather, it was mournful. His gaze dug into her, as if he were looking down to the very matter of her, to each piece that made her up, immortality and all.

"It is fitting that he should see what true loyalty looks like before he dies," he said. He dragged his fingers along her cheekbones, then down to her jaw. "How wonderful it would be to never need sleep. To never die."

Corinna looked at him. His burnished golden curls shorn short in mourning, his once-bursting charisma long gone, his ambition turned to avarice, this was a man she no longer recognized.

At a loss for words and trying to put the slaughter of Glaucias out of mind, Corinna could only think to comfort her king. To serve him as she had always done.

"We will stand by you. No matter if you need sleep. No matter if you—" She faltered. *If you die.* "Forgive me, your Highness."

Alexander's hand dropped from her face. He tilted his head up to look at the stars, and Corinna followed his gaze. The blazing torchlight blotted out the night above them. He sighed, then turned his attention back to her, smiling. No happiness reached his eyes. Only sorrow. Corinna felt for him. She knew firsthand how it ached to lose so much in such a narrow span of time, but she would help in whatever way she could, for however long he let her. Even if what he asked unnerved her.

"Thank you," he said. "For everything you've done.

16

AD FIDELIS

Nikias hauled out Lycus and Corinna's domukardi, childlike grin wide and alive on his face.

"The rest of us got a good look at ours last week when you were gone." He stopped and straightened, leaving the box to rest at their feet. His thin frame was deceptive, baby-faced appearance concealing the fox in human skin. He wasn't the strongest among them, but it was for his wit and ability to move unnoticed that this smiling youth had been chosen. "Figured we'd let you guys in on it. I'm sure we'll pass some mortal who can open this for us."

"Explain?" Lycus asked with an up-tilted brow.

Both he and Corinna leaned up against the stone walls as golden light spilled in from above, dust motes fluttering down and verdant ferns swaying with the sigh of the wind. They had been absent from the most recent in a string of funerary banquets, instead hanging Glaucias from the city's battlements per Alexander's command. She'd done her best to ignore his pleas, to ignore his insistence that he *had* seen to Hephaestion and *had* done everything within his power to save him, before she broke his neck. Swift. No one who saw him swinging from the walls would think to check if it was in fact the hanging that killed him. It was a small mercy, but the only one she had to give.

At the banquet she and Lycus missed, the Cohort spent the night letting liquor flow like rainwater and had decided to see their domukardi. After they'd wrangled a mortal serving girl into opening it for them, they'd found it worth the trouble. A fascination. A strange marvel, they'd said, and no less so when they were inebriated. Nikias worried the two of them had felt left out, and said he wanted to give them that same moment of awe..

"It's been years since we last saw this," he continued. "Aren't you curious? Excited? Even a little?"

"I guess," Corinna said. "But it feels strange."

"It's your own heart. If anyone should be able to see it, it's you, right?"

She shrugged, but did have to admit her curiosity was piqued. "What was it like?"

"You'll know for yourself in just a moment."

A faraway look twinkled in his eyes as he bent down to run a hand over the domukardi's metal beveling. He stroked its surface.

"You sure we can't just open it ourselves?" Corinna asked.

Nikias shook his head. "I wish. We certainly tried, but no success. I'm sure we can nab one of the maids on the way to the kitchen."

"Hard to believe a box is worth stealing out of the royal armory," Lycus said. "And that's coming from a former thief."

"How can you be so indifferent?" Nikias asked.

Both she and Lycus shrugged. It was a wonder, yes, but it had been years since they'd taken so much as a peek at them, and they had almost begun to take their immortality for granted. Now was as good a time as any to revisit their domukardi and keep themselves humble. Or, at least herself humble. She didn't think Lycus had the capacity for it.

"If you say it's worth the risk," she said, hands braced on

Death of an Immortal

her hips. Otherwise, she worried she would crouch over the thing and eagerly try to open it on her own. "That amazing, huh?"

"It was, good gods, it was indescribable. It was—"

Nikias disintegrated into a puff of ash.

Corinna and Lycus blinked. Stumbled back.

They turned to one another with eyes wide, then back to the new pile of cinders and fine white dust, bits of him, of warm-souled Nikias, still fluttering to the ground.

In that fraction of a second before he'd burst into soot, they'd seen an unspeakable anguish, a flash of realization, and then the microcosm of his very being disintegrate into nothingness, forever lost like a breath on the wind.

A pallor crept over their faces. Horror clawed its way up her throat. They had seen this before, just once. Years before in the back room of a temple, only then it had been a chicken's death wail she'd witnessed as its heart was deliberately removed from the golden elixir.

Someone killed him.

She and Lycus exchanged terrified glances. Corinna had looked forward to seeing inside the box as a reminder of her mortality, yes, but it had been too long since she had *feared* for it. It was a luxury she and Lycus hadn't expected to lose.

None of their comrades had, either. Her stomach lurched into her throat.

They had to warn the others and secure the storage room —wherever it was the domukardi were kept. The location changed with each new region they drove into, and security measures on top of that made it anyone's guess. But if anyone could find it, it would be them. They hadn't thought to ask Nikias, but Alexander had to know. Roshan too. Without a word, Lycus hoisted up their domukardi and held it close, the closest his heart had been since living in his chest. Corinna and Lycus raced through the maze of halls adorned with frescos of foreign gods. It wasn't her time to meet them yet.

Should that day come, she prayed it would be on her own terms, however rapidly dwindling a possibility it seemed.

"We pass our barracks on the way to command," she said.

Lycus grunted in agreement behind her. Both broke out into the open air and past the groves of broad-leafed date palms, then into a separate compound closer to the city center where they and their comrades had been housed.

"Enyo, Myron!" Corinna yelled as she swung inside the doorway. They were the only two in the lounge, the rest likely tending to business. She lowered her voice in case their attacker was within earshot. "Someone's killed Nikias."

Enyo's eyes darkened, anger roiling up as she stood, followed by fear. She shook her head. "That's not possible."

"Domukardi," Lycus panted. "Someone must've—"

Myron crumpled to the ground with a yelp, clutched his ribcage, and burst into a plume of ash.

Corinna's breath scraped to a halt in her throat. Whoever this did not seek just one kill. No, their target wasn't Nikias alone, but each and every one of them. Enyo's eyes connected with hers for a long moment, and in them Corinna saw a humanity she'd never found before, a vulnerable and scared child who'd clawed her way to refuge—just like Corinna herself.

She knew what was coming. Enyo clasped Corinna's forearm with hers, and in the next second clutched at her own chest with a rheumy gasp.

"Give them hell," Enyo strained. With the snarl of a feral lynx, she stumbled to the ground and exploded into nothing more than cinder.

Despite herself, Corinna's eyes welled—but they didn't have time to mourn or warn anyone else. They had to get to Alexander fast, before any of their other comrades fell.

"Run!"

Corinna grabbed Lycus by the hand and yanked him onwards, speeding around the corners and archways. His bone-white fingers tightened around the domukardi as they ran. Window frames full of green-necked pheasants flashed past them, wall hangings and overflowing sacks of wheat no more than blurs. Five corridors down, the shatter of heavy glass met their ears.

Corinna skidded to a stop. The lump rising in her throat pressed tears into her eyes. Whether from rage or fear, she didn't know. Breaths shallow and tense, she took a step forward and put her ear to the door. A domukardi's straining hinges squealed. Lightning shot down her limbs and snapped her into action. With a nod to Lycus, they both wound back and kicked the door in, short swords drawn and ready to cut the killer down where he stood.

"Stand back! You—"

Corinna stopped, blinked, dizzied at what she saw.

There stood Roshan and Alexander, hands dripping in gold, shards of thick crystalline glass at their feet, and to the side were discarded chests with her Cohort's hearts left on the ground, suffocating in the open air like fish torn from water. Her king and his alchemist looked up, their gazes hardened and dead as ice. Their eyes tightened as they saw what lay in Lycus's arms. The air whooshed from her chest.

"My king," she said. "I—"

She what? What did one say to *this*? *Thank you, for everything you've done,* he'd said. Was the last thing he wanted to wring from them their own death? This had been no mistake, no necessary sacrifice. The disdain in Alexander's eyes showed clear enough that killing them off had been nothing more than a jealously calculated move. How dare any of his own live as a higher being than he himself?

Was anything he had said to them genuine? His thanks or praise, was it all just to gain enough of their fealty for him to cast this die?

Before the king made so much as two running strides across the room, Corinna and Lycus ran. There was no other option, not if they wished to protect their box and battle their once-beloved ruler at the same time. Even running might not preserve them.

"Outside!" Lycus hollered as he hooked right.

"Thieves!" Alexander bellowed after them, guardsmen clustering in his wake. "Barricade the exits!"

A voice she'd heard and followed a hundred times. She could almost imagine they were back at their war games, training and nothing more. If only.

They burst out into the daylight. The roar of men grew behind them as the pair swung past one of the many arcades, this one nearest the Euphrates' river docks. The chaotic street life swelled and swayed, a mass of textiles, the surge of vendors and buyers, the wafting scent of toasted cardamom pods and hazy incense. Before they could be spotted by their pursuers, she yanked Lycus towards a stack of barrels and barley sacks. They crouched behind them.

"You okay?" he asked at a whisper.

He rarely asked her anything so personal. Mission updates, inventory, sure. Anything personal, affections or worries, he communicated physically. But, no situation had ever before been so dire as this one. Lips tight, she could only nod, even though they both knew their world was fracturing beneath their feet.

"You?" she asked.

He nodded too, likely a lie as well, but they were in one piece. It was all they had left.

"The river runs less than four-hundred meters away from here," she said. "We could make it."

"What, just hop on a ship and leave?"

"You have any other ideas?"

Guards began toppling over carts and pushing through the crowds, chickens squawking and sellers protesting, but the square was packed enough to give them a few seconds more. Lycus shook his head.

"Take this." He handed her the domukardi and took a burlap sack into his dark, corded arms. "We split up but stay close. They won't know which of us has the box, and they can't hurt us without it. I'll buy us what time I can, but you're faster. Get that thing to safety. We'll figure it out from there."

She yanked his mouth down to hers for a brief second, a taste of what she may never again have, then they were off. He darted out nearer the guardsmen, hunched over to obscure their view of whatever he did or didn't hold, and drew their attention as she ran through their blind spots.

Four-hundred meters, just four hundred meters. Could Alexander somehow halt the boats? Corinna wasn't the praying sort, but she threw up a desperate plea all the same. She would have to find a way to misdirect him and his men.

The glittering green waters of the Euphrates' length shone ahead of her, slanted piers like outstretched fingers.

"He's just got bloody grain!" someone yelled in frustration.

"Where did she take it?" came another commander's voice.

She gulped. Lycus's ruse had been discovered, leaving them one less card to play.

"There!"

Corinna pushed on as Lycus came up behind her, just close enough for her to lob something his way. *Something.* Their pursuers were closing in, shoving past produce carts and baffled passersby, not agile enough to follow the path cut for a single, dexterous person. She looked to the rapidly approaching city bastion and the many merchant carts that went to and fro.

"Lycus!"

Following her line of sight, he nodded. As she chucked the shining bronze box high, arcing across the pierfront, he spread his arms wide and caught it with a grunt and a tinny *thwap*. The guardsmen following her veered off after him, trying to regain lost ground. He raced up the wooden slats of the citadel's walls as Corinna darted past the barbican towards the waterfront. She looked over her shoulder to see her partner at the wall, guards no doubt almost upon him. Lycus all the way up there, and with no one tailing her down here.

"Ready!" she yelled.

From on high he threw the domukardi down and wide, and she scooped it up to continue her frenzied run, sights set on the docks ahead.

"Stop her!" barked a guard from behind.

Any hope to catch her was futile. By the time she'd taken off with the domukardi, they were still scrambling down the stairs.

Only one ship was actively leaving the port, and from that same stretch of pier pulled away a donkey-driven cart, its back piled with crates and dark sacks of tubers. Her legs coursing with fire, she pushed ahead, box clutched tight to her chest and vision fixed on her target. But it was not the ship.

A full ten paces ahead of even their fastest man, her muscles glinted with sweat, focus honed. The water grew brighter as she neared. Packed earth turned to wooden slats under her feet. She couldn't hear Lycus snarling and fighting in the background, couldn't even hear the gulls or sailors barking at one another, her focus sharpened to the one vessel her hopes rested on.

The cart driver gave a yelp as she swerved around him. Darting behind and out of the guards' sights, she dumped the box between the hauler's wares and snatched up one of the bags of tubers.

She ran to the ship. Its bowed sides scraped against one of the decks as it parted, now just ahead of her.

Corinna seized the bag in her throwing hand as she ran—making a split-second judgement where it would land—then hurled it towards the ship's banners towering many heads above her own. Packed tight and tied off at the top, it looked dense enough to be mistaken for the box at a distance.

A *thud* met her ears. A few crewmen looked to one another, then shrugged and returned to adjusting the ropes and sails.

The din of pursuers clamored back into her ears, right on her. They didn't so much as glance at the cart carrying away the domukardi, the modest donkey and master carrying away that gleaming beacon of all she had to lose, all that her friends had once been. In a blink, it disappeared from view.

Before anyone could lunge for her, Corinna dove headlong into the brilliant green waters, a rush of pleasant coolness singing on her skin. Bubbles surged behind her as another figure exploded into the water. The plain garb trimmed with yellow fabric, just barely distinguishable through the cloudy water, told her it was Lycus. She grabbed his wrist and kicked to dive deeper, heading under the pier and disappearing from the view of those above.

They broke the surface far under the wooden pier, the space between the deck bottom and the water leaving less than a foot of air for them to gasp in. Even though her lungs didn't need it, they still burned for air, a reflex, something she'd never not done. Lycus shot up alongside her and gave an audible gasp.

"Ssh!" She clapped a hand over his mouth as the guardsmen's yells rang out across the waterfront. Half of them were a jetty or two away, unsuccessfully trying to halt the ship.

"What now?"

"They'll go after the ship," she warned. "By the time they catch up to it, they'll have realized their mistake."

He looked to her, brow furrowed. "It's not on the boat, is it?"

"The cart driver didn't look like he was from the city.

Looked foreign. Even once Alexander spreads word of his hunt, the driver will be long gone."

"Corinna." A pause. She knew him well enough to know that if he weren't treading water, his head would be slumped into his hands right about now. "Where was that cart headed?"

She swallowed. "I don't know."

"How do we find it?"

A deep but shaky breath, in and out. "We don't."

"We *don't?*"

"There was no other option. We had a better chance of surviving with it lost to Alexander completely—even if that meant losing it ourselves."

He muttered a curse under his breath. "So now what?"

If only she knew. Why the sudden betrayal? Why now? Why exacted upon such loyal, dutiful soldiers? They had given their lives to him, their mortality as well. No one could call them innocent, but they'd been acting on Alexander's command himself. Surely he wouldn't damn them for his own demands. The camaraderie they shared had gone on far too long to be a ruse, all of them too close to just be some fabricated ploy. Though as the distance had grown between him and his people, so too had it been with the Cohort.

Corinna felt a wrathful burning lick up her spine—and yet, there was also the hollow of the unfamiliar. The world she'd assumed a spot in, the structure she'd clung to and been grateful for, all disintegrated in the span of mere minutes. If it had ever been real to begin with.

But she'd escaped. More than the others in her Cohort could say, spirited away into no more than dust. She still saw Nikias' beaming face, falling, falling. Enyo's mask of bitter resolve. Myron's anguished contortions. How the others had fallen, she would never know, but her imagination gave her enough. Too much.

"Corinna," Lycus said, calling her back to reality. Again, he asked, "what now?"

"Now?" She bit down on the inside of her lip as her thoughts churned. Was she being rash? No, it was justice. Betrayal such as this *demanded* justice, god-king be damned. "Now we kill Alexander."

17

A HAWK FROM THE GAUNTLET

Roshan straightened the sheaves of parchment on his desk with a sigh, ran his hands over his balding scalp. The candlelight did little to warm the chill that had settled into the room, the golden flicker and overflowing ferns doing nothing to ease his apparent anxieties. Corinna watched on from above, hidden in the sill of a high window. While better than any position he'd likely ever occupied before, the stresses of this job looked to be wearing at him. She couldn't imagine anyone had taken his alchemic abilities as seriously as Alexander—though no one ever had as desperate a need. Even she had raised a brow at first. Yet now he had all the tools, all the resources, all the books he could ever need. She wouldn't begrudge him that. The needleless moral compass he served, however…

Roshan dipped his face into both hands with a sigh, and she silently jumped down from her hidden position.

"Scream and I'll cut your throat."

From behind him, she pressed cold steel against his Adam's apple, right over the delicate web of pounding veins. Roshan slowly raised his hands in surrender.

Death of an Immortal

""I'm a scholar, nothing more," he began to beg. "I mean no one harm—"

"Pretty words," she spit.

"Honest, I'm being completely hon—"

Corinna padded around to face him, knife still trained on his jugular and eyes burning like gold in the forge. Roshan looked as if his bladder was about to loosen.

"You'd do well to remember me. One of the two you couldn't kill, if you recall?"

"I didn't—I was acting on orders," he stammered. "I swear it, I never meant to kill—"

"Orders? We *all* acted on orders." She pressed the blade's edge even more firmly against his throat. "And look where it's gotten us."

Whatever pathetic words Roshan had to defend himself with seemed to stick in his mouth like tar.

"Why'd you do it?" she asked. Pointed, blunt, but honest. She was on a mission. While she could've spent time making him grovel and plead, wanted to make him suffer, nothing could undo the king's deeds. Besides, he was just as much of a pawn as they had been. How long until Alexander would try to axe him, too?

"Alexander commanded it."

Betrayal and anger coursed through her, but the initial sting wasn't there. That much she had already known. "Why?"

He swallowed, chewed his lip, but one look from her made the words come spilling back out. "He wanted immortality for himself, but I didn't know—the formula I created only works in one batch at a time. I couldn't recreate it, at least not in working form while your Cohort remained alive. It wasn't until I'd reexamined the Emerald Tablet that I'd even considered... But if the formula wasn't in use, any similar batch made after would work. So, you, you had to die.

He didn't want to do it until he had to, but with his men threatening mutiny—"

"Mutiny *we* protected him from! When he killed one of his cavalry and the poor boy's father, we stayed by his side. When he killed his friend Cleitus, we did not question him. When he tortured and killed his own pages and royal historian, still we remained faithful. And we would have continued to do so." Her words came out as a growl, slamming his back into the adobe wall with each sentence. Through grit teeth, she pushed down her surging anger. And her burning guilt. How blind she had been. She had to stay focused, even as Glaucias's pleas of innocence rang in her head. "Are you saying the old formula would've worked for him?"

He nodded, hands still raised.

"What does he have you doing now?"

"I'm searching for an altogether different concoction, one that would work simultaneously."

"How likely is it you'll find one?"

She saw his throat bob. His voice came out at barely a whisper. "It is an unthinkable task. I did it once, yes, but it nearly drove me mad to find a formula that worked. To do the impossible a second time…"

Corinna watched him for a long while, wheels turning. "So Alexander is still mortal?"

"Yes. While you and your partner remain, yes. Or until I find a different formula."

Even though she was shorter, she still somehow looked down her nose at him. "For a servant to the king, you certainly spill information fast."

"I'm a Persian working under a Macedonian. I have no allegiance but to knowledge itself."

"Convenient." Her gaze remained unwavering. "Hand over your notes and your poisons."

He blanched. "Please, don't make me—"

Death of an Immortal

"Not for you, coward," she said. "But I won't let you go free with them at your disposal."

"You—you'll let me free?" He almost jumped up with relief before fat drops of blood beaded at his neck.

"If you hand over everything to me first. You can flee and start again under a new master, study elsewhere." The sting of the blade seemed to prick at his senses as she pushed further. "Unless you'd rather die here."

"Any notes of use are here on this desk, everything." Holding his neck and torso still, he raised a hand to the side to rest atop his crinkled yellow papers. "I swear it."

"As for the potions? Serums, tinctures, I want everything."

His eyes darted to the periphery. "They're in a trunk. Under the bed."

"Go get them."

Corinna withdrew her knife and stepped back, then gestured to the other side of the room. He dashed behind her. That she made no move to stop him should have been warning enough, but his mind was no doubt awash with that intoxicating mix of fear and panic.

He flung open the door only to have a wall of muscle push him back. Lycus. Roshan cursed.

"Been too long, Roshan," he purred as he locked the door behind him. "Five days, if I'm right?"

"Not that we'd forget," she said.

Roshan swallowed hard, again surrendering with palms up. "I'll do whatever it is you want."

Corinna snorted, but there was nothing victorious in it. "Damn right."

"All your goodies," Lycus said as he leaned against the door. "Fetch."

Roshan's eyes darted to the window, too high for someone like him to escape through, and there was no way he'd be able to make it through the door either. Corinna knew that defeat in his eyes, and stowed away her sense of satisfaction for later. Cornered cowards were always the easiest to manipulate.

As Roshan went to haul the trunk from under his bed frame, Corinna pulled out a flint spark stone and stood over the desk. She struck it once, twice, and a spray of orange flares spit up on the pages. Their edges curled as she nursed the flames, his evils disappearing into the ether for good.

"Hold on!" he said.

She didn't bother to look up from her tiny inferno. It was hard enough to keep herself from striking him already. "You're in no position to expect anything different. Certainly none to bargain."

Roshan pursed his lips. The room went hazy as smoke wafted up and up, his life's work being quietly destroyed before him. His formulas, his equations, his research. She heard his breath tighten, saw him bite his inner lip. That alone brought her ire boiling back up. Her Cohort had their very lives ripped from them. Certainly he could endure the loss of some notes.

"No dawdling." Lycus picked at his nails and remained up against the door, but through his relaxed demeanor Corinna could still read the hatred in his eyes.

Roshan knelt down and opened the trunk to reveal rows upon rows of glass vials and jars, all with aqueous mixtures inside, some shimmering liquids and others a muckish brown with floating clumps. He gave his collection a long, hard look. Would he find anything, even one piece of knowledge worth giving his life to protect? Or had he truly done nothing so worthy in his many years?

Lycus stopped picking his nails, face hardening. "No. Dawdling."

"Here," he said, looking as if he were about to faint as he righted himself. "Everything I've made, save the solution inside your domukardi. They are marked according to their uses. Do with them what you wish."

A moment of silence passed between them, Corinna's hands clasped behind her back and sights fixed on the trunk's contents. The scales teetered within her, calculating, and she turned her gaze back to him with a flex of her fingers. The color drained from Roshan's face. Taking a step forward, she drew her dagger.

"Now hold on!" Roshan backed up against the far wall. "I gave you everything! Everything you wanted!"

Corinna slapped the blade of her elbow against the soft, exposed flesh of his neck, and his eyes popped. "Merely because we survived to ask it of you. Have no illusions that you did us a kindness."

He swallowed a gasp, eyes wide like a goat brought to slaughter.

"My companions received no better," she said. "From dust to dust, isn't that what you said?"

"Believe so." Lycus straightened with nostrils flared. "And back to dust you go."

Corinna clamped a hand over his mouth and thrust the knife into his gut, strangling his cries as hot blood slicked down Roshan's abdomen. He shoved back against her but she didn't budge, the one vertebra of backbone he had left writhing under her heel. His lips moved against her palm, but her forearm crushed what words he had left to die in his throat. Prying at her hands, he squirmed and fought for what ounce of life he had left, only speeding his death along as the blood poured from him even quicker, soaking through his shoes. She yanked the blade out and swung again. Again. Again. Ten stabs for ten dead friends. Ten people who would have died for Alexander time and again, who had no allegiance but to him, all struck down by the man they protected. A man who had called them friends.

Again she swung forward, this time landing at Roshan's jugular in a deep slice. He bit at Corinna's hand, but she and her knitting flesh remained unbothered, her eyes cold. He deserved no better. A red stain pooled at their feet.

Roshan crumpled to his knees with a gurgle. As the light faded from his eyes, Corinna picked out a single vial from his trunk, closed the lid, then shoved it back under the bed.

Poison in hand, she watched Roshan die.

ALEXANDER'S GARRISON remained on high alert ever since he found Roshan dead, slit belly to throat with his corpse torn to pieces. They had done their best to keep the news quiet and frame it as a xenophobic slaying, but his men were still distrusting and on-edge, even after they began their march back home. The Cohort's week-and-a-half long disappearance had been left a mystery as well. At first, Alexander told his commanders they'd been sent off on a need-to-know assignment. Few bought it. Trust was slim within his ranks these days, a seed of resentment and wariness germinating in every mind.

Let them mutiny, if they dared. If his men believed themselves strong enough to try it, he was stronger still to see them hanged. He'd done it to men more powerful before, framing them for any crime that would stick and sentencing them to a public death. He could remain untouchable.

Could have, had Hephaestion not died. Had the protests and constant threat of revolt and the churning bitterness in his ranks not overwhelmed him. Men used to fall over themselves to be called one of his own, yet now he could hardly command the obedience of any. Ill-fated battles or failing weapons, those were the things he had expected to loom over him. Not disloyal men. If there was a thread that could make the whole rug come undone, that would be it.

At every turn, people only continued to disappoint him. His letter petitioning the oracle to make Hephaestion a god was denied, and the conciliatory title of 'divine hero' he'd been granted instead wasn't enough. He deserved honors as great as Patroclus's.

Alexander could hardly even concentrate on his supper, a plate of well-roasted mutton, figs glazed with honey, and tender eggplant spiced with cumin and sumac. It might as well have been ash in his mouth. Chalky. Dry.

Not even the new serving hands could draw his attention. The maid came to drop off his food, sweep his tent clean, polish his replacement warhorse's saddlery—he had lost Bucephalus years before to battle wounds, yet another piece of him this campaign had taken—and spoke not a word. A veiled woman, he had averted his eyes, though more out of the desire to avoid conversation than chivalry.

He sighed and settled into his chambers for the evening, thoughts still whirring as he tried to escape to sleep. Returning home did not mark him a failure. He was still going home with an empire in his pockets, from his Macedonian throne to the Nile to the Ganges. He had still conquered. Every battle had been his victory to claim.

So why did he feel so empty? Why this hazy smoke clouding his heart and mind's eye? With a heavy sigh, the king flipped onto his side.

Stars screamed across his eyelids as blinding pain shot through his intestines. Vomit spurted from nostrils and gaping mouth as acid surged up and out his stomach, and he propped one shaking arm beneath him as he heaved over the side of the bed. The patterned rug, formerly a thing of beauty, now showed him his own dinner, a disgusting ecru heap.

"Sohrab! Payam!" he called to the guardsmen standing just outside his door. Persians. Far too many Greeks had become disillusioned with him, their own kinsman, to stay, and he had to fill their positions somehow.

They ran in, arms drawn in alarm. Alexander shook his

head, which felt so dizzy and light he could imagine simply floating off earth's surface altogether.

"Physician," he muttered. It was all he could do to keep his bile down, nonetheless his wits about him. "Now."

The stocky Payam ran out, and Sohrab retrieved a rag from Alexander's wash basin. "My lord, is there anything else I can fetch you?"

"Water." Even to his own ears, his voice sounded like a garbled mess. Disgusting.

Sohrab grabbed the waterskin wrapped around the post at the foot of the bed and poured some of its contents into a bronze cup. Alexander swished it around in his mouth before spitting it back out onto the rug. If he was repulsed, Sohrab hid it well. He grabbed its clean edges and folded it up, then took it out of the room.

"What is it that ails you?" asked the physician as she shuffled into the room, back bent, hands gnarled yet practiced. Her dark complexion hid her age well, save the wrinkles hanging from her jowls, and her still-bright eyes flashed wisdom.

He couldn't do more than shake his head. She pulled up a footstool and rested a hand against his temple, then the upper right quadrant of his abdomen. She gave a light push to his stomach and he yelped.

"An imbalance in the bile humors. You've begun to sweat as well." Her heavy brows pressed together as she looked over him. A minute passed, her silent assessments lingering as her face continued to darken. "A priest will be in to pray the Yashts over you when the sun rises, when it reaches its peak, and when it sets, and I will begin brewing you a restorative tonic."

"How bad is it?" he asked, words slurring. Shame burned his neck.

She shook her head, wrinkles swinging. But no one could deny the king an answer. "It seems to be the same condition that ailed Hephaestion, my lord. But we will not fail you."

A lie. Without Roshan or Hephaestion or his Cohort or the support of his men, people did nothing other than fail him nowadays, the betraying and scheming and incompetent lot of them.

As he fell back against the down of his bed, he thought that maybe when all was said and done, drifting up and away wouldn't be such a bad thing after all.

BLOOD POUNDED sluggishly through his veins. One would've thought he'd been left out in a rainstorm by how thoroughly sweat drenched his bedclothes. Pleasure in food had forsaken him for two days now as well as his ability to keep it down, and yet his stomach had swollen painfully outwards. The priest's chants had done nothing. The tonics and brews, nothing. This evil heat searing him from the inside out couldn't have cared less about the lands he had conquered nor the titles he had been bestowed. It just kept on burning.

Even tossing and turning was beyond his energy. Limp and pale, he laid sprawled out on the bed as one of the veiled serving girls entered with a basin and rag in hand, the flickering torches casting a dim light across the room. She came to his side and sat on the edge of his bed. He lacked the will to turn over, to let her wash his face.

Instead she tilted his head upwards, and he swallowed whatever was in the cup she pushed to his lips. Her hands suddenly dropped him back to the pillows. Even through his haze, his eyes widened at her sudden carelessness.

"Not feeling so well, are we?" Corinna said.

His eyes snapped to her as she drew back her veil and let it fall around her shoulders, golden eyes both cold and aflame all at once.

~

Corinna looked upon the man she once so admired. Now crazed. Paranoid. Weakened. If he thought mere walls and some Persian guards were enough to save him from her, then he had forgotten how his Cohort had been trained.

"Wh— You?" The shock on his colorless face was plain to see.

"If you're surprised, then I'm disappointed in you." She snorted, though she felt no mirth. Instead, there was only the single-minded drive to make him suffer as he'd done to her once-companions.

Alexander opened his mouth to holler for his guardsmen, but she clamped a hand over him and held firm. Struggle though he may, the malaise and fever had already taken their toll, rendered him weak. She had seen to it with every meal he ate and sip he took, all sprinkled with one of Roshan's powders, one that would drain the vigor from Alexander bit by agonizing bit. As she fought, she relished in every push he gave against her, in every gasp he tried to take from behind her hand. Pictured him taking out each heart jar and smashing it to the ground. The unremorseful eyes he'd trained on her when discovered.

Corinna bent over him, eyes narrowed to dagger slits. "If you have any gods other than yourself, I advise you make your peace with them."

He went still. After a moment, she loosened her grip. The man must know his fate, know that he was lying upon his very deathbed. Even if he managed to call in his men, she would cut them down. Could easily do so. Finally Alexander's ghosts had come for him, and she would be their hand.

"My empire will endure," he hissed up at her. "My people will find out what happened and they will hunt you like a boar."

"Perhaps if you hadn't alienated your own countrymen.

Or do you think I just waltzed into your camp unaided?" She shrugged. "You have more enemies in your ranks than you know, and you created every one of them."

He sputtered, but through his fumbling lips it came out as if he were drunk.

"We would have protected you. Even as you became a monster, we stayed faithful to you." She leaned closer towards him, feeling only icy fury bubble up in her. Vengeance. Something she'd never sought herself. Before, she killed on command and to protect, for something higher than herself. Now, she killed for a justice that couldn't be found any other way. "But now, I will ensure that every last piece of your empire dies. That your lands are carved up. That your heirs suffer the same fate as Enyo and Myron, Nikias and Acteon, Galene and Bakchos, Dimnos and Zoilos, Polemon and Hermias. I will destroy every last shred of your memory so thoroughly that humanity will not even be able to find your tomb."

She heard a gurgle in his lower intestines, and his eyes flickered backwards as they rolled in pain. She could almost imagine that she heard the leaden thump of his pulse, a drumbeat announcing his death. Could he hear it too? Alexander gasped for air. Justice sweet on her tongue, blood singing in her ears, Corinna clamped a hand over his mouth for the last time and held her face above his own, a handbreadth away and voice as sweet as the hiss of a black asp.

"Does it hurt to die? I wouldn't know, but my Cohort, *your* Cohort, they did. You saw to that. Yet while you may think yourself and everything you touch invincible, it is I who am immortal."

He scratched at her hand and wrestled under her grip, a mouse against a lion, but she held firm. He thrashed. Struggled. Panted for air he couldn't gulp down as beads of sweat ran from his temples. Even after everything she'd done for him and the wide ends of the earth she'd traversed at his command, the things she'd witnessed and done in his name, no part of her mourned the man she now murdered. Where she once felt adoration and devotion, now she felt only the cold.

Within minutes the light in his eyes extinguished, and Alexander of Macedon was dead.

NEWS SPREAD FAR and wide of Alexander's death, to the edges of his already-crumbling empire and then a leap further. His once-loyal generals had begun the process of portioning the lands for themselves, but after Corinna and Lycus had set those wheels in motion they couldn't be bothered to stick around. Their revenge had been exacted, their reason for staying dead.

Sitting around a weak fire one night, they'd decided to head north. Trying to find their domukardi was futile. If not even Alexander's men could recover it, it was long gone by now. Besides, what would've been the point? No mortal held the code, and none would be so drawn to a plain, unadorned chest.

They wandered from the Scythian foothills, a smoky green landscape with lakes shimmering over each crest, to the Xiongnu state out east where they wandered with the nomadic bands, yurts and goats in tow. They traversed the Satavahana empire by the far Erythraean sea, where the temples were a burst of vivid color and fruit and incense were piled high on altar plates. They then found passage across the ocean to arrive on the African shore of the Axumite empire, where blocks of salt as wide as Corinna's chest were slung over the backs of camels for trade. Everywhere they went, a new sight, a new taste, a new tongue.

Neither she nor Lycus kept count of how many years they'd been gone, drifting from place to place. They had lost track of how many winter solstices had passed somewhere around the forties and hadn't bothered re-tallying since. It wasn't as if their bodies knew the difference. Corinna's hands were just as they had been since the day her heart was cut from her ribcage, Lycus's jaw just as firm. No sunspots, none of the deep lines of age. No children to watch grow, no land either one of them could call home.

At first their abundant vitality had been a wonder. A liberation. A thing as expansive and limitless as they themselves. They could go anywhere, do anything without a single worry. And they did. Trek after journey after pilgrimage, and it was thrilling. Weeks in bed together, feasts and feats, all intoxication to the soul.

In the moment. While it lasted.

But in the creeping years, however many it even was, the weight of time began to hang upon her bones, threatening to tug her down. Was this life? Chasing one thing after the next only to be freed by the release of death?

But then, what of her? Even the empire she was born under no longer stood. After a new fledgling city-state named Rome began to expand, its domain swallowed up nearly all of what Alexander had considered his own. She hadn't even needed to obscure Alexander's tomb. Time forgot it on its own. The winds had already shifted, the march of technologies and men and moral faults continuing onwards, onwards, as the world she'd known crumbled, reshaped, then crumbled again in a cycle as unrelenting as nature itself. And within what seemed to be the blink of an eye, her blessing of long-life no longer seemed as auspicious as it once had been. Still an incredible thing, still it had given her much, but the realities that had come with it…

Alexander the Great, as they now called him, would have never withstood the cruelty of immortality. He craved it, but such preservation would've been the unraveling of any man as vainglorious as he. After his empire's inevitable fall, he would've been damned to watch new visionaries take his place and lead the charge for their kingdoms, each convinced —much like him—that they were building an enduring thing. An immortal thing. And then he would watch each and every one crumble as his own had. He would see the rise and ruin of nations play out over and over again on the wheel of time, around and around. He would be forced to watch as his kin died, one, then two, then ten, for as long as his untouchable life lingered on. And then he would watch as his memory became nothing more than dust choking in the wind, until his very name died to leave only his vessel.

But the yoke of immortality was not Alexander's to bear. It was hers.

With her commander gone, with the falconer dead and no glove left to land on, there lay only the wilds ahead.

In some small corner of her heart, Corinna sighed as she looked up at the stars, and wished her mother had never sent her to hide in the crop fields those many eons ago.

18

LOST EONS

Lycus hadn't shown up. Neither of them had been particularly excited to go out into the English springtime, the warming weather still too cool for their Mediterranean natures, but this wasn't any regular job, either. There had been a wave of anti-semitism roiling towards the north, and it wasn't until tensions reached a fever pitch that a land-owning Jewish man had requested protection for his family. With hundreds of Jews living around York, and with few able to afford a hired blade, she had few reservations in lowering her fee. She'd seen many a frothing, bigoted horde throughout her days, too often to imagine that this one would end any better.

But Lycus, who had been helping her guard the family, was absent today. He'd woken up alongside her, and through her foggy half-sleep she'd seen him readying for the morning, but nothing beyond that. Nothing to indicate trouble either, which she supposed was just as well. After planting a kiss on her forehead, he'd dressed and left without a word. Though he wasn't the most dedicated of workers, preferring to work only for himself after Alexander's betrayal, she wouldn't imagine he'd stop working altogether. He liked pilfering his employers' spices and jams too much for that. Perhaps he had merely gotten himself into trouble again, but she didn't have time to go looking for him today. He would show up eventually.

The side door burst open, one of the two domestic servants entering out of breath and with her face sheet-white, burlap sacks from the market still in hand. So much for it being a quiet day.

"Tell me," Corinna said, mincing no words. Her accent in this tongue was bad, but people could still understand her.

"Riots," the woman panted. "Coming this way."

Gods. Was that what Lycus had been diverted by? Had he tried to direct the masses away? As an immortal he'd be fine, but she worried after him all the same. "How many among them?"

"I couldn't say."

"How many?" she pressed. "Guess, if you must."

"I—At least a hundred, if not two."

Corinna's stomach twisted. Rioters would make quick work in tearing apart any normal edifice, especially one of thatched reed and timber. She looked out over the hillside where plumes of smoke began to gather and cursed inwardly. *Out of all the days for him to not show.* She could certainly use an extra set of fighting hands today.

"You should run. Leave me to look after the household and go," Corinna said. "Now, while you can."

The girl nodded, and Corinna turned on her heel to rush down the corridor and into the main sitting room. Out the window, the man and lady of the house were craning their necks to watch where smoke gathered on the horizon.

"Out back," she commanded. Even though the man, Gershom, was more agreeable to taking orders from Lycus, the looks exchanged between him and his wife told her they weren't about to protest. "Now."

Faces panicked, they swept up their three children and

headed to the stables, Corinna ushering them along the whole way. The yard chickens gave strained, nervous clucks as they passed them, the birds hiding in the bushes. The lady of the house tried to turn back for a pocketful of their nicer possessions, only to have Corinna force her onwards with an exasperated huff.

"Riches do no good if you're dead."

She directed them to the horses, not even sparing time to tack them. These beasts were work animals, not used to being ridden but broke nonetheless. Wheels turned in her head, cogs trying to find where they best fit. There was a castle not too far off where they could shelter behind a barricade. The Jewish here were protected as vassals of the Crown, living in the area to tend the land. There was at least a better chance at safety there. Corinna hoisted herself onto a dappled mare and instructed the two young twins behind her to hold on tight. With the reins of the husband, wife, and other son's steed in hand, she squeezed her legs around her horse's barrel and they were off.

It was a short ride to the warden's gates at York Castle, but each minute weighed on her as if it were ten. She should have been used to it by now—the chaos, the turmoil—but it had been ages since the last time she'd seen battle, not to mention that the mother and father, the children and farm animals, it all reminded her too acutely of a scene she'd walked away from long ago.

No, she wasn't used to it. Would never fully be. How some people not only endured this kind of anguish and fear, but reveled in it, escaped her.

Already the sky was turning a dark slate, as if the smoke from the rioters' torches had blotted out the blue heavens itself. With her charges close behind, they broke over the horizon to see the fortress, a welcomed sight settled between the grassy slopes. A brief glance told her they weren't the only ones seeking refuge there.

A cacophony met them at the walls, men and women and their young pleading to be let in, a man on the other side shouting for silence and order. Corinna nudged her mount forward to cut through the droves, grip tight on the reins of the other animal.

"The warden will see you and your own into the sanctuary of Clifford's Tower, and no further than—"

At that their voices swelled, a ray of hope in the dark. The portcullis was pulled up with the groan of wood and metal chains, and as soon as its teeth were a mere foot off the ground people began wriggling through. Corinna motioned her wards towards it only to be stopped by the gatekeepers.

"No livestock may come through, only those in need of shelter."

She cursed under her breath with a nod, and swung down to whisk the two little ones off the mare. Then, their mother and the older boy. The father was able to handle himself, even if his face had gone pale and sweaty. The sun sank below the horizon in full, all light now gone save for the rioters' torches just atop the nearest hill crest, like the spitting tongues of dragons.

"Go." She pushed the group on through the barbican, and hesitated as she saw the gatekeepers begin to lower the portcullis. Assuring both the durability of the gate and tending to her charges would be easier if Lycus had shown, but she couldn't afford to get ensnared in hypotheticals.

The throng of people surged towards the base of Clifford Tower, wooden slatted walls high and strong. They were nothing like the walls the Qin dynasty had built, nor the Walls of Constantinople, but maybe it would withstand the masses. Maybe. She chewed her lower lip. The roar of voices swelled as the mob drew nearer, until finally they were hissing and cursing right outside the gates, no better than feral mountain cats.

"Crusaders," the lady of the house whispered.

Death of an Immortal

Anti-semites already. The Third Crusade had all but begun, a spark feeding the flames of hatred for anything and anyone Jewish. Why her mortal kin couldn't see the meaningless cycle—slaughter then regret then, inevitably, yet more slaughter—was beyond her. Human suffering meant little in the larger scheme of things, the universe brutal and unflinching as it was, but every instance chipped away at whatever light remained in her. Smaller and smaller it grew, and she wondered if one day there would be nothing left at all. Then again, she wasn't one to talk.

The outer walls began to reverberate as rioters banged against them, screaming for conversion or death. Corinna circled her charges in tighter, waiting for the rage to cease.

Deep down, she knew better.

The night sky became a thick blackness, a blazing orange halo from the torches shining up behind the parapets. Minutes slid into hours, painstaking, and yet instead of tiring the crowd grew even more feverish. It was a scene she felt she'd witnessed a hundred times.

Some of the Jewish leaders converged towards the center of the huddled masses, their heads bent together and brows heavy. Corinna turned away. There was nothing that could be said or done to stop this, save an act from a long-absent god. She went to usher the family closer to the middle.

"Bring 'em out!" someone shouted.

She clenched her teeth. The more eager they got, the more vocal and unruly, the sooner this would all go to hell. There would be no negotiations or appeals for de-escalation.

"Corinna!"

Hope jolted through her. She knew that voice well, had come to know it so intimately over the eons that it was like a fixture in a childhood home. She spun her head in its direction, eyes scanning for him in the crowd.

"Lycus!"

"Over here!"

"Stay," she said to the family, leaving them in the center of the crowd. It was the safest place they had for now. Pushing her way to the walls, she hollered his name through the wooden panels until she saw a sliver of his golden eyes and impressive height.

"Where have you been? Are you alright?"

"I'm alright," he said, nodding. "We need to get you out of there before this all goes to shit."

"Nowhere else nearby is safe, and there's no way we can get five people out of here without drawing attention."

"Leave them, then!" he hissed.

Corinna looked at him, as gob-smacked as if he'd struck her across the face. They were immortal. What did they have to fear from standing against mere rioters?

"Are you joking? Lycus, this isn't the— How could—" She shook her head, then smacked at the wall as if he were able to feel the sting of it. "Get over here *now*, damnit, and help me protect these people!"

"Cor, sweetheart." He wiggled two fingers through the slats to grab hers. Despite herself, she laced hers with them. "Look, do you really want to live like we have been? Relying on someone else's purse?"

Her brows knit together. "What are you talking about?"

"Leave here. With me, like we've done before. When we come back, there's going to be more land and more money. More for us to get in on."

Those words, so simple and muddled in the chaos—but she understood the meaning weaved into them.

"We can't!" she exclaimed at a whisper, checking over each shoulder to make sure no one else had heard. She yanked her hand free.

"I'm not saying we become Crusaders! We don't have to watch this, don't have to be a part of it, but if we just walk away we can reap the spoils once we're back. Or do you want to keep living in a thatched hut and running mice out of our rooms?"

Corinna took a step back, shaking her head. Ice crystallized in her blood. She knew Lycus had a love of the material, but she never thought it'd warp into this. Sure, she had caught him pocketing others' things before, and sure, she had seen him sell out people for coin, but this was a new layer she'd never imagined. Had Alexander's betrayal sown this seed? Taught him he should look out for himself at the expense of all others?

"We don't need money or land," she said. "We are *immortal*. We need nothing else!"

"Nobody *needs* anything," he said, voice soft despite the madness around them. "But it sure makes for a better life, yeah? We've got an awful lot left to live."

She could hear the inexplicable calm laced into his voice. He'd *known* this was going to happen. Known and not told her, not raised the alarm or even tried to spare the one family they were tasked to protect. Corinna spewed off a string of colorful words at him as she attempted to assemble her thoughts into coherence, but the rising din soon made anything else impossible to hear. She raced back to the family.

A scream pealed out behind her, and she wheeled around to see a man stab deep into his wife's jugular. Dread built in her bones. *No.*

A mercy kill, a surrender. Saving themselves from slaughter by choosing death at their own hand. The man moved to his children next.

A wizened and bearded man, a Rabbi from the looks of it, began calling for those assembled around the tower to sacrifice their lives before giving up their faith, proclaiming it better to kill themselves than to be torn to pieces like animals. Panic rolled throughout the yard, men turning on each other as their children shrieked and their women wept, others protesting as they were borne down on with blade and rock.

Corinna turned and pushed the children behind her, parents on either side, sweat beading down their temples and upper lips. Were her heart still in her chest, she was sure it would've beaten up her throat by now. They were good people. They did not deserve death, and certainly not in this way.

"Look away," she ordered the trembling family, her blade at the ready in case anyone drew near.

Smoke tickled her nose. Sudden crackling sang in her ears. The far corner of the walls shot up in a blaze as the Rabbi threw himself onto the conflagration he'd ignited, ending himself and breaching their only defense in one fell swoop. Opening the dam. Bleeding piles of family members littered the open space yet still about forty remained, determined to survive. The fire spread and she could hear the mob move towards the flames. Boards snapped as they kicked at the fire-ravaged walls. She swore. The mother behind her began to sob, and the children clinging to her skirts wailed. They'd be overrun in a matter of minutes.

"Hold onto me and follow, now," Corinna commanded, looping the mother's hand around her leather belt. The oldest child walked close to his mother's hem, the young twins each carried in their parents arms, their father bringing up the rear. Corinna weaved through the hysterical crowd back the way they came, and the portcullis came into view. The guards were nowhere to be seen, likely having abandoned their posts in the turmoil. And the gate, lowered. She would need more manpower to get it back up.

"Gershom, grab with me and turn." She grasped the wooden wheel controlling the gate and began to crank it back. Setting the girl he carried into the mother's arms, the father's ruddy, uncalloused hands then joined hers. Even through his stoic facade, she saw him fight the tremble in his hands. Her stomach tightened.

The little girl shrieked. Corinna whipped her head over

Death of an Immortal

her shoulder to see the mob spill through the charred walls and stone those whom the fire hadn't already claimed. Corinna grit her teeth and pulled harder, muscles searing as part of the swarm broke off towards them. The portcullis came up by a few inches. Then a foot.

"Crawl under," she ordered between gasps. "Quickly!"

Their mother crouched to her knees and egged the boy through, and he squirmed through the dirt on his protruding little belly—until a pair of hands wrapped around his ankles to yank him back.

The gate came down with a thunderous crash as Corinna tore out her short sword and dagger, a blade in each fist. Her heart sank into the slippery bile of her core. A group of five men stood at their backs, Lycus off to the side with a grimace and eyes begging understanding. Gershom managed to wrest his son back from the zealot, but Corinna didn't hold out hope they'd withstand them for long.

"Why?" It was all she had to say, all she could think to ask him.

"We've endured enough, love."

"What of them?"

"All mortal things die. I can't stop that, and you can't either."

There he went again, twisting words, acting as if he weren't complicit. A bystander who happened upon a boon. She had known this side of him existed, the side that went out stripping armor from the enemies' war dead before bandaging up comrades, the side that pocketed an old widow's silver while pretending to check on her, but never thought it would turn around to bite her. Never thought he would sell innocent souls. How short sighted she'd been. They were supposed to be different sides of the same coin, and while this was a man she recognized, it hurt to look at what he'd become. Was she worse for it, too?

"That's not an answer," she spat. "Tell me *why* you've done this."

"Same reason we joined Alexander. For a better life. We knew we were gonna have to get our hands dirty, but it was worth the price then like it is now."

"We're not the one's paying it!"

"We never are. Yeah, this will be a tragedy, but a necessary one." He looked down and kicked at the dirt beneath his boots, as if he had the right to play self-effacing. "Nothing new to either of us."

Corinna often wondered how terrible things continued to happen, over and over again, before looking at her former partner and realizing men like him were the source. The people who convinced themselves of necessary sacrifices they'd never be made to pay, and who called tragedies inevitable.

One of the men with Lycus let out a barking laugh, like an animal with a bone caught in its throat. Corinna wanted to beat that wicked grin from his face, wanted to crack those teeth so he'd never smile again—but she stayed planted in front of the family.

Her once-partner flashed regret-filled eyes her way, but the set of his shoulders was nonchalant. In that moment, she saw Lycus for what he was. She felt stupid. This guile didn't spring from nothing. He must've done this before. How long had she been sharing her bed with a monster, or had he been a monster all along?

Lycus tested her with a step forward, and she flashed her canines. There were plenty of people, entire groups all at once, whom she could easily go up against. But Lycus knew her tricks and tactics as well as he knew himself. They'd stalemate one another. They were two blades of the same twin set, each moving as seamlessly as the other's shadow.

The four men he was with descended, not sated with the carnage they'd already wreaked. Corinna moved to block

Death of an Immortal

them only for Lycus to cut her off. His arms were outstretched as if to hug her, to wrap her up in his grasp and hold her still until it was all over. With a snarl, she dodged Lycus then hurled a knife at one of the attackers to bury it deep in his meaty shoulder, but in his animal state he tore it out, went after the mother and her two youngest. Corinna's absent heart seized.

She threw herself in front of them, letting the assailant bury his spear into her gut. Corinna cried out, agony blinding against the metal piercing her intestines, but still she pushed on, fighting her way up the length of the pike to slash the man's neck. He toppled over, and she pulled the weapon through herself.

"Take it!"

Corinna handed the spear to the gaping woman, but she took it with unsure hands. Her grip was all wrong—but Corinna didn't have time to teach her. Being armed with something was better than nothing.

The men glanced at her with wary eyes, then shifted to Lycus.

"I'll contain her," he said to them. With a sombre gaze, he rolled up his shirtsleeves. "Do what you have to."

Sensing what was coming, Corinna leapt out of his reach, but he quickly caught up. One of the men advanced, this time circling Gershom and his eldest child.

"No!" she cried.

Gershom ran to cover his son, but it was too late.

She tried to feign a dodge to the left then hook Lycus's ankle and toss him backwards, but he didn't fall for it, standing instead like an impenetrable wall. A stalemate, sure enough. She fought against him, thrashing and toppling him over anytime he grasped onto her, trying to outmaneuver him when he blocked her path to the family, but he knew her tricks. As the men approached the mother and two remaining children, she dragged Lycus down by the hair and jammed her last knife into his kneecap, but didn't make it more than two steps forward before he clasped onto her calf and yanked her back.

The mother and children's screams came to a sharp end. Corinna cried out, throat hoarse from her screams and vision beginning to blur with tears.

"It's okay," Lycus whispered. "It's okay."

As she crumpled to the ground he pulled her down against him, holding her tight. Corinna's tears seeped into his shirt. Memories and nightmares consumed her, indistinguishable. An adobe home flashed through her mind. Tall fields, wheat tickling her cheeks and smoke in her lungs. The mangled wails of her family. Heinous men.

She shoved against his chest and broke free before snatching up the now-discarded knife she'd lodged in his leg. Pinning him to the ground with her knee, she stabbed into him. He didn't fight back. Not now that he'd gotten what he'd wanted.

Somehow that made her even angrier.

Corinna stabbed him again and again, each time Lycus yelping and gasping, but he did not stop her. Ten, twenty, fifty times. She only grew more tired with every swing, her rage twisting into grief. Not only for the family annihilated before her or the many more dead in the smoky tower remains, but for the man she thought she'd known. Thought she'd be able to spend the rest of her endless days with. Thought that, surely, would never betray her.

She had been so very wrong.

News of the pogrom at York went down in bloody infamy. Over a hundred Jewish parents and children, poets and farmers, elders and lovers died that night, either by their own hand, the fire, or the mobs. She was sure Lycus's profits from the following Crusade were immense, but even the war itself became old news throughout the centuries, blurring into the mass of yet more atrocities and bloodletting. She could only guess which ones he had his fingers in.

She left after that day. He had tried to convince her to stay, tried to woo her with jewels and silks and spices no doubt pinched from the dead, but Corinna simply left. She wished she could kill Lycus for what he'd done. Wished she could string him up and slaughter him in a public square, but—short of bricking him up in a tower he would end up escaping from anyhow—he remained just as untouchable as her.

As for herself, Corinna had given up. Leaving behind Europe and the Arabian plains, she voyaged east. The blue-capped peaks and throat-singing nomads soothed her soul, the yak milk and toasted spices healing what her physical self was unable to regenerate. While always partial to that stretch of land, she couldn't bear to get too attached to any one patch of dirt. The continent was massive, certainly enough to keep her mind and feet busy. And so she wandered.

It was within a grotto nestled in a stretch of valley where Corinna thought she found herself, some long-lost center. Rows of meditators sat within, shaved heads like the first fuzz of a peach, polished rosaries like knowing eyes, robes making the people look like carnations springing from the rock. She wasn't sure if the nuns sensed the fractures within her, or the strangeness, or the emptiness, but they took her into their fold all the same. Peculiar though they deemed her, she was welcomed.

As she watched the calm minds around her and listened to the deep vibrato of bells, the longer she spent here, the less guilt and despair sat like a noose on her collar. The more she sat with her own mind, the places where she had gone wrong appeared as black spots on the map of her mind, now laid out as clear as day. Attachment, desire, clinging to the past and the people in it… All of it had ruined her.

Even after ranks of young temple girls aged into bent-backed nuns for years untold, as a torrential monsoon season ripped the temple from the mountainside to leave a heap of sludge and wood and twitching flesh and memories, Corinna quietly stowed away what emotions would let her care.

19

RED HANDS

A RIVER CHURNING yellow with silt carried her body away from the mountains, a thing she only noticed in passing, like peering in a stranger's window to experience their evening meal. The current enfolded her and she bobbed along like driftwood. A living antique, discarded. Trying to forget its own self.

It wasn't until she heard a tinkling voice that she realized she'd hit shore, her back warm against the sun-heated earth.

"Hái hǎo ma?"

Bleary-eyed, Corinna strained to blink in the intense sunlight. The outline of a woman, hair woven into a thick black loop, was silhouetted against the sky.

"Dǒng bu dǒng wǒ shūohùa de?" the woman asked.

The lilt of the words was familiar, guttural and cutting all at once, but Corinna's brain was too waterlogged to make any sense of it. She sat up, spine like jelly. Before her stood a slight girl in a broad straw hat, muddy sleeves rolled up to her elbows and with a net of waxy winter melons slung over her shoulder. It took a moment for the water to leave Corinna's ears.

"Jiào Yōng Lìwěi."

Her name. It's Liwei Yong. That little bit, the pleasantries, Corinna still knew.

"Jiào Kòurùinà," she stumbled. She'd long given up on conquering the mechanics of Mandarin, but it was close enough.

The girl, Liwei, lit up. "Xūyào bāngzhù mā?"

Corinna blinked. Myriad languages rose to her lips, but most of those tongues had already died out. Latin, Cuman, Khitan, Khazar, and more, but she had abandoned learning different tongues as she saw their use die over and over again with their civilizations and people. Nothing lasted long. Nothing. Except her.

Liwei rocked back on her heels and chewed on her crescent-shaped lower lip. Corinna knew she looked like hell, but why was this girl so insistent on tending to her? She offered her a hand up, and Corinna took it despite herself.

Attachment is the root of suffering.

Notice only as a passing shadow.

The beliefs she'd used to calm, to distance herself remained etched into her. Yet though she was wary to keep her emotions guarded, it was difficult to keep her more sentimental side closed off as she looked about the rural village just ahead, settled along the riverside. Strings of faded red lanterns bobbed between market alleyways, where vibrant spreads of lustrous eggplants and fat cabbages, barrels of ripple-scaled fish, and cages of twitchy hares sat on display. Like a lazy smile, the mountain slopes swelled and fell in the distance, blanketed with green and tipping-point autumnal ochre. Farmers and fishermen and weaving grannies milled about, none too wound-up to indulge in a cup of tea or lay down a few tiles in a mahjong match.

Corinna followed Liwei up terraced hills to one of the many earth and stone residences, this one with a hazy fire crackling up in a backyard pit. As red hens bobbed after worms and summer beetles, she was hit with a surge of nostalgia for a place long lost, that of her parents' old patch of land where her family worked what soil they had, ate what little they could barter for, and were happy. Even if the faces of her siblings and parents had become fuzzy, those feelings remained clear as crystal.

"Shì shéi a?" an elderly woman asked, sweat clinging to her drooping brow and jowls.

Corinna couldn't make out where their conversation went after that, but she could tell that she at least seemed welcomed. Nothing beat country hospitality—even if she was undeserving. Even if she couldn't afford to become attached.

After a few minutes of back and forth, the old woman nodded at Corinna, what she took as her being deemed fit to stay, and Liwei took her by the arm to the terraced fields. Liwei worked with what little Mandarin Corinna had at her disposal to tell her that, so long as Corinna helped them with the fields, she could get a hot, regular meal. Something about her parents having gone somewhere, and her being an only child now. Even though Corinna didn't need the food, she missed working with her hands. Some rich soil under her nails and a fresh sheen of sweat might help her forget.

Yet something was different in China. It was a vast country, ever-changing, but this was distinct from her other times seeing the world shift. Traditions and Confucian values had been done away with. She heard of books being burned, heirlooms smashed. Posters with slogans in crimson block prints populated the scenery, though she couldn't read them. Little red books could be found in most households, distributed with a circular red and gold pin.

Unable to read, she gathered bits and pieces from Liwei. Every night as they made sure the hens were in their coops, the kindling was set out for morning, and all the pots of pickled vegetables had been put away, Liwei worked with Corinna's slowly growing vocabulary to tell her what news she'd heard.

While the shifting winds tasted strange on Corinna's tongue, they made Liwei's eyes sparkle.

We won't have to work every hour of every day anymore. We can have enough food, without any more liánghuāng. At that, Corinna had cocked her head. *Famine,* Liwei explained. *When there's not enough for everyone to eat.*

Corinna bit her lip. Enough people had spoken about revolution throughout her lifetime and few ever delivered, but that was hardly news she wanted to break—were she even to have the words to explain her stance. Then again, if anyone was ever to get something done, it'd be the Chinese. Corinna heard that, a few years before she'd been found on the river bank that fateful day, some low-level agricultural communes had already been formed throughout the nation. But it didn't seem that dramatic of a change. Not yet, anyway.

Nai-nai, elder matriarch of the house, tended to agree with Corinna in her low rumbly voice, like an old dog's wheeze. Perhaps it wasn't so bad for things to stay the way they were, even if they were hard. What was life without struggle? Liwei respectfully nodded, though it was evident she disagreed. As the moon rose high every night, and she and Liwei sat shoulder to shoulder on the hearth sharing their usual clay bowl of rice and preserved radish, she began to feel an odd sense of warmth despite the chilly night air.

How long had it been since she'd washed up here? How many months? Was it already a year, perhaps? Sleeping on the thin mats next to these people, sharing meals with them while secretly dumping most of her rice into their bowls, scrubbing clothes in the river, harvesting gourds and beans and cabbages, all of it had knit her closer to them than she'd intended.

Stay at arm's length, she chastised. Despite herself, every night she fell asleep on the floor alongside Nai-nai and Liwei, the cicadas humming in the brisk air, and that warmth only grew and grew, lulling her into something long forgotten. A sense of belonging.

A sense of home.

PEOPLE THOUGHT IMMORTALITY CHANGED YOU. It did, in some ways. The immortal often became reckless and impulsive, but no wiser or smarter. No more enlightened. Did humans ever *really* learn? Were people any more certain of themselves at twenty than they were at ten? If her experience was any indication, no.

Humans *thought* they grew smarter, herself included, but whatever new path they'd dreamed up would just as surely fail them as her own had. Humans *thought* they would use their additional years wisely, but they would squander them the same as others. Corinna had long given up on trying to become something she wasn't. She wasn't a sage or a clairvoyant. No amount of extra years would give her that.

But she would forever lament that she hadn't seen the signs before her, the forewarning in the change that worked its way over the Chinese landscape. Some believed it was a new era, and she should have known to call it what it was: naiveté. While things might have been new, they were rarely ever different. Corinna knew that best of all.

Liwei carried her small bowl of rice back from the commune's canteen. The village had been brought together into one unit, all of their tools, their livestock, their everything lumped together for public use. It was a strange way of living, and one Corinna had yet to adjust to. Squealing children ran around in the streets, getting out their last bursts of energy before bed, bellies full enough to sleep and their cheeks ruddy. Parents sat with little cups of hot water by their side, massaging cracked and dusty palms. Corinna had told

Liwei she'd already eaten, a lie, but she couldn't bear to eat their food at a time like this.

Liwei gestured for her to take some of her rice. Corinna shook her head. With a shrug, Liwei scooped up a clump on her chopsticks and popped it in Corinna's mouth as she yawned. Corinna squawked in surprise, then laughed, the bits of sticky white rice threatening to go up her nose. Once she stopped cough-laughing, she elbowed Liwei in the side.

"Try to make me die?" she asked. Her Chinese was passable now, if fragmented.

"Trying to share." Liwei smiled, mischievous and innocent all at once.

Corinna grinned back.

Where would she have landed without being found on the riverbanks that day? Would some other angelic woman have swept in to save what humanity she'd had left? Would they too have stitched her soul back up? Likely not. While it was dangerous to get attached, perhaps being detached had its own harms.

"Thank you," Corinna said.

"Ah?" Liwei cast her a sidelong glance, hair catching the sunset's light like a brush painting of a waterfall. "For what?"

"For—for giving me a home. For finding me."

A tiny smile pulled at Liwei's lips as they stared at their feet. So many words left unspoken, but she suspected she knew the many sentiments, the many '*thank you*'s and more that lingered in her heart. It was the closest she'd become to anyone since Lycus those many years ago, Liwei a world away from the person he'd been. If she could call him a person at all. Corinna pulled her eyes away to look out at all those people with full stomachs and a safe place to sleep, and, seeing them with Liwei by her side, she couldn't help but feel hopeful for the first time in far too long.

∼

By 1961, the floods had come and gone.

The subsequent droughts had taken every bit of moisture it could squeeze from the living.

The anemic crops had failed, and the political maneuvering and corruption had worked the people over until they could bend no more.

As the fields died, died, died, bountiful surpluses were reported to the capital so bureaucrats could gain the Politburo's favor, causing an even higher percentage to be taken to feed city-dwellers. Causing the rural poor to starve. And all the while, those jockeying for power reported that the districts under their purview were excelling, crushing families under their heel with every false word.

Liwei had tried to steal rice from the granaries, just enough to feed her ailing grandmother. Just enough for even one more day. She was caught and beaten by authorities on the edge of the village.

It wasn't until a few hours later that Corinna, off scavenging for anything they could eat, found her bleeding, crumpled up on her back and looking out towards the freshly emerging night sky with dazed eyes. Corinna's heart dropped into her gut. She raced to Liwei and knelt down, scooping the woman into her arms.

No, no, no.

"Liwei? Liwei-ah?" Corinna's voice rose, frantic, head swimming.

Not again. Nikias and Enyo flashed through her mind, and Gershom and the nuns and the many others she had failed.

She wiped away the dirt smudged on Liwei's pale cheek, its former fullness stolen by hunger. Liwei's eyes half-fluttered open, looked up at her. Purple bruising seeped across her skin and thin forearms, her bird-like jaw and twiggy calves, everything she was now reduced to no more than angles. A deeper wound was there too, an internal gush of blood deep in the cavity of her starved organs. Corinna learned to read the signs long ago. Had she been stronger, had she been nourished, she may have withstood such a beating. But not now.

"Tell me their names. Tell me who did this to you."

Faint but still there, she shook her head with a tiny smile. Her heart was as untouched as a closed bloom, as snow still drifting in the air. How she had endured the cruelty of the world without succumbing to it, Corinna would forever wonder. Liwei's head suddenly stopped shaking.

"Don't," Corinna choked between gasping tears, reverting to her mother tongue. "Don't leave me."

Liwei's chest still rose and fell, the sole sign she was alive, yet whether she could still hear her was a mystery. Corinna cursed herself. It had been her mistake to become attached, yet again, to the impermanence of this world. But—no. No. There were some things, some people, worth suffering for. Even if it tore her apart from the inside out.

Cradling Liwei in her still-thick, still-strong arms, Corinna sat there with her until the stars came out in brilliant force. Death's coming took a while for her to learn to see on a human face, but once she did, it was impossible to forget. The far-away look as the heartbeat slowed, the vigor evaporating up with the spirit, the memories… She saw it now, and knew there was nothing left to do but wait.

In the unending blackness of Corinna's life, Liwei had been a sparkle of light. That she would never forget, but not forgetting wasn't enough for her. She had hoped she'd have had enough time, found some way to repay her. Yet no matter what, there was never enough time. Not even for her.

Corinna stroked Liwei's hair, pinned the small flower from a weed behind her ear, and, a few agonizing minutes later,. Liwei died in her arms.

Record harvests were reported that year.

20

DEATH, INTERRUPTED

"I knew from then on, that was always going to be my life," Corinna says, hands knit together, elbows on her knees and back bent over with the weight of a thousand years. "And I didn't want to do it anymore. I've been looking for my way out ever since."

I sit there, breath shallow and hands shaking. A part of me absentmindedly reaches up to take my pulse and make sure it's not too high. Words, anything I could say to give her a piece of my many condolences, they all escape me as I watch her. While I'd guessed at the things she's seen and endured and experienced, hearing about them firsthand is different. For her to have lived them, a world apart entirely. A lump sticks in my throat.

"Did you ever get them?"

"Who?" she asks, voice as flat as her heartbeat.

"The people who hurt her. Hurt Liwei." I feel stupid asking such an intrusive question, but I can't stop myself.

She nodded. "All but one."

"Oh." I pause. "Just one?"

"There's money to be made in revolution."

"Oh." *Oh*.

"Her blood isn't directly on his hands, but he played a part in the larger picture. I suspect we've been on the opposite side of many coins. Where I go, my shadow always follows." She straightens then lets her arms go slack, hands dangling between her knees. From out the open window, Corinna gazes at the faint smattering of constellations and long-departed souls, and the dim light catches like sparks along her dress.

"You really like the night sky, don't you?" I ask.

She nods, and for a moment we sit there, silent. "Everyone I'd known, everyone I'd loved, they're now up there somewhere in the stars. It's all I have left of them." Corinna sighs. "My father once told me they never changed, but now we know that's not true. I've seen them shift. Hell, I've even outlasted some of them. Ironic, isn't it?"

Silver lines her eyes, a brief glimpse into whatever swirls in her mind, her heart. I lean forward and, without thinking twice, grab her hand. Her skin burns on mine. Corinna wipes the wetness from her face with the hem of her dress.

"Since this is the end, someone might as well know."

The end. My heart seizes, but I think I understand her reasons a bit better now. Even if they pain me.

"I wish it didn't have to be," I say.

When I look into her eyes, I see only mystery there. But of the sliver I can read, I see a woman rent apart by her own love of the world, her soul broken into kindling for her own destruction—yet no matter how long she ran and hid and resisted, she never escaped it. Until she found her ultimate way out, her ending of all endings.

But she's so full of life, of vigor and eternities. Routine is all that sustains me, and she is anything but—so how do I feel more than sustained around her? And how can the world continue to turn without her in it?

Corinna leans towards me, and I find myself leaning in as

well. Our lips brush against each other's. I expect my soul to sigh, like a long-tensed muscle finally relaxing, like a warm breath on winter-frozen fingers, but it doesn't. The ache in my chest remains. As we pull back from one another, I see her eyelids still closed, lashes thick and the kohl around her eyes faintly smudged. We don't speak for a long while. The air between us is like sunlight, delicate yet charged with power. I'm not sure how much of it's her maybe yearning for one last intimate act, or how much it has anything to do with me—I'm likely little more than a footnote in her boundless existence—but I don't mind it. Her hand settles on my knee and slides a few inches up my thigh, and we move closer again.

She goes rigid. Her eyes are wide, glued to my chest, and I look down. A tiny red dot sits there against the beige fabric. My brain goes hazy.

Corinna whips around to the door, opened so silently that even she hadn't heard our intruders. She throws herself in front of me with teeth bared. Our two pursuers from earlier stand in the entryway, handguns at chest-level and all patience gone, the woman's hand bandaged in thick gauze from where Corinna bit her. Lycus stands behind them, ire visibly bubbling beneath his skin. Knowing what I do now, he hardly looks human anymore. He's more demigod—no, more devil than man.

"Talented. Clever. But just too sentimental." Lycus walks towards us, jaw tight, white suit jacket still splattered with erupted ink. "You always were."

The muscles in Corinna's back tense as she draws herself up, bracing for whatever may come.

"Where's the domukardi?" He stops in front of her, their noses less than six inches apart save for their difference in height.

"Beats me."

"I'll have your boy shot."

"I'll get in the way."

"With the caliber they carry, the bullet will go straight through you to him." All of the light has gone out of his eyes, leaving only a death-ravenous glint. No jeering, no playful taunts, nothing. He leans closer. "Not to mention, I have two shooters. You gave Nia a nasty bite, but David's shot will still do just fine."

Corinna's lips tighten, her lids pull back as she searches for anything within arm's reach to use against him or distract him with, but we both know it's futile.

"Don't kill him," she says. Pleads. "Don't kill him, and I'll give you the box."

Lycus cocks his head to the side and studies her. "Or I could kill him and find the box myself. Use a little elbow grease on my end. It can't have gone far."

"You'd never have peace another day of your miserable life," she snarls. "If I give you the domukardi, you keep your hands off him. Deal?"

He stares down his nose at her and I can almost see her fiery gaze reflected in his eyes. Despite the tension thick in the air, his face shifts to amusement.

"Deal."

My heart stutters and I release the breath I'd been holding. At least I'm not condemned to the grave—yet. How have I been spared yet again? How is one more life now a price too heavy to pay when she's seen hundreds die? It seems her promise to keep innocent blood from spilling continues on, even now.

"Under the bed frame, right side." Her voice is hollow. At least for now, it's clear she's given up on finding a way out. If she can't find one, I certainly won't be able to.

"Please and thank you." He inclines his head, a mockery of modesty, then waits. Stares at her. "Well?"

Corinna grits her teeth even tighter—I'm surprised they haven't already cracked in her jaw—and steps out from in front of me to fetch it. He watches her move like a leopard circling a guinea fowl, smug and predatory in every way. Disgust rolls through my stomach. She walks back over, grip on the box turning her knuckles white, holding it close to her chest. I see the effort she makes to choke down her tears and blink them away, but I'm not sure Lycus does.

The red dot on my chest disappears with a wave of his hand as Corinna brings the domukardi forward. She glances at me. There, I see the thing she won't say. *It's the only way to keep you safe.* Guilt crashes into me.

If it was watching her loved ones die over and over again that's pained her so, I can only wonder how much worse it's made by being trapped in this endless dance.

Lycus takes the box from her hands, and she loses her heart once more.

WE WERE strong-armed into an SUV Mercedes out front, all swoops and graceful edges, but everything has faded into an unremarkable blur for me, sounds reduced to background static and my movements on autopilot.

Corinna's head resting on my shoulder, her face a portrait of utter defeat, is all I'm able to register.

"I can get you out," she whispers, hardly even a brush of air against my ear. "I can't leave, but I can get you out. There has to be a way to pop the trunk or break one of the windows, and I can I hold them off while you—"

I shake my head, cutting her off.

"I'm not leaving," I whisper back. Somehow, I would get her box back. Somehow, I would return her choice to her. "You made a promise, and I did too."

I squeeze her hand and she squeezes mine. We sit like that for a long while, hands entwined with her head pillowed on the space between my clavicle and neck.

I can't say how long the drive takes us, just that the stars grow more intense the farther away we drive, until a lime green and gold horizon begin to peel back the night, turning over into day. I don't know where we're headed, but I had expected to drive up to a ranch manor or some other similarly-styled country house, not a massive white stucco estate. Its wings stretch out over the hills like the fingers of a greedy skeleton. It's just as unnatural, as jarring in this landscape as Lycus himself.

Finally within their employer's domain, David and Nia shuffle me out of the car first, pistols openly displayed at their hips in a warning for me not to try them, and an even stronger warning to Corinna. Heat sears up my neck. Right now, I'm her one vulnerability. Maybe I *should* have left, if it meant freeing her of my dead weight.

They pull her from the car and lash rope around her ankles and wrists, arms pinned behind her. Just enough slack is left at her ankles for her to walk. She holds her chin high and defiant, her glare as scorching as a dying sun.

"Inside," David says with a jab at her back.

Corinna snarls.

"Please," Nia adds.

There's no reason for me to like Nia, and I don't, but at least she isn't as hawkish as David. Which is an already low bar, but still. What with the bite to her hand, she's the only one we've actually harmed, yet her aggression is more reserved. Only called upon when explicitly asked to. I just hope that Nia's restraint carries over into the uncharted territory we're about to enter. The look on Corinna's face tells me she's less hopeful, but we're out of options.

Together we walk forward.

My anxious nature requires that I know what to do in case anything bad ever happened to me—like if I got kidnapped

Death of an Immortal

or mugged. A bunch of good that did. Regardless, I know the stats, how someone's chance of ever being seen alive again drops drastically after they get in another person's car, how after 24 hours of not being found they usually disappear forever. I passed both of those thresholds long ago. Prepare though I might, no amount of facts can help me now.

We stand in the foyer, sterile yet beautiful all at once; bare white walls, early morning light spilling through the skylight and over the floors, the wood planks so rich that they're almost black. Lycus stands at the wet bar, slate whiskey stones clacking in a thick-bottomed glass. He decants amber liquid, takes a swig, then runs his tongue over gleaming teeth. Taking the glass in his multi-ringed fingers' grasp and not saying a word, he walks over to us. No, to Corinna. He stops a foot before her.

"You've had a long journey," he says.

I see her mouth tighten as she lowers her gaze to meet his. He holds the glass out to her as an offer, but she turns away from it. Lycus shrugs and takes another sip.

"Must be tired," he says.

When she doesn't respond, he reaches up to twirl a loose lock of her hair between his fingers then brings it to his lips. He lowers his voice, but I can still hear him murmur to her. I wish I couldn't. Instead of letting my sights drop to the floor though, I force myself to look forward. I won't leave her to endure this alone.

"Come back," he says. "You don't have to struggle, don't need to fight. We both can be like we once were. Anything you've ever wanted, say the word and I'll give it to you. The liberty to do whatever you want is yours. You just have to take it."

"Death is the truest liberty." Straight-backed and despite the world crashing down around her, she's unwavering.

He sighs and brings both wrists to rest on her shoulders, hands dangling behind her shoulder blades as the fingertips of his free hand draw small, lazy circles there. His nose butts against hers, but she remains an unmoving statue. A shot of fury courses through my bloodstream, followed by uselessness. I have as much power here as an ant in a henhouse.

"Don't you remember how we used to be?" he asks. "We can live a comfortable life, together again."

"Comfort isn't worth sacrificing an eternity for. Even if you hadn't—even if you had been by my side all those years, even if you hadn't sold yourself, your *soul*, for coin, I would still want this."

He shakes his head and blows air from between his teeth, brows raised in disbelief. After a moment, he goes on. "Pretend I care, and answer me this. What is your problem with living?"

"It's our time. It should have been a long time ago." She snaps her shoulders to throw his hands off her.

He stands there for a silent moment before throwing his head back in a cackle.

"You live for nothing but yourself," she continues. "You're empty. Hollow."

"Get a hold of one too many after-school specials?" Lycus asked between gasps. She didn't respond. "I asked what *your* problem with living was. Not mine."

"Fine then, it's *my* time. I've seen too much and endured too much. You glut yourself on the suffering of others then find a way to profit from it. It'll do the world a favor to no longer have a leech like you in it." Her lips curl back, eyes daggers, and tongue spitting rage. "I have no problem taking you with me."

His laughing cuts off, face turning dark. "You're never gonna get the chance, sweetheart." He turns on his heel to drop onto one of the leather sectionals. "Lock them up."

David grabs Corinna by her bound wrists, Nia taking me, and leads us through a winding hall. Whatever sense of direction I have tells me we've entered a new wing of this monstrosity. I look for hints and clues of a way out, but no such luck. At the far end of a corridor, Nia punches in the security code on a panel beneath a doorknob, and its steel frame clicks free. She shoulders it open and we enter. My stomach turns.

Inside is what looks like a jail cell with its bars speared into the tiled floor. A drain sits in the middle of the enclosure, and a wash of red clings to its rusty edges. If that is in fact rust. There's only one sort of room this could be—and it's nothing good. My nerves fray. Sweat begins to bead on my palms and upper lip.

"Relax." David sounds exasperated, as if perturbed I'm making him expend the effort to speak. "It's a secure place until Lycus decides whatever his next step is."

"Secure for him," Corinna hisses.

"Yes, that's the point."

David shoves me into the cage with little resistance and I stand in the far corner, expecting Corinna to follow. Nia tries to haul her forward, but Corinna slams her spine into her, refusing to be herded like cattle. David sighs and draws out his pistol, then aims it at me.

"You know how this goes," he says. "Don't make it any harder than it has to be."

"You want me to just lie down and take it?"

"You want me to shoot him?"

"David," Nia warns.

"You're bluffing," Corinna says to him. But I see the hesitation on her face, the almost imperceptible way she tenses up.

He pulls back the hammer. "Want to take that bet?"

Corinna bites down hard on her lip before moving forward, resigning herself to the cage. I drop my gaze to the floor. She'd already have what she wanted were it not for me. The guilt isn't any less intense this time around. Nia shuts the metal door, locks it, before leaving. She returns with the domukardi.

"One of the bottom drawers will do fine," Nia says as she takes a dense ring of keys from David, then unlatches the bottom part of a filing cabinet. She looks over her shoulder at us once, then twice—and, unless I've lost my mind, appears torn. It's gone as soon as I glimpse it. Some corner of me clings to hope for one bit of mercy, however small.

"Give it a rest, Nia." David settles into a swivel chair, the same as you would see in any office. A strikingly ordinary touch in a place like this. "You always were too soft."

Her face tightens and she mumbles a creative string of curses at him, then stomps out. Her footsteps echo down the hall.

"Do you even know who you're working for?" Corinna asks our remaining sentry as she presses up against the bars. Even for someone as small as her, it'd be impossible for her to slip through. I wonder if Lycus designed this place with her in mind. From what she's told me, it's not hard to imagine.

"Not my job to know." David picks at his already bitten-down nails, grey hair the only sign of his age. He crosses one ankle over his knee and pops his back, twisting this way and that. "Might as well get comfortable, kids."

"How long do you plan on keeping us here?" I speak up, surprising myself. For once, whether from adrenaline or fear or lack of sleep, I feel a sense of agency. I surely can't make anything worse at this point.

"Through the night, at least. Lycus wants to rest up and then we'll see where he goes from there. I have a few ideas." He shrugs with a sigh. "But, don't know for sure."

She spits at him, but he dodges to the side. If this guy is as unflappable as he looks, it'll take Corinna actually laying hands on him to get any information of use.

"Nice aim." Unperturbed, he pulls out a beat-up paperback of the Iliad.

Nia comes back with two duffel bags—our bags, I realize—and dumps their contents out on the glass-topped desk. It's mostly balled up clothing with unmatched socks, multigrain bar wrappers, crinkled receipts, and loose ammunition that tinkles to the ground like the sound of wind chimes. As she sorts through it all, I untie Corinna's bonds. In here, our guards aren't likely to care. We're trapped no matter what.

After checking the pockets, Nia hands us our more casual clothing through the bars.

"Here," she says in a weak gesture of something akin to kindness, or at least a facade of it. I'd prefer her over David any day.

Corinna doesn't take it. With a resigned roll of her eyes, Nia chucks it to the ground. David chuckles. She doesn't bother to fire back at him. Whatever their relationship is like, I assume this is the typical dynamic. She moves to walk away.

Corinna lashes out through the bars before Nia has the chance to pull back, grabbing for Nia's collar and the hand she'd bitten into hours before. Corinna yanks her towards herself, and Nia's jaw slams against the metal with a ringing *crack* of bone on steel.

I see David tense, but he doesn't get up. Doesn't even uncross his legs. Corinna snakes an arm around Nia's neck, and though Nia tucks her jaw to protect her throat as best she can, this is a beast Nia has to know she can't outsmart.

Corinna looks to David.

"Keys. Now."

He turns his eyes back to the book. "Do what you want. My orders are clear."

"David!" Nia shouts, breath strained.

As if supporting her outcries, Corinna lowers her teeth—the only weapon she has—to hover just above Nia's jugular in threat.

"I'll do it," Corinna says.

"I'm sure you will. But it doesn't change what I'm hired to

do, which is to not let you out." He gives a conciliatory glance to Nia and flips to the next page. "Sorry."

"At least give—" Nia strains as Corinna crushes her neck even tighter, applying pressure on the back of her head now too. "Help me!"

I stifle a gasp. Though I jerk forward, I don't pull them apart. Nia is the only person here who's shown anything like kindness to us, but I trust Corinna. I trust that she knows what she's doing, even if Nia doesn't deserve this. Whatever sympathy she'd had for us has now probably gone out the window.

"Ma'am," David says, looking up at Corinna, "all due respect, but my hands are tied. Do what you feel you gotta do, but I can't budge. Rough her up, kill her if it'll get all that energy out of your system, but don't expect it'll get you those keys."

Corinna holds his gaze for a moment, then two.

She releases Nia and lets her drop to the ground with a desperate gasp for air. My heart breathes a sigh of relief. Nia stays there for a long moment, massaging her throat with wide eyes, but as soon as she regains her bearings she's upon David with every foul utterance I've ever heard, and even some I haven't.

"You absolute piece of shit!" she exclaims. "You didn't—"

"I'm not allowed to give her the keys." He talks to her as if she were a child, which appears to only further enrage her.

"You still could have helped me! Tried to pry her off or something!"

David rubs the bridge between his eyes. "Look, she didn't kill you, did she?"

"That's not the point—"

"It *is*. From what Lycus told us, she," he gestures our way, "doesn't have the stomach for that kind of thing anymore. That's why she's in there, and we're out here. You're fine, okay?"

"No thanks to you, *partner*." She spits out the word as if it's rotted in her mouth.

"I'm sorry," Corinna whispers. I'm not sure if it's directed to Nia or me or herself, but none of those sit well with me. She has nothing to apologize for. Caged for trying to do the right thing, hope again stolen from her, what she did is understandable. Though I'm sure Nia wouldn't mind an apology.

Nia's brows knit together for half a second, bewildered at Corinna's words, before she returns to quarreling with David. Corinna turns her back on them and walks over to the far side of the cell, grabbing clothes off the ground as she goes.

"Cor." I reach out to her as she goes past, but she's distant, and not only because this enclosure is big enough for ten men. She shakes her head, unreachable.

Nia, bitter and betrayed, leaves, and David stays absorbed in his book. The room goes quiet, only the sound of the A/C and worn, crinkling paper accompanying us. David pulls out a map of what looks like tiny island chains and cross-references them with his book. At least someone is able to take his mind off things. I feel my jaw tense. How he's able to sit there, nonchalant while we languish less than five feet from him, bewilders me. Not only that, but if he's willing to risk even his own partner, I'm certain he'll do worse to Corinna and I. Where I expect to feel rising fear, I instead find a cold and resigned anger.

I take in a deep breath in an attempt to calm myself. The room smells like bleach. Normally I'd worry about the damage such strong fumes can do to my eyes and skin, but my day-to-day anxieties are silent, graver ones focused instead on imagining *what* they would need to clean up in a room like this. The answer unsettles me, but doesn't surprise me.

After Corinna and I have both changed—modesty isn't at the forefront of my mind right now—we sit on the tile floor, backs against the cold stone. She doesn't talk, doesn't move. Just stares ahead at the empty walls. Almost as if she were staring into an empty eternity itself, unending and unrelenting.

I wrap an arm around her shoulders. She tilts her head back as tears gather, and closes her eyes.

21

SPARROW SONG

Squealing metal wakes me. I jolt up, a dull ache in my head from my awkward sleeping position against the bars, and I see Corinna awake as well. While she doesn't need sleep, I read the lack of it in the dark smudges under her eyes, her tousled hair and hanging shoulders. Something moves in the corner of my eye, and she snaps into sudden clarity as David pulls the domukardi from a cabinet and locks it back, empty.

"What're you doing with that?" she asks, a venomous edge to her voice. When he doesn't answer, it comes out as more demand than question. *"What are you doing with that?"*

He shuffles through a leaf of papers on the desk. "Lycus is moving it."

"He just got his hands on it." She rises to her feet and grips the bars. "He wouldn't toss it after all this time."

"With you around, he would. Hopes to hide it somewhere even you won't find it." After setting the box on the desk, David packs a wad of dip between his lip and gum. "Think he's burying it, actually."

Invisible hackles bristle along her spine. If the domukardi gets buried, she'll never find it again. Not ever. The earth only gets deeper over time, sinking people and their possessions and histories further into the depths with age. It had taken centuries to find even with it above ground. Below, it would never be recovered.

Corinna lurches towards David. The bars keep a healthy distance between them, but still she struggles, trying to squeeze what portion of her shoulder will fit through as she swipes at him with a roar, stretching fingers like the talons of a hawk. He steps back only a bit surprised, then rehardens his face into an annoyed sneer. Picking up the box, he makes his way to the door. It swings open and Lycus walks into view, flanked by Nia. Corinna's shouts come to an abrupt halt as the former Cohort pair lock eyes. The reality, the finality of everything crashes over me.

"Don't do this," she begs.

"Oh, I will." He steps forward and takes his prize from David. Balancing the box against his hip, Lycus rakes his hungry gaze over me. "And when I'm done, I'm coming back for your boy. Tie up loose ends."

The following silence threatens to shred my very eardrums. Everything Corinna has hunted for and worked towards and dreamed of, now crashing down around her. My life with it. I know what Lycus finishing up his business means for me. The world wavers under my feet.

"Ready to head out?" David asks Lycus as he grabs a pair of work gloves.

Lycus puts up a hand. "I want you two hanging back. This I do on my own."

David nods, and after a moment's hesitation so brief I almost miss it, Nia does too. Lycus turns to go.

"Lycus." Corinna's voice climbs with each plea. *"Lycus!"*

"Don't be so glum, dear." He shoots her a smirk from over his shoulder even as she wrenches against the bars. "I'm saving your life, after all."

Before she can utter another word, he's gone. The panic in

her eyes reaches a fever pitch, and Corinna turns out her pockets. I do the same.

"There has to be something we can use," she mumbles as she sorts through the crumpled receipts and hair ties—but the most threatening thing we seem to have is a mere bobby pin and little else. I see the hope rapidly drain from her, and then up bubble hot tears of disbelief.

David scoffs, but Nia remains quiet as she stares at the floor. My heart becomes a leaden weight in my chest as I sit here, useless. An anchor holding Corinna, holding myself down. I look at her, at the hope that now lays abandoned.

"Why do you work for him?" I ask, turning to face our jailers. Maybe it's seeing Corinna so beside herself, maybe it's knowing that my own time may be drawing near, but I feel a resolve, a backbone I never had before calcifying under my skin. David casts me a withering glare, but I hold his gaze, not looking away. Not backing down.

David chuckles before going back to his book, but Nia's sights lingers on us. Neither answer.

"Is the pay really so good that you'd protect someone like *him?*" Corinna's sobs stab at my chest. I can almost swear that it's my own shoulders heaving, my own ribs shaking with gasping cries. Watching her, unable to do anything, heat stings my throat and expands into a lump. I rise to my feet.

Though she hesitates at first, Nia steps farther into the room. "It's not that the money—"

"Nia, don't." Warning laces David's words.

"Try to tell me what to do one more time, I dare you," she snaps back.

"I'm not going to take insubordination." His leathery face creases as he gets to his feet and draws himself to full height, but they're of equal stature. With youth and sheer fire, I'm sure Nia could overtake him in a fistfight. "We have to cooperate here."

"Cooperation didn't mean much to you earlier when I was close to getting the life strangled from me."

He purses his lips with a scowl. "That was different."

"Always is, isn't it?" She turns her back to him and walks closer to the cell, despite the position she got into last time. She jabs a finger at Corinna. "Our prisoner, her, she treated me with more respect in five minutes than you have in all the time I've been here."

"She bit your hand. You remember that, don't you?"

"We were chasing after them!" She whirls around. "Given the circumstances, I can't blame them."

"Given the circumstances? Do you know who we're dealing with?"

"Do you?"

Corinna's sobbing drops off, and I see her watch the scene unfold before us. Slow and silent, as if careful to disguise the threat she can turn into, she gets to her feet, the squeak of her boots' rubber soles the only noise.

"Do *I*?" David asks. He throws his hands up. "We have a job to do, Nia, and it's time you get your head out of your ass about it. It doesn't matter who they are."

"How can it not?" She points to where we stand behind the bars, watching. "How can you not see that something is wrong here, David? You always said I was a good judge of character and that I could read people. Hell, that's why you pushed Lycus to hire me. If you trusted your judgement then, trust mine now when I say that something isn't right."

A pause.

"You're soft," he says with a tone of dismissal. "Have always been soft. That's why I'm here, to keep you in check. We work as a *team*."

"A team." Nia snorts with a shake of her head, box braids swinging. "You don't care about teamwork. Stopped caring a long time ago. You'd do anything for a dollar, isn't that right? You keep your head down, bury your nose in your little book to distract you from what you're doing, then collect."

David looks her up and down with narrowed eyes, then spits his dip into the trash can by the door. It leaves a greasy brown film on the plastic lining. He picks up his book and looks half-prepared to give her a piece of his mind—then I jump in.

"I can't judge you for doing your job. But we have to get out of here. *She* has to get out of here." The words pour out of me, and I'm unsure whether or not David will throw a hand at me for talking, but I put my arm around Corinna's shoulder and draw her close. "If anyone knows Lycus, she does. All she wants is to call the shots for her own life, which anyone should be able to do. That's all she wants, and she's waited so long for it. Too long. She almost gave up everything, *did* give up everything, just to keep me safe. She didn't want what happened to Brendon Watts to happen to me."

Nia's eyes narrow. "We didn't do anything to Brendon. Shook him off our tail, but that's it."

"He's full of shit," David says.

"Turn on the news. Look on the internet. See for yourself, but I'm telling the truth." I swallow. "A .45 caliber, execution style. Near the intersection of Wells Branch and Howard Lane, in the back alley of a strip mall."

Nia's pupils shrink. Here, this is where I've finally found my mark. Seems my proclivity for stray facts has found a use after all. David shifts beside her. A moment passes and slowly, ever so dangerously slow, Nia looks to the .45 holstered on his belt. Her gaze ignites like fire.

"You," she breathes. David opens his mouth, but she cuts him off. "You absolute *snake*."

"Now hold on, Nia, nothing has changed—"

"Nothing's changed? The fact that you lied to me, that you killed a boy in cold blood doesn't change anything?"

"We tie up Lycus's loose ends! We always have!" His face

remains hard, but he backs away from her. Backs towards the cage bars.

"A kingpin or crook or shady bureaucrat is a world of difference from a child," she snarls. "When did you do it? *When?*"

He grinds his teeth together, but spits out the answer anyways. Hiding it would only damn him further. "Once the girl was gone. You were trying to find her, and I did what had to be done."

Nia purses her lips. Puts her balled fists on her hips. "After they were no longer together, that's when you killed him. Once he wasn't even with the person we were looking for anymore. Is that it?"

"You already know."

"I want to hear you say it."

David sighs. He stops moving backwards just within arm's reach of us. From the corner of my eye I see Corinna straighten as she watches the scene unfold, thoughts no doubt whirring.

"Yes," he says. "I went out, found Brendon, and killed him. As per our orders."

I jump forward. With a handful of David's collar, I yank him against the bars, and the metal smack reverberates against my skin. Before he can pull away, Corinna dives in and wraps her arm around his exposed neck, then holds tight. His eyes bulge. He's unable to tuck his chin in time, leaving his windpipe to be crushed, the air escaping him only a pitiful wheeze.

Nia blinks at us, the divide within her clear on her face. The next action she chooses could damn or deliver us. She takes a step forward and cracks her knuckles, sights trained on me. I swallow. David's shoulders relax by a hair.

"He didn't help you, Nia," Corinna warns. "Don't expect that he—"

Nia slams her hand into the sides of David's neck, and at

Death of an Immortal

first I fear that she's trying to pry Corinna off—until I see her fingers like a vise over each carotid artery, cutting off the blood flow to his brain. Within seconds, he's slumped in Corinna's arms. She still holds him though, just in case. Nia looks at him, rage and despair and guilt and a hundred other emotions I can't name flooding her face.

"I didn't know," Nia stammers after a pause. "I didn't know."

"I believe you," Corinna says. "I know what people like him do to those around them. Lycus is my own David, only he's been hurting people for hundreds, if not thousands of years longer."

I hold my breath as the woman across from us shifts from one leg to the other. She meets our gaze, warm eyes searching ours for some lie or deception, but she won't find any.

"Please," Corinna says, so quiet her words are barely audible. Her lips quiver, but she keeps herself together.

Nia casts a sidelong glance to David, likely knowing how little time we have before he regains consciousness.

"Well," she finally says, "I suppose it's time you stop him."

She looks to the desk and the key ring that sits atop it. My heart leaps in my chest and Corinna's eyes widen—but we don't dare believe our fortune, not until we're out. Nia flicks through the keys for the right one, and a rueful grin lights her face.

"I used to be a boxer," she says. "A good one, too. My problem was that I could read people, and I might not've had a problem beating on jackasses, but I got soft when it came to people who were alright. Cost me my position, of course, but I never regretted it." She finds the correct key and hurries back over to the door of the cell. "As far as I could tell, Brendon was a good kid. Someone who orders the death of children isn't someone I'll work for." The lock pops free. "Damn the consequences. And you can tell Lycus I said that."

I step out from behind the bars, expecting someone to come out of the shadows and yank me back in. No one does. Corinna takes his gun and phone off him, then tosses him onto the floor of the cell before she slams the door behind. Nia locks it.

Despite what just happened, Corinna keeps her back away from Nia, eyeing the exit and whatever else is within arm's reach. They look at each other. Nia swallows—and then Corinna extends a hand.

"I will, Nia," Corinna says.

"Nia Johnson."

"Nia Johnson, then." Corinna's mouth quirks up and they shake hands, their grip like that of long separated comrades. "May you live a long and happy life."

"But not too long," Nia adds with an impish grin.

Corinna's smile grows and this time the fire, the full and wild soul in it has returned. Gold eyes once again reignite, her spark again catches flame. My heart lifts, and she snaps back into the seasoned warrior she's long-since been.

"We need to go," she says. "Nia, tell us how to get there."

"This way." Nia ushers us into the corridor. We race through the hallways that led us here, conscious of the limited time we have to work with.

In the foyer, she opens an oak box and hands us the keys to one of his undoubtedly many cars, then from the coat closet tosses us our duffel bags. Metal clangs from within them, heavy with our returned weaponry. At a jog, Corinna unzips both to check and nods. We make for the garage, passing scattered collections of Lycus's abundant hoard. Mink coats, purple silk wall hangings, cut gems, and carved ostrich eggs are piled on racks and in corners, coveted, possessed, and then forgotten. Nia pockets a handful of verdant stones as we stride past.

"Severance," she says.

Death of an Immortal

Corinna doesn't bat an eye. Her mind is likely far away, piecing together our next move.

Nia gives us her work phone with Lycus's location pulled up in the tracking app, we slap each other on the backs one more time, and then Corinna and I are in the car speeding towards the horizon. The sun begins to lower into the sky. We don't have more than an hour of daylight left, and finding him in darkness will be near impossible.

I look over at Corinna and try to ignore the sinking hole in my chest as we race onwards, towards the edge of the world and the monster that lies there.

22

MAGNUM OPUS

"How're you going to find him?" I ask. The world passes us in a blur, and I can't make sense of where we are. The vast unclaimed stretches of dead Texan wilderness were never something I'd exactly set out to memorize, and I doubt Corinna has either. Even though scrubby brush and packed earth and rocky outcroppings mark the landscape, they do nothing to help distinguish one place from the next. Not to me, at least, but I rarely venture outside. The risk of chiggers or poison ivy or heatstroke in a climate like this has always deterred me. "His location hasn't updated at all in ten minutes. Do you think he left it in his car?"

"Doesn't matter." Corinna blows through an out-of-place stop sign. "I can track him."

"You're sure?"

"I know him too well for him to hide."

I believe her. There are few roads this far out save for trails carved by animals, so a general heading will at least tell us which path to take. As for the rest... Well, her instincts have brought us this far, haven't they? We drive on for another fifteen minutes in relative silence. Only the hum of the car engine and of tires gliding over rough asphalt meets our ears.

She doesn't give me instructions, doesn't make small talk. Nothing.

Should I say something? What would I even talk about, and would it be for my own sake or hers?

"He can't die, but he can feel pain," she starts. "Once we get there, we'll need to do everything we can to slow him down, so take this." Corinna fishes out a small handgun from the bag draped over the center console. Driving one-handed, she presses small brass bullets down into the magazine like she's loading a Pez dispenser. "The safety's off, so keep your finger away from the trigger unless you need to shoot."

I put my palms up. "Nope, not going to happen."

"Now's not the time, Eugene."

"I don't know how to use one, and it won't do me any good anyways. It's not like I'll even be able to hit him."

She lets out a frustrated sigh. "So you want to be a sitting target?"

"No. But I don't have much of a choice."

Corinna bites her lip. She flicks the safety on, tosses the gun aside, and meets my stare. "Then if you see him first, if he comes after you directly, get behind me. Understand?"

"Why're you worried about *me?*" I ask.

Her brows knit together—for a moment I think she's going to hit me with another of her quips—before smoothing over, and something spreads across her face. I would almost dare to call it peace.

"Being reminded of the kinds of people who could make life worth living, the people who live their simple, beautiful lives," she sighs, a sigh of relief and contentment, utterly unlike those I've heard from her before. "That's something that should be protected. That entire adventure should be. And you, Eugene, god, you still have so much of that ahead of you."

I give a half-laugh, or what constitutes as one through my nerves. "I'm not sure I'd call my life an adventure."

An impish grin. "Are you sure?"

"Well," I hesitate, and I realize I'm not so certain anymore. While still very real and very present, my anxieties no longer eat up the forefront of my brain, not gone but at least quieter. The rigid path I'd set out for myself no longer seems so necessary. Constricting, even, a defense I'd put up in fear of the world. And now I've had the worst happen. I have been kidnapped, been hunted—yet here I stand, alive and well. While I feel more resilient than when this all began, maybe that strength was always there. Maybe all it took was that one fateful night in that parking lot to make me realize the kind of person I could be after all. "Maybe it is."

Though I'm sure she can see what lies beneath, I grin at her, and Corinna smiles back. A hint of sadness is there, too. I grab her hand and give it a gentle squeeze, a silent admission.

"I'm not going to let Lycus destroy what you have left ahead, Eugene. Not like he's done to so many others, not this time." She straightens, and I do too. "Now I'll be able to set things right."

I look at her for what feels like a long while, though it's likely no more than a second or two. I won't ask how she feels about our time together. I know my own heart, and that's enough. Whatever it was was reciprocal enough—she kissed me back, hadn't she?—but I'm a mere speck of gold dust reminding her of the shining treasure she used to have. Happiness, freedom, and a lifetime to drink it in.

And me, us, whatever this thing is that we're a part of, we are a reminder of things once had and days since passed.

I'm okay with being no more than that. Already she's given me more than I could've asked for. Hearing about how much she's seen change, witnessing for myself the changes that have taken place over these few mere days, I no longer fear the impermanence or unpredictability of this world. The fleeting now seems that much more beautiful, if only because it's here one moment and gone the next. Like her.

So long as this is a journey she still wants to finish, I'm behind her. Even though I get the feeling, however slight, there's a small part of her afraid for everything to end.

She jerks the wheel sideways and swerves off the road. I yelp out a curse, banging my head against the window, and bite my tongue as I hold back a handful of choice words. Through the fog clouding my mind, I look up to see Lycus's sleek Benz from earlier parked on the side of the road. *Of course* he'd bring something this lux out into the wilds. At least he stays on brand.

I turn to Corinna whose eyes remain fixed ahead, her hands clenched around the wheel with knuckles bone white. I see the hunger there. Leaning over to touch her shoulder, I think better of it and draw back. To my surprise, she snatches my fingers up and gives them a squeeze.

"Let's go get the bastard," she says. "Ready?"

I close my eyes and take in a deep breath. I feel a newfound resolve harden under my skin. "Ready."

That long since ingrained soldier-mode takes over as she checks the safety on a hefty .45, then loosens the laces on one of her boots to tuck it inside. From the duffle bag she pulls out a knife and tucks it into her other boot. The leather interior of Lycus's car, without a stain or crack or even a mote of dust, is as fine a place as any to prepare for what lay ahead, even though it's at odds with the woman before me. A delicate newness against her enduring strength.

Corinna turns her gaze away from me to scan the blazing horizon. The sun throws off streaks of pink and orange as it sinks into the earth, a tapestry of color and light.

Her eyes tighten.

"I see him."

Ice jolts into my veins as my sights follow hers and I see movement by a rocky crag, so minute I would've missed it had a trained set of eyes not pointed it out. Sure enough, the closer I look the more evident his garish clothing becomes against the tan, dusty landscape. From the cadence of his movements, he seems to be digging a hole or a shallow grave. An ironic difference, in this instance. At his feet sits the domukardi.

Corinna nods to me and we get out of the car.

"Take these," she says as she drops the car keys into my palm. "I'm carrying enough as is."

I tuck them into my back pocket and we're off, breaking into a jog and pacing ourselves. There's no point in trying to hide, nor in trying to rush up on him. He'll see us coming either way. The land here is so dead and open, there's no way that he wouldn't, even with the meager cover of outcroppings and pebbly detritus. But he's alone and there's two of us. For once, I actually help tip the scale.

"Remember the code," she says. Our steps quicken. "3-7-1."

"I need to get close enough first."

"You will." She grimaces. "He's going to have it out for you."

I almost laugh. As if we don't already know that.

"Stay behind me as much as you can. Once we get close, I'll draw him away from the box, you open it, then get it to me."

"Can't we just throw the damned thing or something?" I feel sick even saying it, but now's not the time to get emotional.

She shakes her head. "It's padded on the inside. Only reason it's survived after this whole time. That, and even if you were to throw the jar itself, it takes a lot of force to break the glass."

I nod, and my temporary mirth blends with a surge of anxiety. Only this time, unlike so many others in my life, it's warranted. Blood hums against my eardrums, singing into my throat and limbs with every pulse, and the edges of the world begin to fade out as I focus on the task ahead.

"You with me?" she asks.

She probably thinks I'm slipping right about now, losing my resolve to do what I'd promised her. But I'm not that person anymore. Golden light catches in her hair and glimmers in her eyes. She's an utter work of creation—yet I look not just at her face, but deeper down, past the superficial to that wild, tender soul.

I give the best smile I can muster, no matter how sad it may be.

"Until the very end."

WE RACE TOWARDS LYCUS, arms swinging, blood pumping, ready. Thank whatever god is out there for my regular exercise routine, because I doubt I would be able to keep up with her otherwise. It isn't until Lycus looks up from his digging that he sees us. Even from this distance I can see his shock, then anger. So long as we stop him here, Nia will never have to fear his vengeance. I try not to think about what'll happen if we fail.

He picks up the box and bolts, just as Corinna predicted. Works just fine for us. He can't hide it and run at the same time. Lycus tears up one of the crags, digging his shined oxfords between its limestone cracks for purchase to reach the top. Corinna pushes faster and her legs propel her onward, a stallion from the gate, a hawk from the gauntlet, and she outstrips me to race ahead. She takes the back way around to run up the rocks and cuts in front of Lycus with a smirk just before he reaches the top, before he can escape our line of sight.

"Someone's gotten soft off a life of luxury," she says, voice carrying the hint of a victorious smile. "And it's not me."

His lips tug downward. "Try me."

She strikes out at him and he blocks the first blow, but the second lands hard on his jaw and snaps his head to the side. Livid fire leaps in his eyes, and he drops the box behind him to punch back, a blow for his pride. Corinna's knife glints from within the cloud of dust their tumult has kicked up, and while Lycus is armed with only his teeth, he uses them as weapons all the same. All snarls and fists and fangs, equally matched with one another. Where their slashes and blows land, the wounds instantly begin to knit back over, spurring them on to even greater damage in a bid to outdo the other.

I rush up the rock to move towards his undefended side, and just as I reach the top Lycus whips around to face me, crouching over the domukardi like a wolf over a carcass. Corinna wraps her fingers through his hair and kicks his hips to throw him off center, then yanks him backwards onto his spine in one fell swoop against the rain-smoothed rock. As she jabs and claws at him, trying to keep him down with limbs locked and pinned, I rush forward and grab the box. My fingers close around it. The thing is heavier than I'd remembered, and not just for what it represents.

Corinna yelps as Lycus bites into her ribs and kicks her off, then he rushes me. I freeze. I'm not going to lose the box. I refuse to. But I also don't want to be a sitting duck. I hoist the domukardi up into my arms and prepare to run.

Lycus swings for me. Stars explode across my vision. His punch threatens to knock my teeth free, the sheer force of it reverberating into my bones. I topple backwards but keep the box clutched to my chest, arms wrapped snug around it and kicking at him with my legs, trying to push him back. Corinna strikes the pit of one of his knees to get him off balance, then throws him sideways. Seizing the fabric of his shirt, she drags him backwards.

I right myself and wipe the blood from my busted lip. I crouch over the domukardi, still protective, still not believing that we finally have it. Still not believing everything is about to end.

Hands trembling violently, I click the first wheel-like button to 'III'.

I could still walk away.

'VII'.

But I made a promise, and the choice isn't mine.

'I'.

The lid pops open, flecks of grime and patina crumbling free as the old hinges squeak. Before me sits a hand blown glass jar, its inch thick walls showing every ripple and imperfection, sloshing full of the scintillating golden liquid she'd told me about. Old wool and feathers cushion it against the box's metal walls. Submerged inside are two hearts as healthy as the day they were ripped from their masters' chests. The muscles twitch, pumping the liquid through its valves and veins. A living thing.

My hands feel as cold and detached as a dead man's as I pull out the sealed jar. I can almost feel the hearts' shudders shake the glass. The jar itself takes both hands to hold, not that I would dare handle it with any less. I grunt and heave it out, then inspect the evening light that filters through it to cast the colors a bright amber.

Corinna screams, a cry of anger and panic.

I spin around to see her tumbling down the rocks, bloodthirsty triumph on Lycus's face. Without wasting a second, he dashes towards me. My soul threatens to leave my body, but I hold firm. And I will continue to. Securing the jar tightly in my arms, I run.

Down the slopes and with my eyes on Corinna, who has now skidded to a halt at the bottom of the crag, I hurry in her direction.

"Your back!" Corinna roars.

White-hot pain screams behind my eyelids as Lycus's fist connects with my skull. He seizes me by the shoulders before toppling me backwards, and I barely tuck my chin in time to keep my head from busting open across the stone. Blow after blow lands on my jaw, my abdomen, my forearms, as he attempts to pry the jar from my grasp, and still I don't let go. The tang of blood meets my tongue.

I let it wash over me. The pain. His fury. I watch it pass me like rolling plains out a car window, even as the corners of my vision begin to blur. But I don't worry. The truth of Corinna's promise rings in my ears, even now.

A knife flashes behind Lycus and dives down to slit his throat. Skin fillets open and his mouth contorts in agony, his full hands leaving me to clutch at his butchered neck where pink cords of flesh peek out in an attempt to hold him fast. Corinna seizes her moment and stabs him again. But when I meet her eyes, there's nothing triumphant there. Instead I find sorrow. Knife still in Lycus as he fights like a shark on a line, she yanks him backwards and away from me.

In that moment of opportunity, I heave the jar away and throw it over the edge of the slope.

My breath catches in my throat.

Corinna and Lycus seize, but remain standing.

She blinks. Her eyes connect with mine, despaired. I scramble to peek over the edge and see the jar, brought to a halt by a cluster of scrub brush. Our gazes meet, and the color leaves her. Glee breaks across Lycus's face as he begins to fight against Corinna once more, and she is just barely able to hold him. I push myself to my feet. The slope is steep, but not too much to ease down it and retrieve the jar.

"Go," Corinna says.

I blink and turn back to look at her, convinced I misheard. "What?"

"Go," she presses. Slowing his recovery, she slams her heel onto the nape of Lycus's neck with a gut-twisting crack. "Leave the jar, take the car, and go. You've already opened the box. You've done your part. I can take care of it from here. But, if I fail, then the farther away you are from all this, the safer you are. Go home and even if this goes sideways, so long as Lycus has the jar, so long as he has me, you'll be safe. But you need to leave *now*."

The air rushes from my aching lungs. The keys weigh heavy in my pocket. Finally, here it rests before me. A way out. I've opened the box and held up my end of our promise. I could wash my hands of this and be done.

But, while I'm here for one heartbeat and gone the next, if this fails then she'll be doomed to endure and endure, spinning out into darkness. She could try again in another 80 years, if the box isn't under firm lock and key by then. Which I doubt. But she could, suffering all the while.

On the other hand, if she succeeds, then I will have to watch her die. But I will not let her die alone.

I shake my head.

"No," I say. "No. I'm staying here."

"*Eugene—*"

"Until the very end."

If anything she's shown me throughout our time together has stuck, it's that suffering for those you love is worth it. No matter where it may lead.

Hearing a grunt from below, I look down just in time to see Lycus roll out from under Corinna's boot, his head still lolling to the side at a grotesque angle as it straightens, bones cracking back into shape. He swipes a paw towards me before she pulls him back by the hair.

If we're to seize our chance, it has to be soon.

Without thinking about how one misstep could send me sliding down into a patch of cacti, or about the rattlesnakes that like to live in the crevices of these outcroppings, I inch down and keep my body as flat against the rock face as I can. I block out the sounds of the scuffle above me and, reaching the jar, look down. Even if I throw it from here, the angle of the slope makes no guarantee that the jar will actually break. The other side could very well have the same problem, and the glass is too thick to smash to pieces at our feet. Getting it to her is our only chance.

I scoop the jar up and tuck it against my chest. Next to my heart, ironically. Worming my way up and pushing into every foothold I find, I reach the top again.

"Corinna!"

She hooks Lycus's calf and topples him backwards, then spins to face me with open arms, hands raised high. Now. It has to be now.

"Eugene!" she shouts.

I don't think. I can't. I just nod.

Infinite possibilities and years clutched in my grasp, I aim right for her palms and use all of my might to throw the jar into the air. It arcs towards her.

Corinna's hands drop. She doubles over as Lycus delivers a ferocious kick to the pit of her stomach, her head smacking against the ground with a crack. He catches the jar, his many rings tinkling as they meet the glass.

The world narrows to a single point. My lungs drain of air. My heart stutters, clenches. A stalemate. That's all this can end in now—which for me means a swift death at his hand. Corinna rights herself, but doesn't move to strike.

"You tried, I'll give you that," Lycus pants with a laugh, all bone-white, glittering teeth and a poison-black voice. He hugs the jar to his chest like a long lost child as his neck crunches fully back into place. "But I've lasted this long for a reason. All the people you've grabbed onto have only ever met an early grave, but not me. Try all you want, your boy won't even make it to tonight."

His gaze on me turns predatory. Cold sweat beads up along my spine, nausea roiling like a pit of snakes in my stomach.

"Say your goodbyes," he sneers at me.

Click.

I look to his left and my eyes go wide. He turns to look

too. There Corinna stands, arm raised high and the heavy-weight .45 she'd snuck in her boot now in hand, its barrel level with the jar. I don't move quick enough to process what I'm looking at, what her plan is.

She pulls the trigger.

The glass shatters into a thousand shards, gold fluid spraying into the air as their hearts leap upwards from the impact, muscle spasming, the gunshot splitting in my ears. Lycus flails backwards then tumbles to a gurgling, twitching stop as Corinna's knees give way.

No.

I run forward to catch her, one arm wrapped around her back. Even though I use all my speed, all my vigor, I feel trapped in slow-moving molasses. I never noticed how small she was, looking only at her strength. Now, she seems almost tiny in my arms.

No, no, no.

After a glance over my shoulder to make sure Lycus is truly dead and not somehow still clawing his way towards us, I see the fractured jar. Already his heart is crumbling to cinder on the dry ground, no liquid protecting it. He lays in a heap. Corinna's heart is still in the broken base of the jar, the remaining inch of elixir giving her her last breaths. I sink to my knees and pull her into my lap.

"Corinna?" I can hardly hear my own voice, still deafened from the gunshot. Words are no good now anyways.

Her eyes flutter open and I breathe a sigh of relief. She's still here.

"Thank you." Her voice is already weak.

I hadn't thought it would happen so quick. Too quick, but also painful in its slowness, in the stretch of each individual second. There has to be some way to slow it, just long enough to say goodbye, to say what I need to. I look down at her. Corinna smiles, one last ray before the sun sets.

"Thank you, Eugene."

"I— You're welcome." I lack the strength to say any more. I want to tell her so much, about how grateful I am, about how she deserved so much better, but I don't. There isn't anything I have to say that she doesn't already know. "Thank *you*."

"Promise me," she says, voice barely above a whisper now.

I feel her slipping away like sand between my fingers. Out of the corner of my eye I see Lycus's form dissolving into ash, her fate in a minute's time. Too fast, this is all too damn *fast*—

"Anything," I sob. "I'll do anything."

"Promise me you'll live a good life." Papery, dusty flakes begin to crust across her skin. Shaky breaths rattle in her chest, and what vitality she has left drips out of her like a punctured warship leaking shimmering oil. "No matter how long or strange or extraordinary it may be, you only have one."

Hot tears cut trails down my face through the blood and grime. I don't care about hiding them. I'm not ready, not for this. Her head slumps back a bit as she looks up at the rapidly darkening sky, yet the sun still shows a sliver of itself just above the horizon. The golden hue drains from her eyes to reveal a beautiful earthen brown.

"I think I can finally see the stars," she breathes.

I look up. Even squinting through my blurred vision, I can't see a single pinprick of light. My heart sinks into my stomach.

"Yeah." I look down at her. "I can too."

If there is one thing I can control at least, it's that she isn't going to leave this world alone. Looking at her, one of my newly-roughened hands cradling her head, the other holding her up, I kiss her forehead.

She disintegrates into a cloud of dust.

23

AN AUTUMN DIRGE

I sit on the shower floor, the water having long since gone cold as droplets bounce and splatter across the white tile. It's one of the few things that distract me, drought restrictions be damned. The dull roar of the shower, the spray across my skin, it all mutes the pain somehow. One would think I've had enough time to think about everything, to process what all happened. I haven't.

A week seems both an eternity and a blip on the radar, but it's been a week since I dragged myself from that rock face either way.

I hadn't known where to go. Hours after the stars had come out, I dragged myself to the abandoned car we took and drove to the first crappy motel I saw. Even though Corinna was no longer with me, I still found myself securing the doors and windows. It felt strange not to. After a day of laying numb on the scratchy sheets, I borrowed someone's phone at a Walmart. From there, I called my sister Moira.

"Where have you been?" she'd asked, a mix of fury and relief in her voice. "You didn't answer your phone and the door was open and—"

"Can you pick me up?"

"I— What? Are you okay?"

I had cried. I told her some of what happened—what was believable, at least. I told her I had gone off on a spontaneous road trip and my phone had been destroyed and now I was alone, without any idea how to get home. She was on the road within fifteen minutes.

Throughout the many hours it took to come get me and the hours it took to go back, I knew she was somewhere between furious and concerned the whole time—and, when I broke down in tears, shocked. My sobs, ugly and sniffling and shoulder-heaving, were something she rarely ever saw. But she didn't say a word. Didn't yell at me or threaten to tell our parents, at least not until they returned from Spain. After handing me crumpled napkins to dry my face with, the only time she pushed me to talk was to ask if I was safe, if anyone had hurt me, and when we picked up some drive-thru chicken. Nothing else. My mind churning through a hundred thoughts a minute, I'm not sure I could handle anything beyond that.

Did her last moments hurt? Should I have told her how I felt? What more could I have learned from her when I was instead wrapped up in my anxieties, and what did those damn things gain me anyway? A piece of me tucks the feeling away, resolving to make an attempt at change, however small.

Whatever was going through Moira's head, she had to know this was nothing she could fix for me. Her presence was enough. For her part, she'd always encouraged me to indulge in the same crazy teenaged antics that she had, so I suspected that's all she chalked it up to, if an extreme scenario.

Even when I had arrived back home, I wasn't able to shake the weight from my shoulders. I'm still unable to. A hollow space has been carved out from my chest. In a cruel twist of irony, it's through her death that I've been able to empathize more, to know what it's like to be left behind after those you care for are torn from you.

Death of an Immortal

I was only gone for five days, yet somehow that narrow window seemed like even more of an eternity than this past week, like a speck under a microscope, stretched out and lengthened ad infinitum. I wonder if that's how Corinna feels —*felt*, about it all. Not to mention the many questions I still have. Yet even if she were to pop out of thin air right beside me, I wouldn't ask them. Each and every one now seems trivial.

My grandmother died when I was eleven years old. I was too young to go to her funeral, so it didn't seem real to me. I simply wouldn't see Nana again. My mom though was so torn up that I didn't think she'd ever get out of bed again. Then one day, five weeks later, I woke up to find the house filled with the aroma of pancakes and coffee—the creamy hazelnut kind, not my dad's black, instantly-sprouts-hair-on-your-chest kind. She had her favorite lipstick and perfume on and was smiling as if none of it had ever happened, save a few additional crow's feet for the hardship she'd gone through. Was that how it happened? Did you just wake up one day and the pain was gone?

I turn the shower off and dry myself, a monumental effort. It's unlike me to bathe any time before evening—the post-shower drop in body temperature mimics the drop associated with sleep, making it ideal to shower before bed—but routine and rationale be damned. Damn all of it, in fact. The most I'm able to manage before dropping onto the couch is putting on boxers and a loose shirt.

Above my head, I watch the fan *click, click, click* with each lazy rotation. Cyclical and unchanging. I both do and don't envy it.

It's not that I miss her because I was in love with her. The rational part of my brain says that love isn't something you fall into so quickly, but the other side of me clings to the notion. Either way, I cared about her. I loved the way she lived, fierce and unyielding, ever charging forward even in the face of so much heartache.

At the very least, her life was as full as anyone else's ever could have been. She'd done more, seen more, been more than even Alexander the Great. She'd outlasted empires and peoples and languages and nations. And I suppose, just as she had outlasted the world around her, it was her turn.

I rub to the left of my sternum. It aches, a dull thud. I didn't think your heart could actually hurt unless it was from a heart attack or plaque in your arteries, but I was wrong. The faux-antique clock on the living room wall reads 5:27 and I'd usually be at one of my jobs right now, in the thick of the evening rush. Had I not gotten fired.

When I hadn't shown up for work the day after Corinna whisked me away, my manager had apparently called me eight times with no response. At first he'd been worried. He called my emergency contact, Moira again, and she came by the house to see where I was. After reading the note, everyone had assumed I'd just taken off—even if it was unlike me. I had led them to believe as much. Once I was back home several days later, alive and well and claiming it was all just a road trip gone awry, my work breathed a sigh of relief. Then fired me. I can't blame them. If anything I told them had been true, I wouldn't have been pleased with my negligence either. But I wasn't going to divulge her secret. It was all I had left of her, that knowledge and experience wholly mine.

Two weeks ago, losing my jobs would have seemed like the collapse of the world. Now I know there are much worse things, and much bigger ones too. Let that be one lesson I've learned. One of many.

It was a miracle to witness her, like a soaring comet or a red moon. Seeing all of her rage and passion and fire, shifting the very earth under her feet instead of bowing to it, she forged her own meaning. Accepted what sorrow fell, yet still faced the future. Found beauty in the world even after it hurt her, again and again and again.

In that parking garage, Corinna could have taken the domukardi and left me to the wolves, but her love of humanity kept her coming back to save us. Then for once, after so many years, she put herself first.

I tip my head to the side and look out the window, smeared fingerprints on it. Need to clean that before my parents come back into town this Sunday. I need to do a lot of things, but we'll see if I actually get around to them. The sun still beats down with absurd heat for this time of day, but a rare band of clouds blocks most of its glare from view. We'd even gotten a sprinkle of rain last night. Beyond the windows, I look out to the crunchy lawn and plants on the patio that've soaked up the water, reinvigorated and flushed with a new wash of green. With new life.

I sit in unbroken silence and stare at the shrubs and pink crape myrtles. Such small things. Some would say insignificant, but every piece of this bright and terrible and beautiful world matters. Then, ever so slowly, in the cavernous space of my chest the pain lessens. Just by a fraction, hardly perceptible, but there. As I look out to that unending sky and this strange world, I feel it again.

There, something hopeful and unafraid begins to grow.

I REST my textbooks on my knee, one copy of a book on Papua New Guinea's Huli tribe, another on the Berber people of central Morocco. Listening to the lecture, I scrawl bits of information across my journal—without caring whether or not it follows the Cornell note taking strategy. How much I retain isn't important. This class does nothing to further my career plans or get needed credits out of the way. No, I'm taking it out of personal interest—very unlike me. Or the old me, anyway. Some of my anxieties are still a part of my life, but working on those will take more time.

The lecturer goes on to draw an upwards sloping line and marks it at a few different points.

"Anthropologists used to think a culture wasn't yet developed until it reached certain milestones, like making pottery or constructing settlements. The fewer milestones that culture reached, the less developed it was considered. Can you think why this might lead to miscategorizing a society as primitive?"

She turns to look at us, the usual eager-learners with their hands raised and the usual quiet students shifting in our chairs.

"Someone I don't often hear from." She scans the room from behind the ruby spectacles that magnify her pupils.

My heart thunders in my ears as I get ready to raise my hand. I breathe in, and the thunder fades. I've been through worse.

"Yes, Eugene." She points to me with a whiteboard marker.

"Not everyone needs pottery or buildings."

"Are you so sure?"

I nod, though with an ounce of hesitation. "What about nomads? Pottery would just break, and building in one place wouldn't fit their lifestyle. Not everyone needs to live the same kind of life."

"Very good." Wrinkles pull around her widened smile. "We can't put the same expectations on different societies when each has varying needs and values. Anthropologists and sociologists incorrectly thought societies inevitably moved from bands of hunter-gatherers to industrially developed nations. They believed it was a one-track line."

She turns back to the whiteboard, smudges from poorly erased lessons still visible. I ease back in my chair as a dark-headed girl gets up to leave early. My heart has since stopped lurching at every bronze skinned, black-haired woman who passes me, has stopped searching for golden eyes.

My phone vibrates in my pocket. Sneaking a glance at it, I see an email notification from the community college that the deadline is approaching to sign up for next semester's classes.

Were this before I'd met Corinna, I would have been begging some academic advisor to allow me to take more hours so that I could get more credits so that I could transfer to a university so that I could get my degree sooner so that I could get a job sooner so that I could keep rushing, rushing, rushing through life. Now, I have a few tentative classes I'm looking to take, from coding to Mesoamerican history. I'll find where I want to wind up, eventually.

"Your assignment for Thursday is to write 500 words on why the unilinear model of cultural development is flawed, despite having been widely accepted a century ago. Place at least three specific cultures along this line, and point to why they may not have needed or developed these technologies. Good examples are pottery, archery, and metallurgy."

She rattles off a list of pages to read. While I might not know all of the cultures this could apply to, I could write a whole dissertation on myself. After scrawling down our homework prompt in the margins of my journal, I stand and swing my bag over my shoulder. Both shoulders, just to be sure to protect my spine's integrity. There are some nitpicking habits I've forgone, sure, but a kernel of the old me remains, the part that wasn't consumed by paranoia or anxiety.

Finally, I'm beginning to learn just who that is.

EPILOGUE

DIRT AND FLECKS of mixed granite crunch beneath my shoes as I walk up and over the rocky land, the swells and the outcroppings and the packed earth. I'd almost doubted my ability to find my way back here. It's so out of the way that it doesn't have a specific name, at least not one I could find in any of the maps I looked at. But deep down I knew I'd never forget where Corinna's end took place. Not even now, a full year later. Were I to close my eyes, I could remember it just as clearly as ten minutes ago. I can feel the weight of her in my arms, the scent of ash.

It had also been about a year since the Watts family's own personal tragedy. It wasn't just me who'd suffered.

A few days ago I had visited the unofficial memorial that cropped up near the intersection where he'd been slain. Plastic flowers, a sun-faded cross, and laminated photos of Brendon decorated a wooden telephone pole, and an aura of longing, of aching hearts insulated the area like a bubble. From across the street I'd glimpsed a woman with box-braids longer than when I'd last seen her. Nia. She gave me a nod, a half-smile on her lips. Were Corinna still here, I know she would've come to pay her respects on this anniversary too, just like the countless others. Nia's heavy gaze told me she knew as much.

I couldn't help but tear up as I looked back to Brendon's picture, his bright eyes and crooked smile. That could've easily been me. Could've been my own picture at a roadside memorial like this one. The ending of his life had so radically altered the trajectory of my own. I had considered writing to his family and extending my condolences, but given that the police had never closed the case and were still looking for suspects, I didn't want to do anything to draw attention to myself. My sentiments were with them all the same. I left a handwritten note and a bouquet of overly-bright grocery store flowers by his memorial instead.

Out in the wilderness, here was a memorial of my own. Private, for the memory of a soul unlike any other. I walk around the backside of the rock slope, to the top of the outcropping where everything had happened. I still know the feel of that particular patch of earth under my feet. I doubt I'll ever forget it.

Unfolding the vibrant Mexican blanket tucked under my arm, I pop it out into the wind before laying it flat on the ground. The weather has long since scattered the glass fragments, and god only knows where the empty domukardi chest went. Could have been picked up by some hitchhiker or backpacker, for all I know. While I hope the new owner appreciates it, I never want to cross paths with it again. Unlikely I would, on a college campus.

After what had unfolded, I'd taken the rapidly approaching summer semester off for my own sake. My parents were shocked that I chose time away from school, but happy about it nonetheless. They knew something was off, even if I never told them what happened. I know they worried their trip to Spain upset me and that I felt left out, but nothing could have been further from the truth. If only I hadn't been stupid enough to pass up the opportunity to go to Europe—*Europe!*—so that I could work crappy food service jobs. But it had led to everything else. That, I wouldn't regret. Regardless, at some point my parents started believing my consolations, Moira kept what secrets of mine she knew, and then, as the budding sprout in my chest renewed me from the inside out, I started to breathe again.

I place a butter-colored daffodil on the ground beside me where Corinna died in my arms, then lay back on the blanket with a sigh. I knew coming back here would hurt, but the pain is worth it. Some things are worth suffering for. Tonight, I might even stay in a suspect motel just to reminiscence.

The drive here was a full three hours, so I had more than enough time to change my mind, to turn around and go home, but I didn't. Sure, there was homework I could've been doing, extra shifts I could've picked up, but my habit of scheduling every hour of my day has since fallen by the wayside. Thank god.

I watch the sunset, an orange and lime green strip on the horizon, and look up into the sky. The light fades as I lie there, breathing easy, heart quiet. I don't know how much time passes, but eventually the sun buries itself beneath the earth to reveal a pitch dark sky. Save for the stars. This far out they shine like crushed diamonds under moonlight, scattered so thick that any inch of my vision may contain a thousand constellations. A warmth spreads outwards from my soul and radiates to my fingertips. I smile.

My heart sighs, a quiet sound for the woman, the warrior, the once-immortal, the friend who once walked this earth. And as I look into those ancient heavens, I know that somewhere up there, she's among the stars.

If you enjoyed this story, please consider leaving a review. Reviews are the lifeblood of an author's business, and help us reach new readers.

If you'd like to, you can leave a review at your preferred retailer.

YOUR FREE BOOK IS WAITING

It is a lightless world. The sun goddess, Atthar, has long-since been deposed, her light stripped from her by a tyrant and held aloft above his dying city. Eking out a meager existence there is Nasir and his ailing mother, Atthar's former high priestess, who hold secret ceremonies and face routine beatings from the city guards. Nasir prays when his mother asks, but his faith is dead.

Until the goddess calls out to him from the dark, very much alive—and ready to strike.

> Get a free copy of this standalone ancient
> fantasy novella, *Stolen Sun*, by clicking here.

HISTORICAL NOTE

This book was a labor of love, requiring research into fields from hermetic alchemy to Alexander II's campaigns, from museum heists to China's Great Leap Forward. I will be the first to admit that there were times I could not see how these individual threads would come together in the tapestry of the story, but I'm glad that they finally did.

For your own edification and enjoyment, here are some more details on the elements I used in *Death of an Immortal*.

Alexander the Great — Part man, part myth, Alexander the Great is a person we know little about. Though his contemporaries almost certainly wrote about him, no such records have survived. The earliest account we have on him is from hundreds of years later via Diodorus Siculus, though my personal favorite is the Anabasis of Alexander, written by Arrian of Nicomedia about 400 years after Alexander's death. This latter account was one of the first military histories ever written. Arrian also cites all of his sources, though they have since become lost to us. All of the events I wrote about during Alexander's campaign are thought to have happened, with the exception of making a contingent of his warriors immor-

Historical Note

tal, of course. (There is, however, a Greek legend about him seeking—and finding—the Fountain of Immortality, though it is worth noting that he doesn't use the fountain's waters on himself.) It was difficult to cover all of Alexander's exploits in Corinna's chapters, and it could have been a much longer book if I had time to explore it all. However, that is precisely why I chose Alexander the Great. The brevity of time we have with him is part of his story, and humanity's story as a whole. Here, rich in life and detail, and then gone the next moment. Overall, I could write much more on Alexander, his aspirations, his influences, and his ever-changing nature, but ultimately, much of his legacy can be summed up into this: Alexander of Macedon was a very human man who yearned to be something bigger than himself, and who lost himself in the process. His entire empire crumbled soon after his death, and his tomb has never been found to this day.

Warriors of the Ancient World — Though not common, female warriors definitely existed at this time. We need only to look at the Scythian women, whom the Amazons are likely based on. As much as one third of Scythian women are believed to have participated in battle, and though there are no records of women fighting in Alexander's ranks, he is fabled to have had encounters with Amazons. Additionally, at this time there was an elite band of Spartan warriors who fought in pairs, though exclusively male-male pairs. They were frequently lovers, as it was believed that they would fight harder on the battlefield if protecting someone they loved. This band of warriors was wiped out in battle against Alexander's father, and was thus a practice he would have learned about. For the purposes of this story, I combined the above concepts and suited it to my own needs.

Immortal Elixir and Hermetic Alchemy — Were there any factual works on how to make an elixir of immortality, I would be a very rich and very long-lived woman. Alas, I have none at my disposal. What I *was* able to draw from for this book was the lore surrounding the Emerald Tablet, its alleged author, Hermes Trismegistus, and the various fragments of texts ascribed to him, though they have been damaged by time and shrouded in symbolism. Some say Trismegistus dates back to the time of Moses and others say he lived well after Christ, but almost all scholars agree that he is no more than a legend, a combination of the Greek god Hermes and the Egyptian god Thoth. Though in the West we tend to think of a red stone as associated with alchemically-inspired immortality, many other global traditions more closely associate it with a gold liquid. There are also sources that say any elixir of immortality is unique, and cannot be replicated with the same effect.

The Pogrom of York — This is an event so terrible, so gut-wrenching that I debated whether or not to include it in the final draft of the book. There are many events throughout history that—quite frankly—obliterate one's faith in humanity, but I chose this one in particular because it is so often forgotten. Much anti-semitism goes unmentioned in history classes and texts, and though I do not have space here to speculate why that might be, I decided to keep it in the story. The Pogrom of York took place on March 16th of 1190, and it is regarded by historians as one of the worst acts perpetrated against the Jewish people in the Middle Ages.

The Great Leap Forward — I have always been intrigued by institutional failure, but there are few events that have claimed as many lives as the Great Leap Forward. It's often overlooked by the West, either due to sinophobia, ignorance, or something else entirely, but it ought to be remembered. Having lived and worked in China, I can attest that its people are too often—and unjustly—vilified by the west, when in

Historical Note

reality China is home to some of the most kindhearted and vivacious people I have ever met. (Not that it should make a difference either way, but I would be remiss to not say as much.) That is ultimately what is so tragic about the Great Leap Forward; it is a story of a wonderful people, filled with hope, and failed by their government. Rural Chinese life varied greatly as the country's administrative efforts spread across the nation, but ultimately, the suffering and death that ripped through the countryside was unlike anything ever seen. *Bureaucracy, Economy, and Leadership in China* by David Bachman, though dated, lends excellent if heart-wrenching insight into the institutional failures that caused the worst man-made famine in human history. Estimated death tolls range between 15 and 55 million lives lost.

Heists — I consulted a worrying number of texts on burglary for this book, one of my favorites being *A Burglar's Guide to the City* by Geoff Manaugh. Law enforcement agencies are, naturally, hesitant to disclose how criminals subvert security and surveillance systems, and equally unwilling to answer questions about what would and would not work in a robbery. So, instead of positing new ways to breach security, I was left to lift details from well-known global crimes. For instance, the hairspray trick used in Corinna and Eugene's museum escapade was pulled from the Antwerp diamond heist of 2003.

ACKNOWLEDGMENTS

This book took many years and many people to bring it to life. Dreamed up back in 2012, I wrote pieces of this book in my childhood home, when I lived overseas in China, and everywhere in between. It reflects a great deal of my personal struggles with anxiety, confronting my and my loved ones' mortality, and learning to love life in spite of—and, in some cases, because of—those things.

Though I am unable to thank every person who helped me on my journey, I'll endeavor to try. To my father and mother, who fed me a steady diet of fantastical stories throughout my childhood. To Elisabeth Wheatley, who showed me what was possible in this new and exciting world of publishing. To Intisar Khanani, for her writing advice and mentorship. To the support of the online writing community which has helped to fuel me onwards, even at my lowest lows. To the many coffee shops that allowed me to loiter there under the guise of productivity. To the countless researchers and academics whose works I used in the creation of this story, (particularly World History Encyclopedia and JSTOR). To my talented cover artist, Elona Bezooshko of Psycat Studio, who created a cover beyond my imaginings. And to my love, Samuel Choi, who has given me the support I needed at exactly the right moments.

And last but not least, to you.

ABOUT THE AUTHOR

Eli Hinze is a writer with a particular interest in underrepresented eras, peoples, and mythologies. She has lived in China for a time, fought in tournaments, wrangled various farm animals, and worked in tech, but is happiest in her life as an author.

When not writing, Eli studies everything she can get her hands on, draws, drinks a lot of caffeine, and forces cats to snuggle with her.

If you'd like to stay up-to-date with her newest releases, you can connect with her on social media @EliHinze.

OTHER WORKS BY ELI HINZE

Stolen Sun

Queen of Shades
Consort of War
Lord of Blight
Mother of Chaos

www.ingramcontent.com/pod-product-compliance
Ingram Content Group UK Ltd.
Pitfield, Milton Keynes, MK11 3LW, UK
UKHW042002230426
12048UKWH00009B/494